DWIGHT DAVID MORGAN

THE PREMATURE DEMISE OF SONNY B. FEELRIGHT

This is a work of fiction. The events and characters described herein are imaginary and are not intended to refer to specific places or living persons. The opinions expressed in this manuscript are solely the opinions of the author and do not represent the opinions or thoughts of the publisher. The author has represented and warranted full ownership and/or legal right to publish all the materials in this book.

The Premature Demise of Sonny B. Feelright
A New and Dangerous Career

v3.0

Outskirts Press, Inc.
http://www.outskirtspress.com

ISBN: 978-1-4327-9089-9

Outskirts Press and the "OP" logo are trademarks belonging to Outskirts Press, Inc.

PRINTED IN THE UNITED STATES OF AMERICA

Preface

Nancy Black stared with menace across the table at the small cadre of outside attorneys gathered in her Toronto conference room. The senior partner from the law firm had faced many angry clients in his long and successful career, but he had never felt so personally threatened. As he stared into her smoldering black eyes, he sensed defiant hatred, personal hatred, as though he was responsible for the bleak situation in which she found herself.

"Paying out the investors is not an option," she hissed. "This is my fund. I won't let them destroy it."

The attorney gave her a frustrated look while his colleagues leaned back from the table, as far as possible from the brewing confrontation. "Nancy, it's the only option," he insisted. "They're pulling out their money. They don't want to be part of Black Woods anymore, after all that's happened."

"No!" she snapped. "They'll get paid when *I* decide!"

"You know that's not how this works. They have a legal right to their money."

"They're fools!" she ranted. "They'll get pennies

on the dollar! They'll force us to liquidate everything! They'll kill Black Woods! They're taking my money!"

"Nancy," the attorney almost whispered in as soothing a voice as he could muster, "I know this is very hard. It's not how anyone wanted Black Woods to end. But we're out of options. You're being actively investigated by the Securities and Exchange Commission and the Justice Department in the U.S. The Canadian Mounted Police are now involved. The banks are calling your loans. We've already been hit with three shareholder suits. You can't just ignore the investors. It will only make matters worse."

"I pay you to fix things!" she accused. "Fix it!"

"This isn't something you can easily fix."

"You've made tens of millions off of me, just like the investors! Now you're abandoning me, just like them!"

"We're not abandoning you!" he said angrily. "We're trying to keep you out of prison!"

"I'll find another law firm! One that's willing to fight for me!"

"Go ahead!" he dared her. "No one would take you on for all the money in the world! You're toxic right now! Look out there." He gestured to the nearly empty offices visible through the glass wall of the conference room, offices that were teeming with overworked employees just a few weeks before. "Black Woods barely exists anymore. Your team is gone. Your investors are gone. We're the only ones left trying to help you."

Nancy crossed her arms tightly about her chest and began to breathe deeply, almost hyperventilating. Her face went crimson, as though ready to burst into flames. She closed her eyes and began to shake. "Aaaagh!" she screamed with primal abandon, so loud it made all four attorneys wince. They watched her, unsure of how to respond to such rage, as she continued to pant and shake uncontrollably. Gradually, her breathing returned to normal and the shaking subsided. As her face paled to its normal color, she opened her eyes and gazed at the lead attorney. "He won."

"Who won?" the attorney asked.

"Sonny Feelright. He won. He got what he wanted all along. He destroyed Black Woods."

The attorney shook his head in frustration. "Nancy, you were attempting an illegal takeover. You enlisted him in the scheme through forgery and fraud. Sonny Feelright was your pawn, a dupe. You got caught, that's all. We're lucky it ended this way. If he'd gone to the authorities you could be staring at twenty years in prison."

"He won," she insisted.

"Believe what you want. But the past is behind us. Our job now is making sure you still have a future. We need to fend off the governmental investigations and wind down Black Woods. Once the fund is defunct, the lawsuits will disappear because there will be no assets left for payouts, if we do things properly."

She suddenly appeared attentive. "How do we fend off the investigations?"

"I think we'll be able to settle. You'll have to sit out of the industry for a while, probably a year. But it's better than prison time. Then you can work your way back. Start over with a small fund. Rebuild a track record."

"No one will invest with me after all the publicity."

"Nonsense," argued the attorney. "Wall Street is filled with money managers who've resurrected themselves after failures. All will be forgotten once you start doing your investment magic again."

"What am I supposed to do for the next year?" she asked.

"You're a billionaire. You don't need to do anything."

"No," she said after a moment of contemplation. "There are things I need to do."

"So, we have a meeting of the minds on the need to dissolve Black Woods?"

"Do what you have to."

At that moment, four-hundred-and-sixty miles away in a tired office suite in Chicago, Feelright Intelligence Services LLC was opening for business.

Troubled Start

Nearly six weeks had passed, and things weren't going well for Feelright Intelligence Services. Two of its three partners sat and argued in the newly decorated conference room.

"He's fallen off the wagon," accused Charlotte McCardle, her anger-flushed face nearly matching her silken red hair.

"He'll be fine," defended Sonny Feelright. "He's just frustrated."

"This makes two days in a row he's left before noon. You know he's at the Red Swan. You need to go get him."

"Why? So he can sit here with us, staring at the walls? Besides, he's a phone call away if we need him." Sonny ran both hands through his bush of tangled hair, which bounced back happily to its normal unkempt state.

"He's no good when he's drunk."

"What's he going to do here?"

"So, you've lost confidence, too!" she accused. "I suppose you regret this whole venture!"

"No, Charlotte. I don't regret anything. It's just

that things aren't going quite how we planned. I understand why Simon needs a little time away."

They were talking about Simon Courtney, the senior executive of Feelright Intelligence Services, whose weakness for Tanqueray and tonic was a source of constant concern. It was Simon who conceived the notion of starting a forensic accounting firm. It was Simon who drafted the business plan and, using his law background, their operating agreement. And it was Simon who had the extensive accounting and analytical experience to lead the young firm. Now, Simon was AWOL.

They started Feelright Intelligence Services on a wave of optimism. Their business plan projected they would have paying clients within three weeks. Now, with their six-week anniversary approaching, they had no clients and no prospects. They had received not a single phone call concerning prospective business.

Charlotte crossed her arms and pouted, which melted Sonny's resolve like candle wax. "Okay, okay. I'll go and talk to him." She rewarded him with a smile.

As Sonny stood and pulled on his overcoat, his BlackBerry sounded. The chirp seemed shrill in the otherwise silent offices. He fumbled to pull the phone from his pants pocket and eyed it with a surprised look. The number was unfamiliar. He answered. "Good afternoon. This is Sonny Feelright, Feelright Intelligence

Services." It was the first time he answered an official call, and the greeting seemed awkward.

"Mr. Feelright, my name is Stanley Waring. I saw one of your flyers. I understand you do investigative work." The voice had a slight foreign accent, which Sonny could not identify.

"Yes, sir. We're forensic accountants." Sonny winked at Charlotte, who sat up expectantly in her chair.

"Can I trust you to be discreet?" asked the voice on the other end of the line.

"Absolutely," Sonny assured him. "Discretion is essential in our line of work." Charlotte nodded her approval, her hair shimmering as it bounced.

"I'm the business manager of the Lisle Community School District. And I'm afraid some things are going on. Improper things. I'm not sure whom to call." The man hesitated.

"Go on, Mr. Waring," urged Sonny.

"You see, I believe our procurement manager is on the take. I think he's accepting bribes. And the amounts involved are considerable."

"So, why don't you tell the superintendent? Or the school board?"

"Because I believe the superintendent is involved."

"I can see where that would be awkward," Sonny conceded.

"Before I go forward, I need proof. Otherwise, I could be committing suicide from a career standpoint. Can you help me, Mr. Feelright?"

"Possibly," said Sonny.

"I could give you complete access to our books. But it would have to be discreet."

"Mention the fees," whispered Charlotte.

"There would be fees involved," said Sonny.

"Not an issue," the man assured. "We have some discretionary funds for consulting services. It would be money well spent if a fraud is underway. And if everything is above board, I'll at least sleep better."

"So, how do you want to proceed?" Sonny asked.

"Can we meet at my office? Say tomorrow, mid-morning?"

"Let me check my calendar." Sonny grinned at Charlotte as he waited a moment. "How about ten-thirty? I'll bring one of my colleagues. Her name is Charlotte McCardle."

"That will be fine," the man agreed. He gave Sonny the address and hung up.

Late

Sonny scrambled down the dark stairway behind an animated Charlotte, who scolded him as she went. "We're late! You should have made the copies yesterday!"

"The copier broke down. How was I supposed to know?" he argued. "We need a new copier." He glanced at the toner blackened fingertips on his right hand and knew from experience he was marked for at least several days. To obscure the obnoxious stains he switched his battered briefcase from his left hand to his right.

She reached the dingy landing and burst through the exit door into the late November sunlight. A rush of frigid air enveloped Sonny as he followed her. The four inches of snow that fell two days earlier was packed on the concrete walk into a three-quarter inch layer of ice. Wearing Italian loafers ill-suited for the Midwestern winter, Sonny held his arms out like curb feelers to keep his balance. He marveled as Charlotte gracefully maneuvered across the slick surface in high heels. He caught up with her as they rounded the corner into the alley next to the building.

Later, when he recalled the explosion, he couldn't

remember what made him stop – whether it was the sight of the rusting blue dumpster tipped on its side in the alley ahead or the realization that he left his wallet on his desk in the office. But stop he did.

"What now?" asked an exasperated Charlotte, as she turned and faced him, her lightly freckled cheeks radiant in the winter sunlight.

He patted all his pockets. "My wallet. I forgot my wallet. It's on my desk." He turned and, with toddling steps, headed back around the corner toward the door.

Charlotte yanked him by the arm, sending him into a graceless pirouette. She leaned back deftly, just in time to avoid a blow to the face from his wildly swinging briefcase. "I'll get it," she commanded. "You'll take too long." She disappeared back into the building.

Sonny never heard or saw the blast. But he certainly felt it. One moment, he was watching the heavy wooden door close behind Charlotte. The next, he was sitting in the snow several feet away watching his briefcase skitter along the ground like a runaway sled.

Charlotte burst from the building, a horrified look spoiling her beautiful face. He could see that she was yelling, "Sonny! Sonny!" between panicked gasps. But all he heard was a squelching roar. She fell to her knees and held his face in both her hands, her lips moving incomprehensibly. Soon, Simon appeared over

Charlotte's shoulder, sober seriousness etching his craggy face. While Charlotte mutely babbled, Simon peered deeply into Sonny's eyes, then inspected him for any obvious injuries.

"WHAT WAS THAT?" Sonny yelled over the din in his ears, though he could not hear himself speaking. He tried to stand, but Charlotte forced him back down, then wrapped her arms around his neck and hugged him to her chest. Simon disappeared around the corner into the alley.

Sonny welcomed Charlotte's affection until he became vaguely aware of the icy moisture seeping through his pants. With effort, he extricated himself from her protective grasp and she helped him to unsteady feet. She held his arm tightly as they followed Simon around the corner. Her lips worked frantically but emitted no sound that Sonny could hear.

Simon was talking silently on his cell phone as he stared down the alley. A torn and twisted heap of metal rested where the blue dumpster sat minutes earlier. A lingering cloud of smoke and dust hung over the shapeless sculpture. The neighboring building bore a scorched patch on the brick, and the 2888 West Harrison building, home of Feelright Intelligence Services, suffered several cracked bricks where the recoiling dumpster struck it. Sonny felt Charlotte go still on his arm as she surveyed the scene. Her silence was now real; she had stopped talking and tears rolled down her flushed and lightly freckled cheeks.

"WOW," shouted Sonny. "LOOKS LIKE SOME KIDS GOT HOLD OF SOME CHERRY BOMBS. IT'S LUCKY NO ONE WAS HURT." He tried to approach the steel wreckage, but Simon waved him back.

Charlotte gave him a look of concern and put her hands on his ears. He watched her mouth the words, "Can you hear me, Sonny? Can you hear me?"

Sonny shook his head. He suddenly found the scene absurdly humorous. He began to giggle uncontrollably. Simon walked over and mouthed, "Come." Simon and Charlotte each took an arm and led a cackling Sonny back up the concrete stairs to their offices.

Concussion

The paramedics were the first to arrive. The van pulled up out front with lights flashing but no siren. The two perplexed medical technicians went from one building entrance to the next, looking frantically for the 2888 address, until Simon slid open the conference room window and waved them down the alley to the back of the building. Charlotte hurried them up the stairs and into the conference room, where Sonny was regaining his senses.

One of the technicians quizzed Charlotte about the explosion. The other began to check Sonny's vital signs. "Is that an injury?" the paramedic asked urgently, pointing at Sonny's ink-stained fingers.

"TONER ACCIDENT," Sonny answered over the ringing in his ears.

Soon the first police car arrived and parked at the end of the alley. Simon watched from the side window as two officers got out and inspected the twisted wreckage of the dumpster below. While one officer went to the patrol car to use the radio, Simon directed the other to the back staircase.

The medic inspected Sonny's eyes and ears with an instrument. "What's your name?"

"SONNY BRIGHT FEELRIGHT."

The medic gave his partner a concerned look, then turned gravely to Charlotte.

"That's right. That's his name," she confirmed.

"You're kidding?" He traded smiles with his partner.

"His parents were hippies," she explained.

"Never would have guessed." Turning back to Sonny, "Where do you live?"

Sonny recited his address, which Charlotte confirmed with a nod.

"Can you hear me?"

"STARTING TO. I STILL HEAR SOME RINGING."

Simon stepped from the conference room to greet the policeman, who emerged through the outer office door into the stark reception area. The technician turned to Charlotte. "He appears to have a mild concussion and he suffered trauma to his eardrums. More than anything, he's a little disoriented from the shock of the explosion. I don't think he has any permanent injuries, but it would be good to take him to the hospital for observation."

"NO," Sonny interjected, now able to follow the conversation over the ringing. "NO HOSPITAL. I'M FINE."

Charlotte gave him a stern look. "You were nearly blown up! You have a concussion! You have to go to the hospital!"

"NO!" he insisted. "NO HOSPITAL!"

"Sonny, you heard him! You have to!"

"No!"

Charlotte's face reddened with aggravation. Sensing an argument developing and his lunch break approaching, the technician intervened. "That's okay. I think he's going to be alright. He just needs to rest for the remainder of the day – no physical activity and no unnecessary stimulation. If he experiences any severe headaches, nausea or blurred vision, bring him in. And if his hearing isn't back to normal in the next twenty-four hours, have his ears checked. I don't think he ruptured an ear drum, but you can't be sure."

"You're just going to leave him here?" asked Charlotte incredulously. "You're not going to argue with him?"

"Not a lot we can do if he doesn't want to go to the hospital," he shrugged. "He's an adult, after all."

"That's debatable," she huffed. She sat down in a chair, crossed her arms firmly and gave Sonny an angry stare. The medic produced a release for Sonny to sign and, with his partner, exited the offices as fast as they had entered.

Bomb Squad

After the medical team departed, Simon ushered the policeman into the conference room and then disappeared back downstairs to the alley. The cop was mid-thirtyish with short-cropped blond hair and a weak mustache; a blond should never wear a mustache, thought Sonny. The policeman had the husky build of an athlete, but his face was growing jowly and his uniform was growing tight as age and lifestyle gained on him. When he saw Charlotte, who was still scowling, he flexed his chest and sucked in his gut.

He introduced himself as Patrolman Madigan. "You going to be alright?" he asked Sonny.

Sonny nodded. "JUST SOME KIDS PULLING A PRANK."

"Not likely. Looks like an explosive device."

Charlotte's expression changed from angry to worried. "An explosive device? What kind of explosive device?"

Patrolman Madigan puffed his chest a bit further and worked to hook his thumbs between his ample stomach and his belt, which held his gun holster, handcuffs and other assorted tools of law enforcement. "We'll know when the bomb squad gets here."

"Bomb squad!"

"Looks like it was deliberately set. Now, why don't you tell me what happened." He pulled a pad and pen from his shirt pocket and began taking Charlotte's statement, completely ignoring Sonny.

Within fifteen minutes, two more police cars and a black police van blocked the entrance to the alley. Several patrolmen and two men wearing suits sequestered the blast site with police tape and conducted a search of the area. A few curious pedestrians looked on from the sidewalk. One of the plain clothes officers, a thin black man who appeared to be in charge, donned rubber gloves and carefully inspected the wrecked dumpster and the blast damage around it. He gathered tiny fragments that were of interest and put them in plastic bags, which he labeled.

Soon, a gangly young woman in blue jeans and an oversized ski jacket appeared in the doorway of the conference room where Patrolman Madigan, now seated a bit too close to Charlotte, Sonny thought, was beginning to ask redundant questions.

"Who are you?" asked Madigan.

"Melody Gothim, CHICAGO TRIBUNE." She poked her glasses up on her beakish nose and pulled a notebook from her coat pocket. "Heard on the police scanner that there was an explosion. Thought I'd swing by and check it out."

"When did the TRIB start hiring minors?" Madigan asked condescendingly

"I'm an intern," she answered. "C'mon, give a girl a break. Give me a quote or something. It would really help me out."

Puffing with self importance, Madigan filled her in on the explosion while she scribbled in her notebook.

"Anyone hurt?" she asked.

"He was shaken up." He gestured toward Sonny.

"Who are you," she asked, her pen poised over her notebook.

"Sonny Feelright."

She paused and looked up at him. "You got a card or something?"

He retrieved a card from his jacket pocket and handed it to her. She inspected it. "You're not kidding. You really are Sonny Feelright. Weird name." She slipped the card in her pocket. "What's the 'B' stand for?"

Sonny ignored her.

"So, what do you do here?"

Already tired of the young reporter, Sonny deferred to Charlotte, who enthusiastically explained about forensic accounting.

"Who do you think did it?"

"There are a number of possibilities…," Madigan interjected, just as Simon and the black police officer from the alley stepped into the room. Madigan stood abruptly.

"What's going on here?" the black officer asked.

"I was just getting a statement from Ms. McCardle when this reporter showed up."

The black officer's faced seemed to go a shade darker. He looked at Charlotte, then Sonny, then the reporter. "We've got nothing to say. This is a crime scene. You'll have to leave."

Melody Gothim pouted, slipped her notebook back in her coat and disappeared. The officer turned back to Madigan. "You got your statement?"

"Yes, sir." He turned to Sonny. "You got anything to add to Ms. McCardle's statement?" With a clenched jaw, Sonny shook his head.

"May I?" the black man asked, gesturing to a chair at the conference table. He sat without awaiting a response. Simon sat, too.

"I'm inspector Robinson, CPD, Bureau of Investigative Services. Can you tell me what happened?"

Charlotte repeated the story she had just shared twice with Patrolman Madigan. When she finished, he turned to Sonny and said, "You're a lucky young man. If you'd been around the corner in the alley you'd be maimed or dead right now."

Charlotte's face went ashen. "Oh, Sonny," she exclaimed, and tears welled in her eyes.

"Where did the dumpster come from?"

Simon, Sonny and Charlotte all shrugged. "It's always been there," Simon answered. "No one ever uses it or dumps it. I just assumed it was abandoned."

"Probably," Robinson nodded. "Was it always tipped on its side?"

"No," said Sonny, now remembering the moments before the blast. "I noticed it for the first time when Charlotte and I rounded the corner, just before we went back for the keys."

"Did you see anyone hanging around the alley? It would have taken a couple of guys to tip it."

They all shook their heads.

"What are you thinking?" Simon asked.

"I'm thinking it was an explosive device, deliberately detonated. A sophisticated device – probably plastic explosive – intended to do serious harm to whoever was in the alley when it went off. That would be one of you."

"My God!" cried Charlotte.

"Do any of you have enemies? Anyone who might want to harm you?"

Sonny gave a chuckle, "Surely not me."

"I can't think of anyone," said Simon.

Charlotte, pale and worried, said nothing.

Adonis

It was past lunchtime when the police finally left. Sonny's hearing was approaching normal, but he had developed a slight headache and a chill. He folded his arms to keep warm. Charlotte, who had been watching him like a mother hen, said, "See. You're not well. You should have gone to the hospital."

"I'm fine. Just a little chilly." He stood.

"Well no wonder! Your pants are soaking wet!"

Sonny reached back and felt his damp behind. He took a step to turn and look behind him and immediately felt a chafing in his crotch. In high school, Sonny ran on the cross country team. Never a standout – his coach joked that he was "slow but earnest" – his most vivid memory of his running career was the unbearable rash he suffered every year as he practiced in the humid Chicago summer. He knew the chafing he now experienced was the inception of a very unpleasant and stubborn rash.

"You've got to get out of those pants," ordered Charlotte.

"I can't. I don't have anything else to wear."

Charlotte stood and ripped several large sheets

of paper from a flip chart on an easel in the corner. She handed him the pages along with a roll of masking tape. "Here, make a skirt out of these. Hang your pants on the radiator to dry."

"I'm not making a paper skirt," Sonny protested.

She gave him a stern look. "Just this once will you let me help you and do what I ask?"

Reluctantly, he took the tape and flip chart pages and, with a bull-legged shuffle, made his way through the outer lobby to the restroom. He slipped off his loafers but left his socks on against the cold tile floor. Stepping from his wet pants, he quickly realized that his briefs also were wet, so he removed them, too, carefully draping them with his pants atop the ancient iron radiator. The cold had shrunk his manhood to the size of a peanut, and he was glad there were no witnesses. He inspected the top of his thighs and wished he had some hand cream or Vaseline for the budding rash, which had the appearance of a ripening strawberry. Finally, he wrapped the flip chart pages around him and fashioned a makeshift belt out of masking tape. The paper skirt rustled like dry leaves as he stood on his toes and inspected himself in the mirror above the sink. The skirt extended to just below his knees, leaving about six inches of exposed shin above his black socks. He added a few pieces of reinforcing masking tape to the outfit, then rustled back to the outer lobby.

No sooner had the bathroom door closed then the lobby door opened and Sonny found himself facing a young man with curly jet black hair and wearing an impeccable dark blue suit. He was singularly handsome, with glistening brown eyes, a strong jaw and a discernable dimple on his chin. Though he was clean shaven, his face bore the manly shadow of a dark beard. He was as tall as Sonny, but not as lanky, with a broad chest and shoulders that tapered to a thin waist.

The man eyed Sonny's paper dress curiously. "This is temporary; my pants are drying," Sonny lamely explained.

The man nodded. "I'm Adonis. Adonis Manos. Federal Bureau of Investigation." He pulled out an ID and showed it to Sonny.

"Sonny Feelright."

"The one who got blown up?" Manos asked.

Sonny nodded, wondering how many Sonny Feelrights agent Manos knew. His paper skirt rustled as he reached out to shake hands.

"Is that from the blast?" Manos pointed at Sonny's ink-stained hand.

"No. Toner accident. It's not contagious." Manos gave the hand a shake.

"I'd like to ask some questions if you and your colleagues have a few moments."

Sonny led Manos to the conference room, where

Charlotte and Simon were still sequestered, speculating about the events of the morning. Charlotte stopped talking in mid-sentence when she caught sight of the handsome agent. Feeling absurd in his paper skirt and black socks, Sonny watched with annoyance as she sized up the visitor.

"This is Adonis," introduced Sonny, suddenly stumbling to remember Manos' last name.

"I'll say," mumbled Charlotte under her breath. Sonny's face pinched.

"Adonis Manos," Manos said. "Federal Bureau of Investigation. I'm here to ask about the explosion."

"Of course," Simon said. "We'll cooperate in any way we can."

Million Dollar Question

Manos took a seat and explained that the Chicago Police immediately called the FBI because of the suspicious nature of the explosion.

"We won't have test results for a few days, but it bore the marks of a professional job. The dumpster was placed on its side to create a 'kill' zone across the alley. The explosive looks to be some kind of plastic – military grade. Probably C-4. We're not sure how it was detonated; it could have been a timer or remote. Either way, it was no amateur."

Simon: "So, who do you think is behind it?"

"That's the million-dollar question. Could be the mob. Could be a terrorist, either domestic or foreign. That's why the FBI was called. That's why I'm here."

"Terrorist?" Charlotte repeated with surprise.

"Can you tell me a little about what you do here? What is Feelright Intelligence Services?" asked Manos.

Simon deferred to Charlotte. To Sonny, still standing by the door in his paper skirt, she seemed all too anxious to address the handsome agent.

"We do forensic accounting," she explained. "When

someone has questions about accounting and finances, they hire us to investigate and sort things out."

"Like auditors," Manos volunteered.

"Not at all!" countered Charlotte. "We do investigative work. We find what the auditors don't. If there's a financial fraud going on, we track it down by studying the numbers trail. If there's a bankruptcy and someone is trying to hide the assets, we ferret out the truth. When elected officials violate the public trust, we're the ones who track them down."

"Impressive," observed Manos. "Sounds like there could be a number of people who might have a grudge. Can you think of any cases, past or present, which might have created enemies for you?"

Charlotte gave him a sheepish frown. "Actually, we're a new firm. We haven't had any assignments yet."

"Oh," Manos nodded. "So maybe the blast was meant for the prior tenants here."

"I don't think so," she responded. "We are the prior tenants."

Manos leaned forward with a confused look, waiting for further explanation.

"You see, this used to be Blake & Company, an investment banking boutique. But Tom Blake – the managing partner – he had some … personal issues … and decided to wind down the firm. The three of us worked for Blake and decided to form our own firm. We assumed the lease on the offices, and here we are!"

"What kind of 'personal issues?' Is it possible the bomb was meant for Tom Blake?"

"Not likely," interjected Simon. "Tom's been in a rehab center in Florida for the past couple months. He had a cocaine addiction and severe depression. Tried to kill himself."

"Did he owe anyone money?"

"Nah. He was flush. We all did pretty well when the firm wound down. We were involved as advisors to Palladium Insurance in the Abbott Chemicals deal."

"Wow," remarked Manos. "That was a big deal. Made all the papers. Palladium really put it to Nancy Black. Congratulations."

"We played a bit part," said Simon, minimizing the role that he, Charlotte and Sonny played in frustrating Nancy Black, the Canadian hedge fund manager known as the Black Widow.

In any of your assignments at Blake & Company, did you cross anyone dangerous? Anyone who might have harbored a grudge?"

Simon waved a dismissive hand. "We were investment advisors. We worked with business people and professional investors. We weren't consorting with violent criminals."

Reminisces

Sonny wasn't so sure. His paper skirt shuffled audibly as he shifted his feet, remembering his brief tenure with Blake & Company. He worked for Blake for less than five months, joining after interviewing with Charlotte at a college recruiting fair. He had just graduated with his MBA from Midwestern University, a B-rated commuter college in Chicago. The economy was emerging from a severe recession, and Sonny's job prospects looked bleak – until he met Charlotte. Seduced by her beauty and fast-talking Tom Blake's promise of rich incentives, Sonny found himself working for a dysfunctional consulting firm in a job for which he was eminently ill-equipped.

The firm had only three other employees – Tom, Simon and Charlotte – and only three active projects. Two of the three blew up in their faces.

They raised money for the expansion of a company called Name Plate, which sold toy license plates made in China. Unfortunately, the license plates were made with lead-based paints, which sickened a number of children and attracted the attention of the FDA. Blake & Company was named in a lawsuit and wound up settling for more than the fee income it earned in the deal.

Gardner Plastics was another client. Dennis Gardner was caught by his wife cheating with an employee of his firm. Mrs. Gardner sued for divorce, and Dennis hired Blake & Company to value his firm as part of the divorce negotiations. Tom Blake promised Dennis a valuation that was a third of the company's actual worth, and Sonny was charged with justifying the numbers under oath in court. In the end, he refused to perjure himself, incurring the violent wrath of Dennis Gardner, who bore the temperament and the appearance of a gangster. It turned out that Gardner was Tom's uncle, and he left Tom bruised and battered in the subsequent "family dispute."

The only legitimate client of Blake & Company was Carmen Milton, CEO and President of MSC, a manufacturer of specialty coatings for steel. Carman was an attractive and willful woman who took a special interest in Sonny – as did her gay administrative assistant, Ken. Charlotte, Sonny and Simon worked hard on the MSC deal and staged a highly successful auction. The winning bid was rich, offered by chemicals giant Abbott Specialty Chemicals. But unbeknown to the trio, Tom Blake was conspiring with Nancy Black and Abbott's own CFO to take control of Abbott in a hostile and illegal tender offer.

Employing forgery and fraud, Nancy Black and Tom ensnared Sonny in their illegal scheme, leaving him with a terrible Faustian choice – either join and support the conspiracy or face disgrace and possible prison time as the convenient fall guy. It was a dark and frightening time for Sonny. But in the end Charlotte, Sonny and Simon banded together to frustrate Nancy Black and her "Evil Empire," as they called the network of conspirators.

The three Blake & Company employees were rewarded with a financial windfall when the company was dissolved following Tom Blake's breakdown and suicide attempt. More important, the experience galvanized them as a team and gave them a collective sense of purpose and power, which led to the formation of Feelright Intelligence Services.

Now, as Sonny stood in his stocking feet and paper skirt, he cringed as he remembered his terrible encounters with Nancy Black. Her arrogant aura of superiority. Her condescending abuse of her advisors and subordinates. Her uncontrolled rage. Her self flagellation. Her violent physical attacks on Tom Blake. And more than anything, her frightening intellect, unguided by any discernable moral or ethical compass.

No, Sonny thought as he pressed down a bulge in his paper skirt, Simon was wrong. The business world can very much produce predatory and violent criminals.

Lost Assignment

Manos spent more than an hour interviewing them. After exhausting his line of questioning about the firm, he quizzed them individually about their past, their affiliations and their families. The family interrogations were short. Simon's parents had both passed away, and he had only one sibling, a sister in Atlanta whom he had not seen for years. Sonny's parents, though still married, separated years earlier, leaving him after high school to fend for himself and work his way through college. Sonny's mother was living on a commune somewhere in Hawaii, while his father had run off to Maine with a younger Puerto Rican woman and their illegitimate son. Sonny had never met his half brother.

Though Charlotte's parents were still in Greater Chicago, she was cryptic when asked about her family, a topic she diligently avoided. She told the FBI agent that her parents were divorced and she was more or less estranged from them. She had not spoken with her father in over two years and not seen her mother in more than a year. She described her father as retired and her mother as a housewife.

Sonny knew a bit more, but he wasn't about to betray Charlotte's past to Agent Manos. In fact, Charlotte's father had been a successful investment banker as well as a controlling perfectionist to his only child. He pushed her into modeling at an early age, and, when she rejected the career path he selected for her, he retaliated by withholding financial support to her. Charlotte endured a bewildering adolescence, loathing and loving her father in equal measure. She'd suffered eating disorders and anxiety attacks, desperately trying to win his approval while all the time searching for a sense of self worth. When her father divorced her mother, Charlotte turned on him and set off to find her own identity and prove that she was capable of self reliance.

It took five months and much prying for Sonny to learn this much about Charlotte's family. Talking with her about the subject was like stepping on eggshells – as were many aspects of their relationship – so he no longer asked.

Manos finished his interviews, stood and passed business cards to each of them. Sonny marveled at the perfect shine of his shoes and the wrinkle-free hang of his suit on his formidable frame. Who looks like that, he thought.

"If you think of anything, anything at all, please call me." Adonis turned and left, the scent of his cologne lingering behind him. Charlotte's eyes trailed him until he disappeared through the outer door.

"This is crazy," Sonny said, as he shuffled to the chair Manos had just vacated. He sat, carefully positioning his paper skirt.

"Pretty crazy," Simon agreed.

"The blast must have been meant for someone else. Maybe someone made a mistake – got the wrong address or something."

"Probably," agreed Simon.

Charlotte said nothing. She suddenly sat up as if stung by a bee. "My God," she shrieked, "our appointment! We forgot our appointment!"

"It's alright," Sonny tried to calm her. "I'm sure they'll understand."

"No! No! We never even called!"

"Calm down," Sonny urged. "I'll call and explain. If attempted murder isn't a legitimate excuse for missing a meeting, I don't know what is."

In fact, Sonny was as anxious as Charlotte about missing the assignment. The first several weeks after starting their business was a giddy time, as they formed the LLC, wrote a business plan and set up operations. They turned Tom's old office into a conference room and upgraded their computers and office equipment – everything but the ancient Canon copier in the lobby, Sonny's own version of the computer demon "Hal."

Charlotte developed a logo and a website for the new firm, along with some ads that she placed in several trade publications. She made business cards, stationery and a three-panel brochure, which looked highly professional.

But the past three weeks had been monotonous agony as they waited for the phone to ring with their first assignment. Each day they met promptly at nine o'clock for a morning staff meeting. At each meeting they strategized about how to garner some business. Charlotte developed a mailer, which she sent to a laundry list of potential clients – law firms, accounting firms, corporations and government entities. And each day they left frustrated and anxious about their slow start, which was turning their ambitious business plan into Pulitzer Prize winning fiction.

That is, until the day before when Mr. Waring called.

Now, seated in his paper skirt, Sonny retrieved Mr. Waring's number from a notepad in his briefcase. Realizing his cell phone was still in his pants pocket in the restroom, he grabbed Charlotte's BlackBerry from the table and dialed. After one ring, an electronic voice announced that the number was not in service. Sonny checked the display while his partners watched expectantly. He double checked the number on his notepad. He had dialed correctly.

He looked from Charlotte to Simon. "I think I wrote the number down wrong."

"Argh!" huffed Charlotte. She snatched the phone from his hand and dialed information, which connected her to the Lisle Community School District. "May I speak with Stanley Waring, please?" A moment passed. Charlotte pressed her lips impatiently as she listened to the receptionist on the other end of the call. "No, I'm sure it's Stanley Waring. He's your business manager." She rolled her eyes at Sonny and Simon. "Oh," she finally said, raising her eyebrows with surprise. "I must be mistaken. I'm sorry." She disconnected.

She slumped back in her chair and cocked her head in confusion. Turning to Sonny and Simon, she said, "There is no Stanley Waring. The Lisle school district doesn't even have a business manager."

"Sounds like the explosion wasn't a mistake," observed Simon.

Sonny's skirt crackled like a burning newspaper as he shifted uncomfortably in his chair.

Ride Home

Simon immediately called Agent Manos and reported the phantom client. Manos called back an hour later. Simon put him on the speaker phone for all to hear. The agent reported that, after checking the phone records for Sonny's mobile, the call from "Stanley Waring" was made from a prepaid cell phone, making it virtually untraceable.

"It appears that someone was trying to lure you into the alley. Again, can you think of anyone who might want to hurt any of you?"

"No," Simon spoke for the group.

"Look, until we sort this out, I recommend you all take some extra precautions," Manos warned. "Pay attention to your surroundings. Avoid predictable routines. Make sure your doors are locked. You might even consider carrying a weapon for self defense."

"A weapon?" questioned Sonny. "We don't know anything about weapons."

"Well, you might want to learn," advised Manos. "Whoever set that bomb knew what they were doing."

The mood in the office was sober for the short remainder of the day. Sonny returned to the restroom and gratefully exchanged his paper skirt for his dry underwear and pants. His relief was tempered by the rash on his upper thighs, which was growing like a Chia Pet. The abrasion on his right thigh resembled the state of Florida; his left thigh was marked by a shapeless blob. He made a mental note to buy some diaper rash medicine, the only thing that could check the rapid colonization occurring in his crotch.

As five o'clock approached and the winter sun surrendered to dusk, the three partners locked up the office and descended the cold stairwell into the chilly evening. Simon led them out onto the icy sidewalk and around the corner into the alley. Charlotte nervously hugged Sonny's arm, her eyes darting about in search of threats. The wrecked dumpster was gone, hauled away hours earlier by the police on a flatbed truck. Sonny was preoccupied fighting to keep his balance while trying to minimize the chafing between his thighs.

They reached the front of the building, where Simon climbed into a waiting taxi and headed home. Sonny and Charlotte made their way to the parking lot next to the neighboring vacant building, where Sonny's BMW was the only car. He let Charlotte into the passenger side, then gingerly walked around and climbed behind the wheel. She grabbed his arm as he reached for the start button.

"Maybe you should look underneath, or under the hood or something."

"For what?"

"A bomb?"

Obediently, Sonny got out of the car and stooped to his knees on the cold parking lot. The underside of the car was a labyrinth of shadows. Sonny was no mechanic. He realized he wouldn't know a bomb from a carburetor if the two were side by side under floodlights. Feeling stupid, he stood, brushed the snow from his knees and climbed back into the car.

"Aren't you going to look under the hood?" she asked.

"Look, Charlotte, if someone wants to hurt us there's not a lot we can do about it. I still think it was all a mistake, or a coincidence, or something." He pressed the start button and the BMW purred to life without incident. Charlotte gave a sigh of relief. He pulled from the parking lot and headed to her apartment.

Sonny drove with a sullen expression. He had known Charlotte for more than six months now, but she still remained a puzzle to him. He was infatuated with her from the moment he first saw her at the university recruiting fair. Through the months, his infatuation grew to something more intense, but she seemed completely indifferent to him up until the chaotic breakup of Blake & Company. That's when they began a romantic relationship – a relationship structured around her sometimes arbitrary rules, rules that they never discussed but that he was expected to instinctively understand.

During the day while at work, her attitude toward him was completely plutonic – except for today, when she showed considerable and welcome affection. He drove her to her apartment every evening, when she transformed into a friend and lover, but still on her terms. They often shared dinner, either at local restaurants or at her apartment. Sometimes she wanted private time, and he returned to his own apartment, disappointed and lonely. She might call him late on such nights, which made his heart soar. Sometimes he spent the night with her, never by direct invitation but by natural occurrence. He lived for these nights.

"Why are you acting so weird?" she asked after a few minutes of silence.

"I'm not acting weird. I guess I'm just a little confused."

"About what?"

"About you."

"What did I do?"

"Nothing, I guess. But you sure seemed interested in that FBI agent."

"C'mon, Sonny. You have to admit he's gorgeous," she said matter-of-factly.

Sonny said nothing.

"Oh, my gosh!" she exclaimed, putting her hand on his shoulder. "You're jealous!"

Sonny frowned.

"You're jealous, aren't you?" she taunted with a grin. She reached up and rubbed the back of her hand on his cheek. He pulled away, annoyed. "You shouldn't be jealous, just because Adonis Manos is gorgeous."

It wasn't exactly the assurance for which Sonny was looking.

She continued, "Let's have dinner at my place tonight – if you feel up to it. You can stay over. I really don't want to be alone after today, and that way I can keep an eye on you after what you went through."

Sonny suddenly felt better.

Her apartment was on the western border of Chicago proper. He pulled onto her street and immediately noticed a black sedan illegally parked in front of her building. He could tell from the exhaust pouring from the tailpipe that the engine was running.

"Any idea who that might be?" he asked as he slowed.

Charlotte peered at the black car. "I have no idea." Her voice was anxious. "Maybe we should turn around."

"No," said Sonny. "It's probably someone waiting for one of your neighbors. Assassins don't wait in illegal parking zones."

As he passed the car and headed for the parking lot next to her building, the driver door opened and a dark figure stepped out.

"Stop!" said Charlotte. "It's Adonis."

"I'll say," responded a disappointed Sonny.

Charlotte lowered her window as the agent approached. "Ms. McCardle, I'm wondering if I might have a word with you."

"Is something wrong?" she asked.

"No, nothing's wrong. I just have a few more questions. Perhaps we could step into your apartment."

"Certainly," she agreed without hesitation. "Have you eaten?"

"No, I haven't."

"Well, I'm famished! Maybe we can grab a quick bite somewhere." She turned to Sonny as she opened the car door and grabbed her purse and portfolio. "You don't mind, do you?"

"No. You go ahead," he said, although he minded very much. He drove away slowly, watching in his side mirror as Charlotte climbed into the sedan with the "gorgeous" Agent Adonis Manos.

Brooding

Sonny stopped at a drug store on his way back to his tiny apartment off of Cicero Avenue near Midway Airport. After a futile search of the aisles he asked the pharmacist, a matronly woman with white hair but remarkably young skin, where he might find some A+D diaper rash medicine. He shuffled painfully after her as she stepped from behind the counter and led him to the baby medicines.

"I'll be," she observed. "We're completely out. That's never happened before." She thought for a moment. "Not to worry. We've got just the thing." She led him further down the aisle and pulled a bottle of medicated lotion from the shelf. "Here." She thrust the bottle at him. "This will work just as well."

Sonny stared at the plastic container in her hand. He felt pathetic. His career had taken a bleak turn. His girlfriend, if Charlotte really was his girlfriend, was now dining with a handsome and chiseled FBI agent – a literal and figurative Adonis. And now he couldn't even find a tube of diaper rash medicine to salve his annoying crotch rash.

She thrust the bottle closer. He took it and inspected the label. "Kind of expensive."

"No price is too high for the little ones, right? So, is it a boy or a girl?" she asked.

"Huh?"

"The baby. Is it a boy or girl?" She nodded at the lotion.

"Oh. Neither," answered Sonny. He turned and hobbled toward the front register without further explanation.

The exterior wooden stairway leading to his attic apartment was slick with ice. A stiff breeze blew from the northwest, penetrating Sonny's blue sports jacket as if it were made of gauze. His angry rash made the climb all the more treacherous. Leaning against the rail to keep from slipping, he dug his key from his coat pocket and let himself in. Before turning on a light, he found the wall thermostat and turned the temperature up until he heard the furnace kick on.

The initial incentive payments upon the break-up of Blake & Company were nearly three-quarters of a million dollars per person – more money than Sonny could comprehend. Another payment of a similar amount was to be made in a year, when the firm was finally dissolved, assuming there were no claims against the company or its assets. When they learned of their windfall, Sonny and Charlotte both assumed they would abandon their modest apartments and find something more befitting of their new wealth. Sonny half hoped that Charlotte might suggest they move in together, but she never broached the topic and he feared that initiating such a bold suggestion might impair their relationship.

But when Simon handed them their checks, the amounts were a third less than they had anticipated after taxes were taken out. Simon cautioned them not to get overly excited about their sudden wealth. "It's not as much as you think," he warned. "And paydays like this are the exception, not the rule, despite what you read."

"All the WALL STREET JOURNAL talks about is the huge bonuses everybody's earning," Sonny mused. "I figured this was par for the course."

Simon frowned, ignoring the humor. "Ninety percent of those bonuses are connived, not earned. If the payday seems too rich to be true, it probably is."

"Gosh," said Charlotte, surprised by the intensity of ever-sardonic Simon's cynicism, "that's pretty harsh. I thought you were a free-market capitalist at heart."

"I am. Keeping the markets free is the problem. Unfortunately, a lot of greedy and amoral people congregate where there are concentrations of wealth and power. And they've proven over and over they're not afraid to bend and break the rules to get more wealth and power."

Ponzi Schemes

Simon continued, "I was working on a project in California in the 1990s when there was a huge electrical power crisis. There were blackouts and brownouts. Rates skyrocketed. People had to make decisions of whether to pay their electric bills or feed their families. In the end, it turned out that a subsidiary of Enron had moved in and figured out how to manipulate the market. It wasn't a power company or distributor. It was just a trading company. They figured out that they could buy up all the power in California at regulated rates and divert it outside the state for more money. Then, when shortages developed, they were able to sell the power back into California at unregulated rates because of a hitch in the state's regulations."

"That's disgusting," sniffed Charlotte.

"Tip of the iceberg," Simon responded. "Enron was a giant criminal enterprise. They created a whole new method of accounting that allowed them to book assets today at some ridiculous future valuation that they invented. Then they borrowed against these paper assets to keep the bonuses flowing. At the end of each year they would do some accounting gymnastics to hide their real liabilities in off-book partnerships."

Sonny: "How did they get away with it? Why didn't somebody stop them?"

"Nobody even tried. They were spreading so much money around that nobody dared attack the golden goose. Their auditors were making tens of millions in fees. Enron's chairman, Kenneth Lay, spent more time handing out checks in Washington than he did running the company. The stock kept going up, so investors never questioned the financial statements, which were too confusing to understand anyway.

"Everyone called Enron 'the new age business model,' but it was just a huge Ponzi scheme, not unlike Bernie Madoff. Looking back, you have to wonder why so many wealthy and intelligent people gave their money to Madoff when the returns he was reporting were impossible. Even the SEC bought the big lie.

"But my point is, if it seems too good to be true, it probably is. And windfalls like we got in the Black Woods fight are the exception, not the rule. Starting this new business will be rough. Don't go crazy with your money. We should keep our seed bins full in case of hard times."

So Sonny and Charlotte both decided to stay put in their modest abodes until Feelright Intelligence Services was on its feet.

Visitors

One indulgence Sonny allowed himself was a more generous use of heat in his apartment. Since occupying the tiny efficiency as a college junior, he carefully marshaled the heat to save money. His winters in college were spent wrapped in layers of clothing. He went to bed early and arose as late as possible, cuddled in his warm bed. Now, whenever home, he cranked the heat until the apartment was toasty.

He flipped on the light and retrieved the bottle of lotion from a plastic bag. Better be good, he thought, as he inspected the price label – $12.98 for eight ounces. He dropped his pants and sat on his twin bed, half of a bunk bed set he'd found years before at a garage sale. He squeezed a healthy dollop of lotion into his hands and rubbed them together. The rich scent of mint filled the small room. He then smeared the goo onto his furious rash and awaited the instant relief he always got from A+D diaper rash medicine. Instead, his thighs suddenly felt as though he had straddled a branding iron. He leaped to his feet and began to dance about the apartment while he waited for the burn to abate. But his vigorous gyrations only seemed to intensify the pain. He could barely keep from screaming.

He raced to the small bathroom and doused a wash cloth in water. He pressed the cold cloth against his scalding rash and tried to wipe the pain away. It was a delicate process – rinse, dab, repeat – because the slightest touch burned like a soldering gun. He found himself sweating and panting with pain. Why had he turned the heat up?

There was a knock at the door. Still without pants, he hobbled over and cracked it open. It was Mr. Wilson, his landlord. "You alright?" he asked. "I heard some jumping. You're face is all red." Mr. Wilson eyed Sonny's blackened hand, just inches from his prying face.

"Copier toner." Sonny slid his hand out of sight. "I'm OK," he panted. "Just exercising."

"You didn't spill any toner in there, did you? That carpeting was expensive."

"No. Happened at work," Sonny answered, as he wondered if anyone would notice a toner blotch on the stained and threadbare carpet in his apartment.

Mr. Wilson peered into his teary eyes. "Well, try to keep it down. Sounds like your coming through the ceiling."

"Yes, sir."

"Did the fellas who were looking for you find you?"

"What fellows?"

"I heard two guys on your steps this afternoon. Asked them what they were doing. Wanted to know if you were the one living here. Told them you were at work."

"Who were they?"

"How should I know? Do I look like a spy?"

"What did they look like?"

"Didn't see them close. I yelled out my door. They got in their car and drove off."

"What kind of car?"

"Don't know. Black. Plain vanilla. Might have been a Town Car or something." Mr. Wilson turned and shuffled down the icy stairway. Sonny watched until he reached the bottom, then closed and locked the door.

The police, thought Sonny, as he closed the door. Or possibly Adonis Manos. He had Manos's business card and considered calling. Then he thought about Charlotte having dinner with the handsome agent and decided against it.

Sonny boiled a hot dog and warmed a can of baked beans for dinner, two staples that sustained him through college and graduate school. He turned on his tiny TV and mindlessly flipped through the channels while he ate. He kept his BlackBerry within reach in case she called. But she never did. Finally, he went to bed, where he tossed and turned as he destructively imagined how Charlotte and Adonis were spending their evening. He last checked the digital glow of his alarm clock at nearly midnight before falling into a fitful sleep.

Fickle Charlotte

He awoke the next morning feeling neither rested nor more sanguine about Charlotte and Adonis. Worse, his rash apparently had taken nourishment from the medicated lotion he applied the evening before. It had grown both geographically and in intensity. He had to waddle to the bathroom, where even the touch of the warm shower felt like flames against his inner thighs. Afterward, he stood straddle legged to let the infection air dry, then carefully slid on his underwear, wincing with every brush of the raging rash. It was the worst he had ever experienced.

He forewent dress slacks and opted for a pair of cotton Khaki's, the baggiest pants he owned. He moved slowly about the apartment as he finished dressing, trying to avoid any unnecessary contact between garment and thigh skin. Once dressed, he made his way out the door and inched slowly down the icy staircase, right foot followed by left, like a toddler. He found his way to the BMW and eased into the driver seat, giving a sigh of relief once he was comfortably settled. He pressed the start button and the engine purred to life.

So distracted was Sonny by his thoughts of Charlotte

and his agonizing rash that he completely forgot the explosion of the day before. He recalled it now, and it seemed too surreal to be true. As he gazed around at the spindly, leafless trees against the gray December sky and the modest but tidy bungalows populating the block, it seemed impossible that anyone would target Feelright Intelligence Services for harm. It had to be a prank, he concluded, a prank that went awry.

He pulled onto Cicero and faced a dilemma: should he swing by to pick up Charlotte or go straight to work? Charlotte had no driver's license and, since starting their relationship, he routinely transported her to and from work. It was done with no formal discussion or agreement. But yesterday, she abandoned him to dine with Agent Manos. And she never called in the evening or this morning. He decided to head straight to the office.

He parked his car and made the agonizing hobble from the dirt and gravel lot two doors down to the back of their building. He picked his way carefully along the icy walk to the shadowy staircase, which loomed above him like a torture machine. He struggled his way up, pulling the rails with his arms to minimize the movement of his chaffed legs.

As soon as he entered the reception area and saw Charlotte's darkened office, he knew he made a mistake. As if to announce his error, Simon walked up to him and handed him his phone. "It's Charlotte. For you. She's asking why you haven't answered her messages."

She was panicked. "Sonny, are you alright? Where are you? I'm so worried!"

"Um, I'm at the office. Just got here," he stammered.

Silence. "At the office?"

"Yeah. I didn't know if you needed a ride."

"Of course I needed a ride. You always pick me up. What made you think I didn't need a ride?"

"Well," Sonny struggled for an explanation, "I didn't hear from you, so I just thought …"

"Thought what?" she demanded, her voice rising.

"I just thought maybe you already had a ride."

"With whom?"

"I don't know … Adonis Manos, maybe."

"You've *got* to me kidding me!" she erupted. "You just figured I'd hit Agent Manos up for a ride because he interviewed me last night? And you presumed this because I didn't call you? Did you think I spent the night with him? What do you think I am, Sonny? Some kind of tart?"

"No, no," Sonny stammered. "I'm sorry. I made a terrible mistake. I'll come pick you up right now. I'll be there in ten minutes."

"For your information, I tried to call you all night! And all this morning! I must have left ten messages. And you wouldn't answer – because you thought I was shacking up with Agent Manos? Like I would try to call you while I'm screwing him?"

"Charlotte, I'll be right over."

"Don't bother!" she spat and ended the call.

Sonny pulled his phone from his pocket and looked at it for the first time since yesterday's explosion. The screen was blank except for a white glow, the dial pad was unresponsive. Yesterday's explosion and its aftermath proved fatal to something – his BlackBerry.

He hobbled back to his car and sped as fast as the morning traffic would allow to Charlotte's apartment. She was not waiting out front, so he parked and made his way across the salted sidewalk to the entrance. He got no response when he buzzed. He turned, stuffed his hands in his pockets and sighed, sending a cloud of foggy breath into the crisp morning air. Yesterday's drama was preferable to this morning's, he thought as he limped back to his car.

It was five after nine when he got back to the office. Simon and Charlotte were gathered in the conference room for their regular nine o'clock meeting. Simon looked disheveled and pallid, his bloodshot eyes circled with tired shadows. It was clear he stopped at The Red Swan on his way home yesterday evening. He was looking down at the morning newspaper. Charlotte was busily writing on a yellow legal pad.

"You're late," she observed cryptically without looking up.

"Of course I'm late! I just drove to your apartment and back looking for you!"

No response.

"Look, Charlotte, I'm sorry! My phone is broken!" He slid the glowing phone across the table toward her and then eased into a chair. Charlotte continued to scribble purposefully on her pad, ignoring his apology.

"Enough bickering," Simon scolded, looking up from his paper. "It's not going to help us win any clients. Even if we don't have a business, we at least made the morning paper."

Charlotte looked up as Simon tossed the newspaper to the center of the table. She grabbed it and looked at the masthead. Page twenty. "Front section," she observed. She searched the folded page until she found the headline. "'Police Investigate Explosion,'" she read.

"'Police are investigating an explosion that destroyed a trash dumpster and did minor damage to two buildings on Chicago's near west side yesterday morning. The blast slightly injured Sonny B. Feelright, a partner in Feelright Intelligence Services LLC, a forensic accounting firm headquartered in one of the damaged buildings on West Harrison Street.'

"'Feelright, 26, was walking in an alley between the two buildings when the blast occurred, according to police. He suffered a minor concussion and was treated by paramedics on the scene. Police suspect that the blast was caused by plastic explosives planted in the dumpster, said a spokesperson. '

"'Feelright speculated that the blast could have been an attempt at intimidation. 'We do investigative work. If there's a financial fraud going on, we track it down by studying the numbers trail. It stands to reason we've made some enemies out there,' he said.'"

She tossed the paper on the table.

"What!" Sonny cried. "I never said a word to that reporter! That's all a lie!"

Charlotte slid the paper across the table at him and shrugged indifferently.

"How can they write that?" implored Sonny, turning from Charlotte to Simon. "We should demand a retraction!"

"They write what they write," commented Simon. "Never pick a fight with someone who buys their ink in barrels."

"Let's get on with the meeting," said Charlotte impatiently. "Now that Sonny finally decided to show."

"Charlotte!" Sonny snapped, "I said I was sorry! What more to you want me to do?"

Her eyes flashed angrily. "Maybe I should seek some advice from Adonis! At least he's a lot more mature than you."

"Enough!" barked Simon. "I can't stand this bullshit!" He stood, grabbed his jacket and left the conference room, trailed by his two partners' surprised stares. Simon turned the lights off in his office and left the building without another word. Sonny and Charlotte turned and faced each other.

"Now you've done it!" she accused. "He's going to the Red Swan. If he wasn't already off the wagon, he's laying ankle deep in its tread marks today, thanks to you!"

"Me! I didn't do anything!"

"And maybe that's the problem!" she retorted before storming from the conference room and retreating to her office. A few moments later, she emerged in her overcoat carrying a leather satchel. Like Simon, she flipped off her office light and headed for the lobby door. She turned before leaving. "Don't bother yourself. I called a cab." And she was gone.

A Client Calls

Sonny slouched down in his chair and closed his eyes, wishing he could relive the past hour. The office was quiet, save for the occasional tick of the radiator under the window and the hum of a fluorescent light ballast overhead. "What the fuck just happened?" he said to no one. He stood and wandered in a bull-legged shuffle out past the dark offices into the tired reception area, wondering if Feelright Intelligence Services still existed.

Noise on the stairway caught his attention. Footsteps. Perhaps Simon returning. Or maybe Charlotte coming to her senses, he thought hopefully. But as he listened, he discerned two sets of feet making their way up the stairs. And they were walking carefully, deliberately. His imagination began to race. Perhaps yesterday's explosion wasn't an accident. Perhaps the assassins were returning to finish the job.

Sonny glanced around the office, looking for a place to hide. He hobbled to the restroom door and opened it, realizing at once that the tiny room offered little protection against a trained assassin. In fact, the entire office suite was void of hiding places or escape routes.

He would have to fight. He grabbed a mop from the restroom and hobbled to the lobby door. Sweat beaded on his forehead as the footsteps reached the upper landing. The assassins appeared to be in no hurry. The brass door handle turned and the door opened a crack. Sonny stood poised behind it, gripping the mop handle like a bat.

"I don't think anyone's here," a voice whispered. A female voice. "Yoo-hoo!" the voice called out. "Is anyone here?"

Sonny leaned the mop against the wall and swung the door open, revealing a senior-aged woman and man looking startled to see him. The couple seemed faintly familiar. The woman was slight in stature and wore a plain blue coat and flowered headscarf tied tight around her face, giving her a mousy look. The man stood behind her and wore a parka over blue work clothes. He sported a pencil thin mustache, salt and pepper colored, matching the thinning hair on his hatless head. The right side of his forehead bore a long scar and seemed to be dented slightly. He hugged a brown cardboard portfolio file to his chest.

"Can I help you?" he asked.

"You're Sonny Feelright," said the woman. It was a statement, not a question.

Sonny nodded.

"We weren't sure anyone was here."

"My colleagues are out on assignment," he lied. "Can I help you?"

"We clean your office," she said. Sonny suddenly realized where he had seen the couple; they cleaned the offices on weekends.

"Right, right. I'm sorry I didn't recognize you."

She inspected his face. "The paper says you got blown up yesterday?"

He nodded.

"It says you do forensic accounting."

He nodded again.

"We need your help."

Sonny led them to the conference room. The woman walked in front, her husband followed sheepishly behind, still hugging the portfolio, his eyes averted toward the ground. They sat with their overcoats on. Sonny was grateful when they declined his offer of coffee, because the coffee in the pot in Simon's office was hours old and starting to smell bitterly strong. He gave them each a business card along with one of Charlotte's printed brochures.

"So, how can I help you Mrs. . . . ?"

"My name is Mary Herkmeier," she began, "and this is Bill. When we read about you in the paper this morning we thought you could help us get to the bottom of some things."

Sonny nodded, unsure of how seriously to take the two odd birds across from him.

"As you know, we have a small janitorial business. Just the two of us. We started it when he got out of the hospital – after his service in Viet Nam."

"I can relate," offered Sonny. "I worked my way through college as a janitor."

Bill Herkmeier smiled for the first time, as his wife continued in a quieter, sober voice, "Bill suffered a serious head injury in the war. He also still suffers symptoms of shell shock – they call it PTSD today.

"Anyway, Bill also is an investor in stocks – a passionate investor. And he's very good at it. Kind of a savant, in fact. Over time, Bill has accumulated considerable wealth with his investing, to the point where we've been independently wealthy for the past fifteen years." Sonny eyed their practical attire and must have appeared skeptical. "We continue to work because it helps him mentally," she offered, tapping her temple with her index finger. "The reason we're here is because Bill has been frustrated lately that some of his investments are acting up."

"Acting up?" Sonny asked.

"Why don't you explain, Bill?" she said to her husband, placing a gentle hand on his forearm.

The man who'd said nothing and appeared nearly catatonic since arriving suddenly came to life. "Yeah, yeah," he said urgently, "my stocks are acting up. They're acting up. You gotta see this. You gotta see what I'm seeing." He spoke with a rapid staccato pace, barely taking time to inhale. He plopped the portfolio on the table and drew out a sheaf of computer charts and graphs.

"See this. See this." He held a financial chart up for Sonny to see. "This is my main portfolio. My main portfolio. Flat. Flat this year. Can't be. Can't be in a recovering market." He grinned inappropriately and yanked the paper away before Sonny could decipher it. He held up another page. "See this. See this. This is Quintuple Technology. Almost acquired by Intuit. Short selling before the deal fell through. Tons of short selling. Someone knew. Someone knew."

Bill yanked the page back and held up four at once. "Same with these. Four companies. Four deals. Four deals. Short selling. Tons of short selling. In an up market. Someone knew. Someone knew."

Bill may as well have been speaking Greek; Sonny was confused not only by Bill's banter but by the substance of the conversation. He grabbed Bill's waving hand long enough to read the names on the four company profiles he held. All were familiar.

Mary put her hand on Bill's arm, which immediately calmed him. He set the papers on the table, leaned back and averted his gaze to the floor again. "As you can see, Bill is quite upset about what he's discovered," she explained. "But we don't know who to turn to about it."

"Have you talked to the SEC or the Justice Department? Insider trading and securities fraud would fall under their jurisdiction."

She reached into the portfolio and pulled out a paper clipped stack of letters. She handed it to Sonny. "We've sent lots of letters to the SEC, the Justice Department and the attorney generals of five states where the companies are incorporated or operate. We've gotten only form letters in return. No one takes us seriously."

Sonny nodded gravely, not sure where to take the conversation. "Private investigations can get expensive," he tiptoed.

"As I said earlier, Mr. Feelright, my husband has been very successful in the stock market. I hope you would never try to take advantage of us."

"No! Never!" Sonny backtracked. "Integrity is what we sell. I'm just wondering why you'd want to spend personal assets on something like this."

"Because investing is his life, Mr. Feelright. And he can't do it successfully when the playing field isn't level. We're here for my husband. It's his life."

Sonny suddenly felt a deep and resonating sympathy for the Herkmeiers. "We'll need to investigate the facts before I can commit. I'll want my colleagues involved."

"So you'll take the case?" she asked hopefully.

"We'll consider the case. I'll need your documentation to review with my colleagues."

"We brought this for you," she said, sliding the portfolio toward him.

When the Herkmeiers left the office, Sonny wandered back to the conference room and looked out the window facing the alley, unsure of how seriously he should take the odd couple. Moments ago he felt compelled to help them. Now, reflecting back on their modest attire and occupation, he felt foolish to even consider their case. Parked below the window was a gleaming silver Mercedes Benz. From the styling he could tell it was new. He watched in wonder as Bill Herkmeier led his wife to the driver side and let her in, then rounded the car and climbed in the passenger side.

Collecting Simon

Sonny pulled out the contents of the portfolio. While he was no expert on securities analysis, even he could see it was a remarkably detailed collection of information. He read through a dozen or so letters that that Herkmeiers had written to authorities. Stapled to each was the responding form letter, acknowledging their complaint and committing to fully investigate. Some of the letters were more than a year old. Also included was a list of all the stocks in Bill Herkmeier's "main" portfolio, including quantities of shares held, recent closing prices and market values. If Sonny was reading it right, the portfolio was worth over twelve-million dollars. "Son of a bitch," he whispered in amazement.

He needed to gather the team and debated whom to call first. Using the landline in the reception area, he dialed Simon, putting off further drama with Charlotte. Simon didn't answer so Sonny ended the call, knowing Simon was terrible about checking messages. He drew a breath and called Charlotte. Also no answer. He pictured her staring smugly at the caller ID on her phone while it rang. "Charlotte," he said when the call rolled to voicemail, "I'm sorry about this morning. I need to talk to you. Please call me back – on Simon's cell. Mine's broken." He stuffed the Herkmeiers' papers back in the portfolio, put on his jacket and headed for the Red Swan Tavern, three blocks away, wincing at the irritation between his legs with every step.

He was nearly frozen and temporarily blinded when he stepped from the bright December sunlight into the dim neighborhood bar, the cardboard portfolio tucked under his arm. As his eyes adjusted to the darkness, he saw that the room was empty of patrons other than Simon, who sat at the bar leaning on his elbows, a half-full cocktail glass in his hand. He was watching CNBC on the TV near the ceiling. Billy the bartender, who was washing glasses in the bar sink, looked up and nodded. Sonny crossed the worn wooden floor and took the stool next to Simon, who didn't acknowledge him.

"You alright?" Sonny finally inquired.

"You here to retrieve me?" Simon asked sarcastically. "Where's Charlotte?"

"Her apartment, I think. She left in a huff. She's really pissed at me."

Simon just grunted.

"Simon, I'm sorry we got into it this morning. I screwed up. We never should have argued at work. But you can't just walk out on us like that. We need your head in the game. We need you at the office."

"We're kidding ourselves," said Simon. "We never should have started the business. It was a stupid idea on my part. We're wasting our time."

"Don't say that!" Sonny protested. "We all knew it was going to be hard getting started. You're the one who told us to brace for some dark days. These are the dark days. We've got to stick together. We've got to keep trying."

"You ever hear of cutting your losses? We had some success in the Black Woods mess, but it was luck. Pure luck. And we got drunk on our own liquor thinking we could make a business out of it."

"That's not true! We discovered the fraud! We stopped it! We brought down Nancy Black! You, Charlotte and me!"

Simon shook his weathered head and took a sip of his drink.

"Simon, we need you," Sonny continued. "We can't do this without you."

"So this is an intervention?" Simon asked.

"No," answered Sonny. "I'm here because I think we have a client."

Simon faced him for the first time, a glimmer of light in his eyes. "A client?"

Sonny related the visit by the Herkmeiers. At first, Simon seemed skeptical as Sonny described the odd couple. He pulled the contents from the portfolio and showed Simon the page about Quintuple Technology. Simon took it and examined it carefully, sliding his drink away to make room on the bar. He flipped the page over and studied it. "You've got more?" he asked.

"There are more company studies, plus a bunch of letters they sent to authorities about their suspicions. Some of them are over a year old. And here's what he called his 'main portfolio.'" He handed Simon the list of stocks.

"Christ," exclaimed Simon. "There are over eighty stocks on here. This guy's running his own private mutual fund. And he's kicking butt. This portfolio is worth millions. You say he's a janitor?"

"Cleans our offices on weekends."

"Let's move to a table," said Simon as he gathered the papers and climbed from the stool.

"Your drink," reminded Billy as they made their way to a table.

"Just bring us a couple coffees," said Simon, leaving his half finished drink on the bar.

Simon poured over the information for nearly an hour, growing more and more animated as he went. "Look at this," he said, pointing to a chart on one of the stock studies. "This guy has created an integrated system for analyzing stocks that combines elements of fundamentals analysis with cash flow valuation and technical analysis. He's able to predict future business performance with incredible clarity. And he sets precise timing points on when to buy and sell."

Sonny looked at him blankly.

"He even factors in external macro trends," Simon continued excitedly, ignoring Sonny's bewilderment. "See this chart? He's identified a correlation between the valuations of the dollar versus the Euro and the Yen and tracked this stock's performance against it. This is brilliant."

"What about their allegations?" Sonny finally asked. "Is there anything to it?"

"There's no doubt that the trading pattern on these five stocks is unusual. Definitely suspicious. But it could be coincidence."

"So, do we take the assignment?"

"Damn right," Simon gave a determined nod. "This deserves further investigation. And I really want to meet this guy. Get Charlotte and meet me back at the office. We've got work to do."

Intrusion

At that moment, the front door opened, briefly bathing the bar with sunlight. Simon glanced up and then returned his attention to the papers. Behind the bar, Billy looked but gave no nod of acknowledgement. Sonny, who sat with his back to the door, the wooden booth obscuring his view, noted a suspicious look on Billy's face. Just then, a figure appeared next to Sonny. It was a man, young, his dark features shadowed in the dim light. He wore a dark overcoat. He was staring at Simon but hadn't noticed Sonny yet.

Sonny saw that the man held something in his left hand. He stared at it, registering recognition and disbelief at once. It appeared to be a pistol. The man raised his arm and pointed the weapon at Simon, who remained engrossed in the papers before him. Instinctively, Sonny struck out and shoved the intruder's arm, just as the weapon fired. The gun, just two feet from Sonny's right ear, made a deafening sound. Simon jerked his head up. Sonny clutched his right ear. The startled assailant turned and raised the weapon again, this time pointing it at Sonny. Before he could fire a second round, a baseball bat slammed into his left wrist, sending the gun bouncing to the floor. As Billy raised the bat for another blow, the stranger sprinted for the door, clutching his wrist to his chest as he ran.

Crime Scene

"God damn punks," Billy spat as Patrolman Madigan, the first to respond to the shooting, surveyed the scene. "I could see he was up to no good as soon as he walked through the door."

"Did he say anything?" Madigan asked. Billy, Simon and Sonny, who still had a hand on his right ear, shook their heads.

"What did he look like?" All three shrugged. Madigan sighed with exasperation, his overstuffed uniform shirt wrinkling with relief as he exhaled. "Was he black or white?"

"Not black," Billy answered. "Maybe Italian or Spanish. The light is dim and he kept his face down."

"How tall?"

"Maybe five-ten. Maybe six foot. It all happened so fast."

The door to the bar opened and a familiar figure appeared wearing a bulky ski jacket. Melody Gothim of the TRIBUNE. She pulled her notepad from her pocket as she strode purposefully up to the small gathering near the table where the shooting occurred.

"You again," she said as she recognized Sonny from the day before.

"You again!" he responded. "Why the hell did you quote me in the paper? I never said any of that! I never said anything yesterday!"

"I'm sorry." The apology seemed insincere. "They weren't going to print it without an angle. Explosions, it seems, aren't all that newsworthy. Vengeance is. I took some liberties." She turned to Madigan. "The scanner said there was a shooting. What's the story?"

Madigan hooked his thumbs on his belt. "Looks like attempted robbery. Probably the time of year. We always get a spike before the holidays."

"Anyone hurt?" she asked.

"Just him," he nodded toward Sonny. "A gun fired next to his ear. May have punctured an eardrum. The guy's a crime magnet."

"Gunfire?" she asked deliciously.

"Yeah. He shoved the guy's arm and the gun went off. Then the bartender whacked the guy with a ball bat. There's the gun." He pointed to a gun lying under the table, then at a tiny hole in the paneling on the wall. "And there's where the bullet lodged. Don't touch anything. This is a crime scene."

Melody pulled a small digital camera from her coat pocket and, before anyone could stop her, snapped a picture of the gun and the bullet hole. Then she spun and snapped a picture of Sonny, who jerked his head against the bright flash.

"Hey!" he protested. "I didn't say you could take my picture."

"Sorry." She tucked the camera back in her pocket. "So, any leads?"

"No," answered Madigan. "It was dark and he kept his head down. Pointed the gun at this gentleman, then Sonny slapped his arm."

The door opened and in walked Inspector Robinson from the day before, with two plain clothes officers in tow. He frowned when he saw Patrolman Madigan talking to the reporter. He gave Melody an angry stare. "This is a crime scene. You have to go." She shrugged and left the building. He turned to Madigan. "We'll take it from here, patrolman. Wait out front and don't let anyone in." Madigan disappeared.

"Trouble kind of follows you," he said, turning to Sonny. "You alright?"

"Can't hear out of my right ear," responded Sonny.

"So, can somebody tell me what happened?"

Billy repeated the story he'd shared with Madigan. One of the detectives accompanying Madigan donned rubber gloves and carefully retrieved the gun from beneath the table and slipped it into a plastic evidence bag. "Looks like a thirty-eight caliber. Cheap. Serial number is gone."

"Street weapon," observed Robinson. "Which way did it fire?" Billy pointed toward the floor by the back wall. The other detective noted a fresh gouge in the wooden floor and traced it up to a small hole in the plaster wall about waist high. With a pen knife, he dug at the hole until a small deformed slug emerged. He put it in a second evidence bag and brought it to Robinson, who inspected it in the dim light. "This isn't going to tell us much."

"Madigan said it was a holiday robbery," Simon volunteered.

"Normally, I'd agree with him," said Robinson. "But after yesterday, I have to ask you both again, do you know of anyone who might want to hurt you?"

They both shook their heads.

"What's all that?" Robinson asked, nodding toward the financial documents still spread on the table?

"Just an assignment we're working on."

"First assignment, huh?"

"Looks that way," said Simon.

Robinson continued to question the three of them for nearly half an hour about the crime and whether it might be connected to the prior day's explosion. "Look," he finally concluded, "this was probably just a random robbery attempt. That's how I'm reporting it. Let us know if you think of anything else or if you happen to see the guy in the area again." He turned to Sonny. "You're either the unluckiest or the luckiest son of a bitch around, I'm not sure which. But try to be careful; I'm getting tired of this street."

Weak Resolve

It was early afternoon by the time Sonny and Simon left the Red Swan. Sonny, using Simon's cell phone, tried again to call Charlotte as they made their way down the block, Simon walking slowly because of age and hard living and Sonny hobbling bull-legged to minimize the painful chafing between his legs. Charlotte did not pick up, prompting an annoyed Sonny to end the call, again without leaving a message. While Simon headed back to the office, Sonny went straight to his car, determined to confront Charlotte face to face at her apartment. His anger intensified with every painful step.

Mid-afternoon traffic was light. He steamed as he drove, rehearsing what he planned to say when he confronted her. He parked in a "guest" space in the apartment parking lot and duck walked to the front of the building. He buzzed her apartment. No answer. He buzzed again. Still no answer. Exasperated, he pressed the buzzer so long that the tip of his finger turned white. The intercom clicked to static. He waited for Charlotte to say something. Silence.

"Charlotte, we have to talk!" There was a pregnant pause, and then the door lock clicked, letting him in.

Sonny's fury dissolved like road salt in a rainstorm as he made his way down the corridor to her apartment. He hesitated before knocking on her door, now fearful of the wrath awaiting him on the other side. He knocked. The door cracked open. He pushed it and cautiously peered into the apartment. Charlotte stood in the center of the living room, her back to the door, head bowed, arms across her chest. "Charlotte, I'm sorry," he almost whispered. He stepped toward her. "Charlotte?" He placed his hand softly on her shoulder. "I'm sorry, I'm sorry," he repeated. "I didn't mean to hurt you."

She spun away and looked at him with tear-puffed eyes. "It's not you!" she said almost angrily. "It's Adonis!"

Sonny tilted his head and stared at the ceiling, completely mystified at how to respond. He stood stiffly, awaiting some clarification from her but unsure if he wanted to hear it. As if venturing into a mine field, he asked, "Did he hurt you? What did he do to you?"

She plopped onto the couch. "He didn't do anything to me! It's what he said!" She buried her face in her hands and cried some more.

Sonny crossed the room and sat beside her. He gently rubbed her neck. She pushed his hand away. "What did he say?"

Charlotte took a wavering breath and looked him in the eye. "He made me promise I wouldn't tell."

"Charlotte, I can't help you if you don't tell me what he said. You can trust me."

"His visit last night. He wanted to warn me. It's about my father." She took a deep breath. "The explosion yesterday – he thinks my father is involved."

"You're father is trying to kill you?"

"No, no! They think someone might be trying to hurt me to get to him. It's got to do with his business."

He shook his head. "This doesn't make sense. I thought your father was retired."

"He consults," she sighed.

"Consults about what?"

I don't know exactly. Investments or something. Adonis wouldn't tell me more. He said he could get fired for telling me that much. He wanted me to know. To be careful." Then she turned toward him, her face suddenly angry. "And you! You think I'm having some kind of relationship with Adonis? How dare you!"

Sonny ignored the attack, still processing what he was hearing. "Who is he consulting for?"

"I don't know." The denial was unconvincing.

"We should call the police. That's what we need to do."

"I can't! Adonis made me promise. Besides, the FBI is involved. What are the police going to do?"

"Then you need to confront your father."

"Never!" she retorted. "I don't want anything to do with him. Besides, what if it's not true?"

"Well, we can't just sit back and wait for the next attack! This is crazy! This is completely nuts!"

She exhaled a shaky sigh.

"Then we need to tell Simon. He'll know what to do."

She shook her head. "I promised Adonis."

"Simon can help. He'll know what to do."

"No." More silence. Finally, Charlotte looked up decisively. "I'll talk to my mother. She'll know what he's up to. You have to come."

"Me? Why don't you just call her?"

"You don't understand. My mother is ... different. It's been over a year since we've spoken. We need to go see her."

"But why can't *you* just go see her? Why do I need to go?"

"Because we'll fight. We always fight. I need you there. To keep the peace."

Sonny frowned. "I don't know, Charlotte."

"Oh, please, Sonny." She gripped his forearm with both hands and stared pleadingly into his eyes. The delicious scent of her vanilla perfume invaded his senses like an elixir.

"Okay," he conceded, "but on one condition. We tell Simon. We're partners and he needs to know."

She gave him a pouty frown and then agreed with a hesitant nod.

Iatrophobia

Sonny remembered why he had come. "Charlotte, we have to go back to the office. Simon's waiting. We have an assignment!"

"An assignment?" she perked up. "What's it about?"

"I'll explain on the way." Sonny stood gingerly and hobbled toward the door.

"Sonny, why are you walking like that?" she asked with concern.

He stopped and turned. "It's just a rash. I got some medicine. Come on. Simon's waiting."

"No, Sonny. You're walking like an invalid. What's going on?"

"Seriously, just a little rash. I used to get them all the time." He turned and resumed his torturous trek to the door.

"Sonny, you're injured. Nobody walks like that from a rash. Where is it?"

"Upper thighs. Not to worry. Started from the wet pants yesterday. Seriously, nothing to worry about. I used to get them all the time."

She stood and marched purposefully up to him. She stared him directly in the eye as he stared back expectantly. Then, as quick as a cat, she reached down and slapped his left inner thigh between his bowed legs.

"Ouch!" he yelled as he crumbled to his knees. "Why did you do that?" He pressed his hands to his groin, waiting for the pain to subside. She stood over him, arms crossed, with a smug look.

"Show me."

"No!" he protested. "I'm not showing you anything. It's just a rash."

"Show me," she demanded with intimidating resolve.

Surrendering, he stood awkwardly and unbuckled his pants. He let them fall to his ankles as she knelt to inspect his affliction. "My God!" she reacted, when she caught sight of the rash, which now resembled raw hamburger. "We've got to get you to a doctor, right away!"

"No!" Sonny protested. "I'll be fine."

"That's not a rash. You probably have leprosy. That could develop into a staph infection. Sonny, this is serious. People die from things like this."

"No doctors, no hospitals!" he insisted.

"Sonny, I won't bend on this. This is serious. We're taking you to the emergency center. Now!"

"Simon's waiting."

She found her cell phone and called Simon, explaining the situation and agreeing to meet in the morning. "There," she said. "Simon says we can meet in the morning. We need to get you some medical help."

Sonny slumped to the ground and hugged his knees, his pants still around his ankles. "I can't," he whispered. "I can't go to the doctor."

"For God's sake, why?"

"I'm afraid." He gave her a pleading look. "I'm afraid to go."

"What are you talking about?" Her impatience was tangible.

"When I was a kid, I had a bad experience. I don't think I can do this."

Her demeanor softened. She sat down on the floor by him, cross legged. She reached out and stroked his bushy hair. "Tell me."

"Growing up, my parents didn't believe in the 'medical establishment.' They were into holistic medicine. If you got a cold, they gave you herbal tea. If you had a sore throat, they gave you honey. Fevers were the worst. My dad would make me stick my forearms in scalding water to sweat it away. Once, I got poison ivy on my arms, and my mom read somewhere that the best way to cure it was to smother it. So she wrapped my arms in cellophane and masking tape and sent me to bed. I woke up the next morning with sleeves of blisters on both arms. I spent the whole summer wearing long sleeve shirts to hide the scabs. I still have scars." He rolled up his sleeve and showed her the faint white scars on his forearm.

She looked horrified. "My God, that's awful!"

Sonny took a deep breath. "I'm about twelve, and I get a cavity. I've never been to a dentist, but my dad meets a guy at a PETA rally who once was a dentist but lost his license for some reason. But the guy is still practicing, so my dad takes me to get my tooth fixed. We go to his house, where he has a dentist chair in his attic."

"That's sick!" exclaimed Charlotte.

"They put me in the chair, and he has this neighbor lady who works as his nurse. She's middle aged, wearing jeans and a sweatshirt. A big woman. The dentist pokes around in my mouth and announces that I have two cavities, not one. Then she pins my arms to the chair while he starts drilling and filling the teeth. With no Novocain." Sonny paled at the memory.

She gave him a horrified look. "That's torture! They should all be in jail!"

"Anyway, by the time they finish with my teeth, I'm covered with sweat and ready to faint. I've never experienced such pain. I didn't go back to a dentist until I was nineteen and my wisdom teeth started coming in. Even then I waited until the pain was unbearable. Fortunately, they put me to sleep when I got those pulled. But I've hated doctors and hospitals all my life."

She stroked his bush of hair. "Sonny, you have to get that rash looked at. It won't be bad. I promise. I'll go with you. C'mon." She stood and reached out her hand. With hesitation, he took it and stood. He pulled up his trousers and, with an awkward shuffle, followed her out the door, a look of nervous resignation on his face.

Emergency Care

Charlotte directed Sonny to an emergency care clinic near her apartment. It was an efficient looking building, modern and glassy. A large lighted sign announced "Emergency Care" in red letters to welcome the sick and wounded. The asphalt driveway let to a drop off circle at the front entrance and then ventured to a neatly lined parking lot. The whole scene projected professionalism and efficiency. Sonny was terrified.

He parked the car and, accompanied by Charlotte, entered the building through an automatic revolving door. The lobby inside glistened with cleanliness and smelled of antiseptic. The large carpted room was scattered with comfortable couches, chairs and low coffee tables. Two ceiling mounted televisions in opposite corners of the space broadcast CNN, the sound turned to a low murmur. A few of the seats were occupied by people casually perusing magazines. None of them appeared terribly sick to Sonny. Charlotte led him to the admissions desk, where a professional looking receptionist greeted them. Her name tag introduced her as Rachel.

"Feeling ill?" Rachel asked with concern as she inspected Sonny, who was ghost white and nervously sweating.

"He has a rash," explained Charlotte. Sonny struggled to control his breath.

"Looks ill to me," Rachel argued. "He's not on any kind of substance, is he?"

"Absolutely not!" retorted Charlotte, while Sonny shook his head.

"Has he ever been treated for a mental disorder?"

"No!" Charlotte raised her voice in anger. "He's afraid of doctors, alright? He's here because he has a bad rash! Now are you going to treat him or continue with this ridiculous inquisition?" The other people in the waiting room turned toward the commotion.

Rachel gave Charlotte a skeptical stare, then extended a clip board with several forms attached. "Fill these out. One is a medical history. The second is a questionnaire on his current condition. The third is a consent form, which he has to sign. I also need his insurance information before we can administer care." Sonny fumbled for his wallet and retrieved his insurance card. Charlotte took it and passed it to Rachel along with a withering stare.

Sonny took his time filling out the forms, like a death row inmate eating his last meal. All the while, Rachel eyed him suspiciously from behind the admissions desk. After a full ten minutes, an impatient Charlotte snatched the clip board from him. "I don't plan to be here all night," she huffed. "You just answer the questions and I'll fill out the forms." Her encounter with the receptionist obviously was a lingering irritant. When the forms were complete, she walked them to the admissions desk and thrust them to Rachel, who accepted them with equal abruptness.

Five minutes passed before a nurse in wrinkled green scrubs emerged from a door. "Sonny Feelright?" Sonny stood and, with an impatient push from Charlotte, headed for the door. "Is that right? Sonny Feelright? Unusual name." pronounced the nurse, as the other waiting patients nodded their agreement. Sonny disappeared with the nurse through the door.

As they made their way along the labyrinth of examination rooms, the nurse studied his chart. "A rash between your legs, huh? Have you treated it with anything?"

"Just some medicated lotion I got at the pharmacy."

"Do you know what it was?"

Sonny shook his head.

"Next time, try A+D diaper medication. It's a miracle salve." She stopped at a scale in the hallway. "Climb aboard."

Sonny stepped on the scale and watched as the digital readout sped to one hundred and ninety pounds.

The heaviest he had ever been. He was mortified. She then pulled a measuring bar down to check his height. "Six-foot one inch," she announced. She motioned him into a nearby examination room and had him sit on a paper-clad examination table, where she checked his temperature, heart beat and blood pressure. "Your blood pressure normally this high, or are you just glad to see me?"

"I'm a little uncomfortable with doctors," he confessed.

"Let me guess -- bad experience as a child. We see it all the time. Not to worry. You'll like Dr. Loveland. Drop your pants and let's have a look at the problem." Sonny obediently complied. "My God!" she exclaimed when she saw his raw crotch and inner thighs, which now resembled a relief map of the Appalachian Mountains. "That's really bad. Let me get the doctor." She left the room and closed the door, leaving Sonny sitting in his underwear on the table.

A few minutes later there was a knock, but instead of a doctor the nurse poked her head in the room. "Mr. Feelright, we have a few medical students with us today and I was wondering -- if it wouldn't be an imposition -- if they could take a look at your affliction. It's such an extreme case." Before he could protest, she opened the door and ushered six young medical students into the tiny examination room – four female and two male. One by one they stooped to examine his crotch, making painful faces as they did. Utterly embarrassed, Sonny stared at the ceiling, sorry that he ever listened to Charlotte and hoping there were no urine stains on his briefs.

Dr. Loveland

"What's going on here?" asked an authoritative female voice from the doorway.

The nurse, who was bending down pointing out some of the more traumatized sections of the rash for the students, jumped up. "I was just showing the students. . . ," she started to nervously explain.

"Out!" commanded Dr. Loveland. A grateful Sonny turned his gaze to the doorway and his savior, a fair-skinned blond who could not have been much older than himself. She waited as the nurse hustled the students from the room and then closed the door and turned to Sonny. "I'm so sorry. I'm Elizabeth Loveland. That had to be awful."

"Pretty awful," he conceded, as he noted that her eyes were an enchanting shade of blue and her face, sans makeup, was fetching. Though her white medical coat hid her figure, he could tell she was petite. He took her extended hand and shook it. Her grip was firm, her skin soft and moist. "You're a doctor?"

She smiled. "A doubter?"

"I'm sorry." Sonny was again embarrassed.

"Don't be. I get it all the time. Actually, I'm doing

my residency. It's like doctor purgatory. I split my time between Northwest Memorial and here. And in my spare time I work as a bartender to help pay off my student loans. Pretty glamorous, eh?"

"I'm impressed."

"What about you, Mr. Feelright? What do you do for a living?"

Sonny struggled to answer. "Well, I was in investment banking for six months, but that didn't work out exactly. So now I'm a partner in a forensic accounting firm."

She raised her eyebrows. "Now I'm impressed."

"Don't be. My foray into investment banking was a big bust. And we just started the new company six weeks ago and haven't made a dime yet. My last legitimate job was as a janitor – a sustainability engineer – while I worked my way through grad school."

She looked at his chart. "Sonny B. Feelright. What's the "B" stand for?"

"Bright." He waited for a sarcastic chuckle.

Instead, she said, "I love it. Sonny Bright Feelright. Fantastic! I'm guessing it's not your real name. Did you change it yourself? That's so cool."

"My parents were kind of like hippies. I owe it all to them."

"Well, Sonny Bright Feelright, you should thank them for a truly unique name. I'm envious."

"Really?"

"Really. Now let's take a look at your problem."

She slipped on rubber gloves and bent to examine his rash. She retrieved a cotton ball from a container on the counter and gently dabbed a few areas. "This is more than a rash," she finally pronounced. "You appear to be suffering an allergic reaction to something. Tell me the history of this."

"Well, it started when my pants got wet when I sat in the snow."

She gave him a quizzical look. "And why were we sitting in snow?"

"There was this explosion," he began, and recounted the entire story of the past two days, including the attempted robbery at the Red Swan, from which his right ear was still ringing. It was a cathartic outpouring and took a full ten minutes to recite. She listened intently, making him completely forget his anxiety about doctors.

When he finished, she shook her head. "That's quite a tale. Tell me, what was the lotion you bought at the drug store?"

"I don't remember."

"Well, when you get home throw it out. You're allergic to whatever it is. I'm going to give you a shot to counter the allergy, along with a prescription for a topical steroid medication to mitigate the irritation. I also want to check your ears while you're here."

"A shot?" he asked fearfully.

"Big baby," she smiled, and his anxiety fled like a cat in a kennel. With practiced efficiency she prepared the hypodermic needle and administered the shot. He grimaced unnecessarily, barely feeling a pinch. "That wasn't so bad, was it? Now let's take a look at your ears." She peered through an otoscope deep into his right ear, then his left. "I don't see any physical damage; your hearing should be back to normal by tomorrow. But you really need to be careful. Next time you're involved in a bombing or a robbery, please consider hearing protection."

"I'll try to remember that," he smiled.

Sonny pulled up his trousers and tucked in his shirt while she made notes on his chart. "C'mon, I'll walk you out," she offered.

She wrote out a prescription and the two of them emerged into the lobby. Charlotte, still wearing a ready-for-combat expression, stood as they approached her. She looked at her watch, pointedly. "I see you survived," she observed.

"Nothing to it," said Sonny. "Dr. Loveland here was fantastic."

"Hi. I'm Elizabeth Loveland."The doctor extended a hand to Charlotte.

"Charlotte McCardle," Charlotte responded as she cautiously shook hands. "Sonny and I are colleagues."

"I would have taken you more for a fashion model, not a forensic accountant."

"Sonny told you about our work?"

"All about it. Sounds pretty exciting. Bombings, shootings. A lot more exciting than interning here." She turned to Sonny. "The steroids should start to heal things in the next twenty-four hours. If it gets any worse, call us right away. Okay?"

He nodded obediently.

"Well, it was good meeting you both." Dr. Loveland turned and disappeared back into the inner sanctum. Sonny and Charlotte both watched as the door closed behind her.

Charlotte turned to Sonny. "Looks like you're over your fear of doctors."

He blushed. "She was okay."

"What did she mean by 'shootings'?"

He swallowed. "Maybe I forgot to mention. Simon and I were almost robbed today. At the Red Swan."

"What?!"

"It was nothing really. We were going over some information from the client I called you about. Some guy came in and tried to rob the place."

"With a gun?! There was a shooting?!"

Rachel looked up and gave Charlotte a disapproving stare.

"Well, yeah, kind of. He came in and pointed a gun

at Simon and it went off when I hit his arm. Then Billy came over and whacked his wrist with a ball bat, and the guy ran off."

"My God, Sonny, when were you going to tell me this?" She was shrieking now. "You tell Dr. Lovelace, but you don't think to tell me?"

"Loveland. And I'm sorry, Charlotte. I didn't think of it. You were so upset at your apartment and all. I'm sorry."

"And what *else* are you not telling me?"

"Ahem," Rachel cleared her throat.

"Alright!" Charlotte screamed at the receptionist. "We're leaving!" And she stormed from the room with a chastened Sonny in close pursuit.

Hazardous Conditions

Sonny awoke before five in the morning after a restless sleep. He was unsettled. His evening with Charlotte had been stressful. On the entire drive back to her apartment he apologized for failing to tell her about the robbery attempt. She eventually professed forgiveness, but remained distant and aloof. She didn't protest when he suggested they grab dinner at a spaghetti house near her place. But she was distracted during the meal. By the end of the evening Sonny was emotionally exhausted and glad when she did not invite him into her apartment to spend the night.

Back in the sanctuary of his own humble abode, he looked forward to blessed sleep. His body and emotions were willing, but his mind raced uncontrollably. He recounted the roller coaster of the past two days. The explosion and robbery attempt. The drama with Charlotte. The bizarre encounter with the Herkmeiers, who, in the depths of night, seemed like laughable caricatures, not legitimate clients. He remembered the six months he spent with Blake & Company, reliving the trauma of his confrontation with Nancy Black. He thought about Dr. Elizabeth Loveland, remembering with a shudder his horrible dental experience as a child. And most disturbing of all, he thought about his weight – 190 pounds. What was happening to him?

He awoke and donned a sweat suit and running shoes, determined to get some exercise despite his rash. He smeared his thighs with the prescription salve, which he and Charlotte picked up at the pharmacy on their way to dinner. Dr. Loveland was right – the shot and medication were already shrinking the relief maps on his thighs. He pulled on his running shoes and left the apartment, picking his way carefully down the ice encrusted stairs. His breath made thin puffs of condensation in the crisp winter air. He jogged on the road, only slightly bow legged, because most of the sidewalks were treacherous with ice. He ran to the end of his street, turned right and crossed Cicero Avenue. The morning was dark and the traffic was light. He ran almost a mile and then turned and headed back along the same route, disgusted by how out of shape he felt.

He was sweaty and winded as he made his way back across Cicero and approached his street. How had he let himself get so heavy? Never again, he told himself. Never again would he let his life get so unbalanced. Never again would he let circumstances dictate his priorities. Never again would he let others control his emotions. Never again would he weigh one hundred and ninety pounds. He determined to take more control of his life—in all things.

He turned onto his street and noted a black sedan sitting across from his apartment, parking lights glowing and engine running. As he approached it, he could see two shadowy figures inside. He slowed to a walk and made his way to the sidewalk opposite the car. As he picked his way between ice patches on the pavement, he watched the car warily through the corner of his eye. His adrenal glands kicked into overdrive. He could tell the two figures inside were men, but he could not make out their features in the darkness. And they were watching him. He was sure they were watching him. He toyed with approaching the vehicle but thought better of it. He resolved that if a car door opened he would run. Relief swept through him when he reached the wooden stairway leading to his apartment. As he began his ascent, the car's headlights came on and it pulled from the curb, making its way slowly down the street and around the corner out of sight.

Inside the car, the man in the passenger seat rubbed his bandaged wrist. "We could have taken him. We should have finished it."

The driver, Kafele, gave his brother Bomani an impatient look. "We were ordered to stand down."

"I don't care! We had him!"

"You fucked up twice!" Kafele snapped. "We can't afford to fuck up again!"

"He was lucky both times. That's all."

"We were ordered to stand down and watch him. That's what we're going to do!"

"But the job . . . ."

"Enough! We'll get another chance! And next time we won't miss."

The Town Car eased into the growing stream of traffic on Cicero.

Double-0-Sonny

Sonny was wary as he left his apartment and drove to Charlotte's, on edge about the mysterious car. Was it somehow related to the bombing? What was Charlotte's father up to, and why would someone try to hurt Charlotte? And if someone really had tried to hurt Charlotte, would they try again? Equally unsettling, yesterday's robbery attempt underscored how random and violent the world could be. As he made his way through the morning rush hour, every car and shadow seemed to harbor a threat.

Normally, he waited in the street in front of Charlotte's apartment for her to walk to the BMW. This morning he parked the idling vehicle at the curb and greeted her as she emerged from the building. She didn't embrace him, not a good sign. "To what do I owe this special attention," she asked as they walked to the car.

"This morning, as I got back from jogging. . . ."

"Jogging? Why were you jogging? You were just at the emergency clinic yesterday!"

"I'm okay. The medicine is working. I just needed some exercise. Let me finish … so, I'm coming back from jogging and there's this black car parked across the street from my place. Its parking lights were on and its engine was running. There were two guys inside, and I think they were watching me."

"Did they say anything?"

"No. When I got to the steps they pulled away."

"Are you sure it wasn't someone going to work?"

"I don't think so. I've never seen the car before and, frankly, not a lot of people on that block are early risers. It's not exactly where the over achievers reside." He opened the door for her and walked around to the driver side.

"What did they look like?" she asked as he pulled from the curb.

"Couldn't tell. Too dark. Plus, I didn't want to stare at them. Maybe we should call the police."

"Sonny, it was dark out. Maybe you're just mistaken?"

He jerked his head. "You don't believe me? I'm telling you, that car was waiting for me! They were watching me!"

"Okay, okay. I believe you." She seemed unconvinced.

More silence. "We should call the police -- or Agent Manos."

Charlotte turned and gave him a pleading look. "Sonny, they'll think it's my father. Something bad will happen to him. I just know it."

"Look, Charlotte, someone's trying to hurt you and they may be stalking me, all because of your father. Let him take the heat."

"I, I, I..." she stammered.

"I don't get it. I thought you hated him."

"He's my father!" she argued.

Her logic made no sense to Sonny, but he conceded anyway. "Alright, we won't call the police. But we have to tell Simon what's going on." She gave a half-hearted nod.

Sonny parked the car in the lot down the street. They both were nervous as they made their way to the 2888 entrance. The dark stairway seemed more menacing than ever, and they were relieved to finally enter the office suite. The aroma of strong coffee filled the air, alerting them that Simon was already at work. They were surprised to hear voices emanating from the conference room. They entered to find Simon sharing a cup of coffee with Agent Manos. Manos rose, looking formidable in an immaculate tailored black suit. Sonny greeted him with a handshake. Charlotte stood back warily.

"Agent Manos was waiting when I arrived," said Simon. "He heard about our episode at the Red Swan yesterday and wanted to learn more."

Sonny made a curious face. "How did you hear about that?"

Before Manos could respond, Simon tossed the morning's CHICAGO TRIBUNE on the table opened to page four. "You're moving up in the world, Sonny. You made it to the fourth page."

Sonny grabbed the paper and was greeted by a two column photo of himself sitting in a booth at the Red Swan. A small inset photo showed the gun beneath the table. A second inset showed the bullet hole in the paneling.

Charlotte snatched the paper from him and stared with surprise at the photo. "My God! Your picture is in here!" She began to read the article aloud:

Narrow Escape for Sleuth, Again

By Melody Gothim

Chicago -- For the second time in two days, accounting sleuth Sonny B. Feelright escaped injury and possibly death when he foiled an armed robbery attempt yesterday at the Red Swan Tavern on West Harrison Street. Feelright, 26, a partner and namesake of Feelright Intelligence Services LLP, was conducting a business meeting in the establishment just before noon when a lone assailant entered brandishing a handgun.

When the gunman leveled the weapon at Simon Courtney, a partner in the consulting firm, Feelright struck the assailant's arm, forcing him to fire into a paneled wall. Before the gunmen could fire a second shot, bartender Billy Walden struck the robber on the wrist with a baseball bat, knocking the gun from his hand and sending him fleeing from the scene. Police are still searching for the suspect, described as a white male with dark hair wearing a long dark overcoat. He was last seen running east on Harrison.

It was Feelright's second brush with danger in two days. Tuesday morning he was slightly injured when a bomb exploded in an alley next to Feelright Intelligence Services LLP's offices, also on West Harrison Street just a few blocks east of the Red Swan. Police believe the bombing was a deliberate attack aimed at Feelright and his firm. There are no leads in the bombing investigation, according to a police spokesperson.

Patrolman Donald Madigan, first on the scene of yesterday's shooting, lauded Feelright for his bravery. "While we don't encourage citizens to resist when facing armed gunmen, Feelright's quick action probably saved people from serious injury or death. He's narrowly escaped extreme danger twice this week. He's like James Bond."

Madigan wouldn't speculate on the motive of the gunman or rule out that the two attacks might be linked.

After Tuesday's explosion, Feelright conceded that his firm had enemies: "We do investigative work. If there's a financial fraud going on, we track it down by studying the numbers trail. It stands to reason we've made some enemies out there."

Charlotte handed the paper back to Sonny. "That's a lot more dramatic than you described to me," she huffed.

"That's ridiculous!" cried an incredulous Sonny. "That's not how it happened at all. Madigan didn't say any of that. He said it was a petty robbery because of the holiday. And I never said anything to her. How can she get away with this?" He looked pleadingly at Simon.

"Definitely an exaggeration," Simon agreed.

"It's an out and out lie!" Sonny protested.

"Look, Sonny," interrupted Manos, "I asked you guys to call me if anything unusual happened. I'd say a robbery attempt fits the bill, even if it was a petty street crime. But we can't be sure of that."

"But the police said they get a bunch of these types of crimes this time of year."

"Simon tells me the gunman never said a word. He didn't demand money."

"Yea, but …"

"He didn't go to the bar, where the money would be. He walked straight to your booth."

"Yea, but …"

"And you said he was wearing a decent coat, right? If he can afford decent clothes, why would he be holding up the Red Swan? And why would he do it early in the day, when the cash drawer is empty? If he was looking for money, why would he even hold up a two-bit tavern? Why wouldn't he find someplace a little more lucrative?"

Sonny had no answers. He sat down, still in his coat. Charlotte sat, too.

"What was his motive, Sonny? I don't think it was money. And I shouldn't have to learn about this from the TRIBUNE. I'm not your adversary. I'm trying to help you. Now, is there anything else you're not telling me?"

Sonny, ready to reveal his encounter with the mysterious car this morning, glanced at Charlotte, who gave him a stern look. "No. I don't think so," he answered.

They all sat in sober silence. "Well, at least we got some good publicity out of it," Simon finally quipped. "Right, Mr. Bond?" His comment would prove prophetic.

Staff Meeting

Manos stayed another half hour, questioning Sonny about the shooting. When he finished, Charlotte walked him to the outer office, where they spoke briefly. Sonny watched from his seat in the conference room as Charlotte gave Adonis a pleading look and shook her head. They appeared to be arguing in low voices. She seemed distracted when she rejoined her partners.

"Let's talk about Bill Herkmeier," Simon announced, oblivious to Charlotte's consternation. "I've studied his data. His research is multi-layered and complex, but he's able to synthesize a lot of data into simple and highly reliable conclusions. I made some notes for us to review." He handed them each a copy of a single-spaced page of bulleted notes. "I only have a limited history of his transactions, but I'm guessing he rarely loses on his investments. His market timing is impeccable."

Skeptical, Charlotte asked, "And this is the janitor, the janitor I see here on Saturdays who flashes that silly grin at the wrong times and can't even say hello?"

"Be careful not to judge a book by its cover, Charlotte," Simon cautioned. "This guy is some kind of savant."

"Then why is he cleaning offices for a living?"

"They live in Hinsdale," Simon responded. "Not exactly a blue collar community."

"And they drive a new Mercedes," volunteered Sonny. "I saw it when they came in."

Charlotte looked from one to the other and then nodded, convinced.

Simon ran through his notes, which described a series of stock transactions and the underlying analysis. His excitement was infectious and he quickly captured Sonny and Charlotte's attention, despite the distractions of the morning. When he finished, Sonny asked, "What about his allegations? Are they true?"

"Yesterday, I thought Herkmeier was overreacting to a few bad bets. But after going through his analysis, I don't think there's any doubt that somebody is trading on inside information. Given his history of success, there's no way he could suffer such losses on a half a dozen stocks in such a period. And the stocks were all involved in some kind of significant material events. Two were planning acquisitions that fell through; two were takeover targets; one was an initial public offering; and the sixth company lost a major patent lawsuit. In every case, the stocks had big swings in value and trading volume *before* the news went public."

"It could be coincidence," Charlotte offered. "Tech companies are volatile by definition."

"I don't think so." Simon handed out another page displaying six computer generated line graphs. "Look at these charts. Somebody knew and was getting in or out ahead of the news."

"Where's the SEC? Aren't they supposed to monitor things like this?" Charlotte asked.

"Good question." Simon produced the stack of letters the Herkmeiers had sent to various authorities. "The Herkmeiers have sent letters to every official with jurisdiction. I guess you only rate form letters back if you're an average Joe."

"So, we're taking the case?" asked Sonny.

Simon nodded.

Charlotte's cell phone chirped.

"Hello," she answered and then listened intently. "Just a minute...." She scrambled for a pad and pen. "Okay, go ahead...." She jotted notes, flipped the page and wrote some more. "Thanks."

She looked from Simon to Sonny. "You're not going to believe this. That was the answering service. We have six calls, all prospective clients. They all referenced the article in the paper this morning. Sue, at the answering service, says you're very brave. She's single and wants to meet you."

Sonny dropped his head and muttered, "I hate Melody Gothim."

"She's the best salesperson we have," remarked Charlotte. "You should send her a thank you."

"Let's change the subject. What do we do about the Herkmeier case?"

"There has to be a common thread among those companies. When we find it, we'll be able to unravel the mystery." Simon proceeded to lay out their plan of investigation – he would study the companies in more detail, looking further back for any signs of unusual trading. Sonny would look at their competitors to see if more technology companies bore signs of mischievous stock trading. Charlotte would look for common connections – law firms, auditors, board members – people who might have access to inside information and be intimate with all six companies.

With tasks assigned, Charlotte gathered her notes and stood to head for her office. "I need to return all these calls. . . ."

"Wait," Sonny interrupted. "There's one more item of business. There's the matter about your father."

Galleon

She frowned at him and then plopped back down in her chair.

Simon turned to Sonny. "What about her father?"

"Charlotte?" prodded Sonny. When she didn't speak, he proceeded to explain to Simon about Adonis's visit to her apartment, his warning about Douglas McCardle, and Sonny's own suspicions of the mysterious black car he saw that morning.

Simon turned to Charlotte, now slumped in her chair. "What exactly does your father do?"

"I don't know. He consults."

"About what?"

"Stocks, I guess."

Simon eyed her suspiciously. "I thought he was a retired investment banker."

"He is. I mean he was. He retired when First Boston imploded in 2001. He looked for other jobs in banking, but there was a recession at the time. A couple years later he started consulting. "

"And you don't know anything about his business?"

"It was when my parents' marriage was falling apart. I did everything I could to avoid them – him especially. All I know is that he's been very successful. As soon as the divorce was final he bought a house and some land on the North Shore. He got a whole new wardrobe and bought a Porsche – a 911 Turbo Cabriolet, brand new. My mom's attorney wanted to take him back to court, figuring he had been hiding assets, but she wanted no part of it. She'd had enough of him."

Sonny made a mental note to investigate the price of a 911 Turbo Cabriolet.

"Who were some of his clients?"

"Institutional investors, a few hedge funds. He had a pretty good network from First Boston. I guess he tapped into it to build his firm."

Simon frowned. "An expert network."

Sonny gave a quizzical look.

"A recent phenomenon in the financial world," explained Simon. "Hedge funds will pay a fortune for any tidbit that will give them a trading advantage. Expert networks are consultants who sell information based on their expertise and experience. They usually have some area of specialty – technology, tax laws, currency."

"Is it legal?" asked Sonny.

"Theoretically, yes. In practice the lines can get blurred. You ever hear of Galleon Group?"

"It's been in the paper," Sonny responded.

"It was a hedge fund started by a guy named Raj Rajaratnam in 1997. He was an immigrant from Sri Lanka. Within ten years the guy is a billionaire with over seven-billion dollars under management. Everything he touched seemed to turn to gold. He's hitting it out of the park and attracting the bluest of blue chip clients, including some of the major banks and pension funds. Now, logic would tell you that his performance was impossible. But no one wanted to look too closely for fear of killing the golden goose."

"Wouldn't the SEC notice?" Charlotte asked.

Simon gave a sarcastic chuckle. "The game is rigged. Wall Street is big on self regulation. In this case, it's the Financial Industry Regulatory Authority that's supposed to keep an eye on things. It's their job to track trading and report suspicious activity back to the SEC. But surprisingly little ever looks suspicious, and it's no wonder, with hedge funds throwing so much money around. They're buying research and paying trading fees to all the other firms on the Street. Not to mention all the money they spend on lobbying."

"Like giving a drug addict the key to the medicine cabinet," volunteered Sonny.

"Raj escaped the notice of the regulatory authorities; he was done in by his own brother. In 2006, his little brother, who ran his own hedge fund, attracted the scrutiny of the feds. During their investigation they stumbled across some e-mails that suggested there might be some illegal information passing between the two brothers. They put a wiretap on Raj's phone, and, low and behold, he's collecting inside information all over the place. He had illegal confidants at IBM and Intel. His most prominent source was an ex-McKinsey & Company partner who sat on the boards of Goldman Sachs and Proctor & Gamble. The guy would call Raj after board meetings to tell him what was going on. When the SEC and Justice Department brought charges against Raj in 2009, his blue chip clients fled like rats off a sinking ship. Galleon was out of business within weeks. It wound up being the biggest case of insider trading ever uncovered. Around twenty people were convicted of crimes. Raj is now doing eleven years in federal prison."

"The biggest case in history and most people don't know about it," Sonny mused.

"Not necessarily the biggest case in history. Just the biggest case ever uncovered. Crooks gravitate to money. Wall Street represents the biggest concentration of wealth in the world. It's like Fort Knox, only without all the security. It attracts the best and brightest. Insider trading is endemic. The bad guys are just being more careful since Raj went down."

Simon turned to Charlotte. "You have no idea who

your father works for?" The question was shadowed with skepticism.

She shook her head.

"Did Adonis give you any clue who might be trying to hurt you?"

She stared at the table, mute.

Simon's eyes flashed with anger and he rose from his chair to stand over her. "Damnit!" he yelled, pounding his fist on the table, "This isn't a game, Charlotte! To hell with your father! What if Sonny had been seriously hurt in that explosion? What if one of us had been shot? Do you want to carry that on your conscience?"

She began to cry and shake her head. Sonny desperately wanted to push Simon away and wrap his arms around her, to wipe the warm tears from her cheeks and assure her that things would be alright, that it was all just a bad dream. But he said nothing.

Danny Byrne

"Danny Byrne," she whispered between muffled sobs.

"What?"

"Danny Byrne." She took a wavering breath. "Adonis thinks it was Danny Byrne."

"Who is Danny Byrne?"

She shrugged. "I met him just before I left for college. He came by our house and dropped off some papers. I only met him once, but he was charming. Adonis says he's a gangster of some kind. He said my father has done business with him. The FBI is speculating that Danny Byrne might be behind the bombing. That he might be sending a message to my father."

Sonny stepped from the room and returned with his laptop. He went on the internet and typed in Danny Byrne. He quickly learned that Danny Byrne is a common name. There were numerous Danny Byrnes on LinkedIn and Facebook. There was a folksinger, a famous English soccer player and an actor, all named Danny Byrne. There was a YouTube video of a teenager named Danny Byrne being pulled by a car on a skateboard. One Danny Byrne managed a blog site. The

Danny Byrne on Twitter billed himself as "the master of Foxhounds."

"Popular name," he observed. "I see some assholes, but no obvious gangsters named Danny Byrne."

Her head down, voice almost a whisper, Charlotte said, "Try the Cleveland Public Library. Newspaper archives." Sonny gazed at her. She obviously had already researched Danny Byrne.

Sonny tapped the keyboard. "Okay, here we go. Looks like he was acquitted in 1975 in a car bombing in Cleveland. He was only seventeen at the time."

"I'll save you some time," Charlotte volunteered, her voice stronger. "Danny Byrne grew up in Cleveland and became a protégé of Danny Greene."

"The Irish mob boss?" asked Simon.

She nodded.

Sonny shrugged his ignorance.

"In the 70s, Danny Greene was a powerful mobster in Cleveland," explained Simon. "He started out as a dockworker and worked his way up to become the Local union president. Longshoreman's Union. After he was convicted of union corruption, he became a mob enforcer and an FBI informant. He started the Celtic Club, a bunch of Irish thugs. Eventually, he got on the wrong side of the mafia, which caused a huge gang war."

"How do you know all this," asked Sonny.

"Because it was national news at the time and I was in Law School, so we studied it. In the 1970s, Cleveland was the bombing capital of the world. They called it Bomb City, USA. In 1976 alone there were 36 bombings – mostly car bombs. A bunch of people were killed, including some innocents. The authorities were helpless to stop it. There were at least eight attempted hits on Danny Greene. A car bomb finally got him in 1977. In the aftermath, Congress passed the RICO statute, which made it easier to bust the mob on racketeering charges. It eventually led to the demise of much of the New York mafia."

"So, where does Danny Byrne fit in?"

Charlotte continued. "He was arrested three times in the mid 1970s, -- for a bombing, for witness intimidation and for drug trafficking. He was never convicted of anything. Just before Danny Greene was murdered, Byrne left Cleveland for Chicago, probably to get out of harm's way. He owns an exotic car dealership here, but Adonis says it's just a front for organized crime. The FBI's been watching him for years, which is why they connected him to my father. That and the C-4 in the dumpster. I guess it was a favorite of Danny Greene."

They sat in sober silence. "I'm sorry," Charlotte finally muttered. "I'll deal with it, I promise." She gathered her notes and stood. "I've got some calls to make." She left the conference room and returned to her office, closing the scarred wooden door behind her, something she rarely did.

"We need to learn more about Danny Byrne," Simon declared when Charlotte was out of earshot. "Sonny, do an internet search. There are services that do background checks. Find one. Meanwhile, I'm going to ask some friends at the CPD about Byrne. And I'm going to check with some of my old banking contacts about Charlotte's father."

IPhone

In the afternoon Sonny slipped away to the Verizon store, where a cocky young salesman, face peppered with acne, examined his glowing Blackberry and quickly pronounced it dead. The clerk led Sonny through the store, showing him the multitude of options to replace it.

"I guess I just want another BlackBerry," Sonny finally decided.

"No you don't."

"I don't?"

"You want an IPhone," declared the salesman.

"I do?"

"Absolutely. The BlackBerry is a dinosaur. A relic. Ancient history. Heck, I'd take a Droid over the BlackBerry any day. But the IPhone is where it's at." The salesman led Sonny to the IPhone display and gave him a five-minute demonstration. "And this is just the tip of the iceberg. There are thousands of aps that will make it do almost anything a computer will do. You definitely need an IPhone."

"Okay, I guess," Sonny acquiesced.

Fifteen minutes later, Sonny left the store with

his new IPhone in hand. He climbed into his car and clumsily dialed his voice mail, instantly realizing the IPhone touch screen would take some getting used to. An electronic voice announced that he had twelve messages. He scrolled through them. The first ten were Charlotte, trying to reach him after her dinner with Adonis. She left a message every hour through the evening and night, panic growing in her voice with each successive voicemail. "Oh, Sonny, please call me back," she begged in the final message. "I don't know what I'll do if anything happens to you." He flushed with embarrassment for ever doubting her.

The eleventh message was a female, but not Charlotte. "Hey, Sonny, this is Melody over at the TRIB. Wanted your take on the article this morning. And to maybe get some material for a follow up. Things are looking good here for a permanent job when I finish my internship. My editor can't believe I'm producing byline stories. Call me back."

Disgusted, Sonny erased the message without waiting to hear the return number. "He shouldn't believe your byline stories," Sonny muttered.

Call twelve also was a female, not Charlotte. "Is this James Bond? This is your doctor. Just got done reading the article in the TRIB. Very impressive, Sonny, not that I doubted you. Anyway, call me and let me know how your rash is doing." Elizabeth Loveland then left her cell number.

Sonny saved the message and leaned back in the car seat, remembering his pleasant encounter with her. He thought about Charlotte and the heartfelt panic in her messages. After a brief internal debate, he dialed Elizabeth Loveland.

"Sonny!" she answered brightly on the second ring.

"Hello Dr. Loveland. Just got your message. Sorry it took me so long. My phone was broken. I just got a new one."

"It's Liz," she insisted. "I read about you in the paper this morning. You made it sound a lot less dramatic when you told me."

"Trust me, the TRIB exaggerates. It was nothing like that."

"Right, Mr. Bond. So, how's the rash? And the hearing?"

"Speak up! Just kidding. You're a miracle worker. The medicine is working great. I even jogged this morning. And my hearing is back to normal."

"That's good to hear. Even more important, what kind of phone did you get?"

"I swapped my BlackBerry for an IPhone."

"Good choice. Very befitting of James Bond. I guess we now have something in common."

"You have an IPhone?"

"I'm an Apple junkie. You'll love it. We can talk on Face Time and see each other. Maybe sometime I can give you some tips and recommend some aps."

"I'd like that," responded Sonny. The admission, while genuine, made him uncomfortable.

"So, we'll stay in touch?" she asked.

Sonny sensed it was an invitation. "Absolutely," was all he could muster in response. Before leaving the parking lot he saved her number, not under Dr. Loveland, but under Liz.

Busy

Thanks to Melody Gothim and her sensationalized accounts in the TRIBUNE, Feelright Intelligence Services LLC ramped from famine to feast overnight. It was hired by a local restaurant chain to recommend ways to reduce liquor shrinkage, an investigation assigned to Simon by proclamation of the three partners. They were retained to search for hidden assets in three separate divorce cases. The owner of a Chicago machine shop hired them to determine if his purchasing manager was on the take. And they were invited to bid on a contract to reconstruct Chicago's capital improvement budget after a state audit determined the accounting records were unintelligible; Simon summarily declined the invitation, calling the dispute between the state of Illinois and its largest city "a titanic battle between evil and evil."

Melody Gothim continued to call. Sonny mistakenly answered the first time, hanging up as soon as he recognized it was her. He saved the number in his contacts under the name "Liar." Thereafter, he let her calls roll into voice mail. Despite his loathing for the woman, he couldn't help but be impressed by her perseverance, as she left message after message, undeterred.

Other than the liquor study, none of the assignments required much field work, just a lot of document examination and report writing. The offices soon were crammed with boxes and computer files of financial and legal records. For Sonny and Charlotte, the days became marathons of reading and calculating. Two long tables were added to the now crowded conference room for sorting and segregating documents. For his part, Simon remained fixated on the Herkmeier investigation, even though it was probably their least lucrative assignment. Overnight, the partners went from impatiently waiting for the phone to ring to sixteen hour days with barely enough time for a working lunch.

But if business was heating up, Sonny's relationship with Charlotte remained cool. She regained her professional demeanor and maintained a torrid pace at work, leading the daily staff meetings and organizing the multiple assignments like a field general. Sonny still picked her up in the morning and dropped her off in the evening, later and later each night it seemed. But she declined his daily invitations to dinner and deflected personal questions, refusing to engage him in any conversation beyond work. She rarely joked or smiled. The more distant she became, the more he desired her.

While the inflow or work consumed them, it was only a partial distraction from the shadowy threat they all felt. There was no further conversation about Charlotte's father; Sonny waited for Simon to broach the topic with her, fearing the confrontation that might result. For his part, Sonny was ever-conscious of his surroundings, especially when venturing outside his apartment and the office. A number of times when driving he thought he saw the mysterious black sedan, which haunted him like a phantom. But it always kept its distance and changed direction if he looked its way, so he couldn't be sure. Every black car he passed made his heart race. He found himself empathizing with Danny Greene and the stress he must have felt waiting for the next inevitable assassination attempt.

Sonny mounted his investigation of Danny Byrne at night from his apartment. He found little more on the man than what was in the CLEVELAND PLAIN DEALER archives, other than his status as president and owner of Exotic World Cars, a broker of vintage and exotic automobiles. Located in Schaumburg, the business maintained an impressive web site, including a video catalog of its vast inventory of cars for sale. If the business was just a front for organized crime, it was a convincing one. Sonny also subscribed to two services to conduct background checks. One specialized in criminal background checks, while the other searched all of the social media sites for information. Neither surfaced a single reference. Danny Byrne kept a very low profile, it seemed.

Decorating

It was Friday morning, just two weeks until Christmas and Sonny barely had time to acknowledge the approaching holiday. Growing up, it was Sonny's favorite, the one time, it seemed, that his parents conformed to normalcy and behaved like a real family. They would suspend their activism in support of various liberal and usually hopeless causes. The three of them would trudge out to a rural tree farm, always when it was raining or snowing, to cut their own tree, tiny Sonny manning the handsaw until his arm ached and his fingers were numb, at which point his father would take over and finish the job with a few manly strokes. Together they would decorate the tree, along with whatever house or apartment they were renting. On Christmas Eve his parents would share a bottle of wine and give Sonny a small glass as well, after which he would lie in bed with anticipation of the gifts that would surround the tree in the morning. Even during his university years, when his parents had scattered and he was on his own, he always made time to erect a small tree and decorate his tiny apartment.

"What's in the box?" Charlotte asked as Sonny retrieved a large and well traveled corrugated box from his trunk.

"You'll see." With the box slung on his hip, he closed the trunk, prompting the BMW to chirp a confirmation that it was safely locked. Then he led her through the gray morning light to the office, which was dark and chilly. While Charlotte flipped on the lights and turned up the heat, Sonny plopped the box on the vacant receptionist desk in the outer lobby and opened it. Crammed inside were a small artificial Christmas tree and a mish mash of decorations. He put the tree on the desk and straightened its squashed wire branches. He pulled out a clumped string of lights and began untangling it. He looked up to find Charlotte, leaning against the door jam, arms crossed, watching him.

"What?" he asked defensively.

"You're so funny." She gave a wistful smile, the first he had seen in two weeks, which stole his breath.

"What?"

"I didn't take you for the sentimental holiday type."

"I love Christmas." He turned back to the tangle of lights as she continued to watch him. He pulled a handful of knotted garland from the box and held it out to her. "Here, help." She sauntered toward him and took the offering. They stood facing each other, the heat in the room seeming to rise. Then she leaned against the desk and began untangling the garland. Sonny sighed inaudibly and returned to his work.

When they were nearly done Simon arrived. He stopped in the doorway and admired the decorations. "Wow. I barely realized it's the season. Good job." He disappeared into his office.

"Sonny," Charlotte said as he stashed the empty cardboard box under the desk and she adjusted a couple of bulbs on the Christmas tree, "I need you tonight."

He turned to her, wondering if he had heard her right, hopeful. "Oh?"

"We're going to dinner with my mother tonight."

He cocked his head, confused.

"You said you would. You promised."

"But, Charlotte, don't you think this is short notice?"

"I knew it!" she flashed. "I knew you'd let me down!"

"It's okay, Charlotte," he assured. "You're right. I promised. You just caught me off guard."

She continued to pout. "She thinks we're coming for the holiday. She doesn't know about the bombing or my father."

"What did you tell her about me?"

"I told her we're colleagues."

Sonny nodded, expressionless, as a weight pressed on his soul.

Exotic World Cars

Sonny and Charlotte left work in mid afternoon so they both could shower and change for their dinner. Charlotte remained stoic all day and seemed to grow more pensive as the dinner hour approached. She was silent as he drove her to her apartment. She turned to him before exiting the car. "Dinner reservations are at seven. Pick me up at six. I don't want to spend any more time with her than necessary." Perplexed, he watched as she made her way up the walk and disappeared into her apartment building.

Sonny looked at his watch, an ancient Timex he purchased with his own money when he was ten years old. As he squinted to find the hands through the scratched crystal, he made a mental note to buy a new watch now that he could afford one. With over an hour to kill, he made his way to the Eisenhower and headed west toward Schaumburg.

Exotic World Cars was easy to find. Near the Woodfield Mall off of busy Route 53, the establishment comprised acres of paved parking space surrounding a multistory glass enclosed showroom attached to a large warehouse-sized garage and service building. The sign in front said "Exotic World Cars, the finest in vintage and luxury pre-owned automobiles." The parking lot was a sea of glistening vehicles, all of eye catching make and model. Sonny pulled up to the showroom and found a visitor space. Before he could shut off the engine, a dapper looking man emerged to greet him. He wore a tailored gray suit and a crimson necktie. His shoes were neatly polished. He appeared to be in his mid-forties and in good physical shape. He had a full head of hair, black with hints of gray, and a strong jaw. Sonny wondered how he maintained his deep tan in the Chicago winter.

"I hope this is a trade-in," the man offered as he admired Sonny's BMW, which was less than a year old. "I'm Robert." He extended his right hand while offering his business card with his left.

"Sonny Feelright," Sonny volunteered as they shook hands.

"So, how can I help you today? What are you looking for?"

Sonny was caught unprepared. When he decided to check out Exotic World Cars he hadn't considered how to approach the visit. After a moment's hesitation, he said, "Porsche. I'm interested in a Porsche. A 911 Turbo Cabriolet."

"Well," the salesman responded with a look of excited surprise. "That's a lot of car. But you came to the right place. Follow me." He led Sonny into the showroom, where some of the most exotic cars were displayed – including several Ferraris, a Lamborghini, and an Aston Martin. He signaled for Sonny to sit in a small cubicle while he searched his computerized inventory. "We have a 2009 Cabriolet on the property," he announced. "It's stored inside."

He led Sonny from the showroom through the pristine service section of the building and into the storage garage. "We keep some of our finer vehicles inside," he explained as he pushed through a large security door. The room beyond was gigantic and bathed in artificial light. The walls were painted white. The floor gleamed with gray epoxy and was neatly lined with fishbone rows of parking spaces. In every space sat a perfectly conditioned and prepped vehicle.

"Wow!" Sonny couldn't help himself. "How many cars are in here?"

"We have fifty spaces inside, plus all of the exterior lot. On any given day we have upwards of two hundred vehicles in stock. Plus, we have a network of sources throughout the country. The Porsche is in space forty-four. What did you say you do for a living?" he probed as they made their way among the cars.

Again, Sonny was unprepared to answer. "Um, investment banking," he lied.

"We get a lot of bankers in here. What firm?"

"Um, Blake & Company," Sonny lied again. "We're a boutique. Very specialized." Changing the subject, "So, who owns this place? You've got a fortune in inventory."

"A gentleman named Daniel Byrne. He bought the business over twenty years ago when it was a two-bit used car dealership. It's now one of the largest exotic car brokers in the country."

"Impressive. Must be quite a businessman. He must really know his cars."

"Yes," the salesman answered, wary now. "Here it is." He gestured to the candy apple red Porsche 911 Turbo Cabriolet, its convertible top down exposing an intimidating cockpit rivaling that of a fighter jet.

Sonny gaped at the car. "Wow," he repeated. It was all he could say.

"It will do zero to sixty in under four seconds. Not really an everyday car. Not for the faint of heart."

"I'll say," Sonny agreed, fearing he was sounding too impressed.

"Also not for the shallow pocket. This one goes for ninety-thousand dollars. Of course, we could cut you a good deal if you're trading in the Bimmer. Care to take it for a test drive?"

Sonny hesitated, awkwardly searching for a believable excuse. He looked at his watch, immediately wishing he hadn't when he noticed the salesman inspecting the cheap relic on his wrist. "No, I probably can't squeeze it in right now. I've got a dinner appointment in a short while. I'll need to come back when I have more time."

"That's fine." Suspicion edged the salesman's voice. "How about giving me a business card so I can call you if someone else takes an interest in the car? Or if we come across any others."

Sonny made a show of patting all of his pockets. "I'm afraid I'm fresh out."

"Then just write down your phone number for me." He thrust one of his business cards and a pen toward Sonny.

As they made their way back through the building to his BMW Sonny asked, "So, what would one of those cost new?"

"You're considering a new one?"

"Just curious."

"Depending on the features, about one-hundred-and-fifty-thousand dollars."

The salesman waited outside as Sonny climbed in his car and pulled from the parking lot, staring at the BMW until it disappeared into the gaggle of traffic on Route 53. He also noticed the black Lincoln Town Car that eased from a neighboring drive and seemed to be following the Bimmer, keeping several vehicles back. He pulled out his cell phone and made a call.

Faith McCardle

Charlotte, huddled in an off-white knee-length coat cinched with a leather belt, was waiting by the street in the fading light when Sonny pulled up. She wore brown heels, on which she was stomping her feet against the cold. Her cheeks were red when she slipped into the car. "You're late," she snapped. "I'm nearly frozen."

Sonny reached out and turned on her seat heater. "Sorry," was all he said.

She guided him through Chicago to the Lincoln Park area, one of the city's most exclusive, where her mother lived in a townhouse. She seemed tense and short-tempered. Sonny gave a soft whistle as he made his way along tidy streets, with their impressive mix of stately vintage brownstones and fashionable town houses. The area bloomed with holiday decorations: delicate strings of white lights webbing the spindly trees along the avenues, graceful garland and ribbons framing windows, and manicured wreaths adorning front doors. The decorations contrasted sharply with those in Sonny's neighborhood, where trends ran toward garish colored strings of lights and inflatable Santa's in the tiny lawns.

"Your mother lives here?"

"She did well in the divorce," responded Charlotte as they glided past quaint shops and bistros.

"When did you see her last?"

"Over a year ago."

"Look, Charlotte, I could use a little intel about tonight. What am I getting into here, and why do you hate your mother so much?"

"I don't hate my mother."

"Well, you're not exactly brimming with affection."

She sighed and slumped back in her chair. "You're right. I've been a total bitch."

Sonny didn't argue.

"I love my mother. But I can't stand to be around her. She's a wimp. When my parents were married she let my father walk all over her. He mistreated her terribly."

"He abused her?"

"Not physically. But mentally and emotionally. And it got worse and worse as time went on. He was the center of the universe, and she had to dance to his tune. He picked out her clothes, the style of her hair, the make and color of her car. He criticized her constantly. I really hated it when they entertained or we went out to dinner because he would ridicule her in public. He insisted on ordering for her at restaurants. It was humiliating to watch. I would get so embarrassed. Just once I wanted her to fight back, to get up and stomp out. But she would just sit there with a stupid smile and take it."

"But that's no reason to resent her so."

She looked at him and gave her head a slight shake. "I resent her because she let him do the same thing to me. When I started having anxiety attacks and the eating disorder, the shrink helped me see that it was all because of him. I'd spent my whole childhood trying to please him, to win his approval, which was impossible. And she was never there for me. She never challenged him or defended me.

"But the real reason I don't see her anymore is because of the men she sees. She started dating before the ink was dry on the divorce papers, and every guy she's been with has used her. They just go out with her because of the money. And when they've gotten all they can get from her they leave. I can't watch it anymore."

"Who is she seeing now?"

"I have no idea. But I know I won't like him."

She directed him to a row of fashionable condominiums – tasteful brick structures that offered a Boston Beacon Street appeal. He found a parking spot on the street and parallel parked. As they walked up the sidewalk, her high heel slipped on a small patch of ice, tipping her against him. She grabbed his arm and leaned on him as they walked. Her vanilla scented perfume captured his senses; he wished they could keep strolling like this past the townhouses and into the night. It was now completely dark except for the glow of the Victorian style streetlights along the street. She led him up the sidewalk to the third unit, slowing as she climbed the marble treads of the porch stairs. She froze before the impressive holiday wreath adorning the front door, which was painted burgundy with a brass kick plate and hardware. They stood for a full minute.

"Are you going to ring?" he finally asked.

"I'm not ready for this." She exhaled a long wisp of condensation into the crisp air.

Sonny reached out and pressed the doorbell. A deep chime answered from inside. Footsteps. He felt Charlotte tense. The door swung open, leaving Sonny taken aback at who greeted him. It was Charlotte. Her face, shadowed by the backlight of the vestibule, appeared to be Charlotte's twin. She was the same height. And she had the same lean build, with slender athletic legs and arms and a long graceful neck.

She opened the door and ushered them in, wrapping Charlotte in a heartfelt hug as soon as they crossed the threshold. "My God, I'm so happy you're here!" she exclaimed as she squeezed her daughter. "I've missed you so much." Charlotte returned the embrace stiffly, more enduring it than enjoying it. Her mother pulled away and, holding Charlotte by the shoulders, stared at her, smiling. Charlotte rolled her eyes to the ceiling.

"Ahem," Sonny mumbled.

"Oh, I'm sorry." Charlotte's mother let her go and placed a welcoming hand on Sonny's shoulder. Facing her in the light, Sonny remained astounded by the resemblance. Only some faint age lines and her hair style –shorter than Charlotte's in a trendy Bob -- distinguished them. "I'm Faith McCardle. I'm such a bad hostess. Take off your coats and come in." They peeled off their coats and handed them to her. She turned and led them from the vestibule into a comfortable living room, tossing their coats on the back of an overstuffed chair.

"There's someone I want you to meet."

Dominic Bindi

The room was tastefully furnished, with a large couch and matching overstuffed chairs. The colors were neutral, the carpeting off white and plush. Some bland abstract prints hung on the walls. Except for a miniature Christmas tree on an end table, the room was devoid of holiday decorations.

"Dom, they're here!" Faith shouted.

"Coming, darling," replied a baritone voice with a discernable Italian accent. A large man emerged from the kitchen carrying a wooden serving tray with a half-full wine decanter and four glasses. His hair, dark and full, was parted on the side and swept halfway down his forehead. His face was fleshy but handsome and sported a neatly trimmed moustache. He wore creased gray slacks, a white shirt opened at the collar and a blue blazer. Sonny guessed the clothes were tailored. The man set the tray on a coffee table and turned to face them.

"Sonny and Charlotte, I want you to meet Dominic," introduced Faith.

"Dominic Bindi," he greeted them with a half bow. He grabbed Sonny's hand and gave it a forceful shake. His hand was huge, his grip so strong it made Sonny wince. He turned and took Charlotte's hand, freezing when he looked at her face. "*Bellissimo*," he swooned, "you are a vision!" He pulled her hand to his lips to kiss it. She violently jerked it back and stepped away, her face an angry mask.

"Um, why don't we all sit down," Faith interrupted before Charlotte could react.

"Good idea," agreed Sonny. He pushed Charlotte to the couch and sat, pulling her next to him.

Bindi, oblivious to Charlotte's cutting stare, bent to pour the wine. Sonny noted the oversized Rolex watch on his thick left wrist and the matching diamond and gold ring on his finger. A sparkling gold bracelet jingled on his right wrist. "Chianti. This is one of my favorites. *Italiano.* From near my home."

"You're Italian?" Sonny asked the obvious, trying to diffuse the nuclear reaction brewing next to him.

"Ha, ha! You noticed!"

"Where in Italy?"

"Milan. Have you been there?"

"No. I've never been to Italy." In fact, Sonny knew nothing about Italy, except that it was shaped like a boot.

"What?" Bindi gave a dramatic cry. "You've not lived if you haven't been to Italy! The art, the architecture, the food, the wine – especially the wine!" He turned to Charlotte. "I'm sure you've been there. Only a beauty like you could rival the beauty of Italy!"

Charlotte stared daggers at him.

"No, Charlotte's never been to Italy," Faith intervened. "Although she had a chance to model there when she was younger."

"Let's not talk about that," Charlotte hissed.

Faith changed the subject, "Dom is an investment advisor in Milan."

"Is that right?" exclaimed Sonny, wishing he never agreed to come.

"Yes. And very successful," she said.

"Wow, impressive. So, what are you doing in the States?"

"A short sabbatical," he offered without further explanation. "But tell me about you. How did you and Charlotte meet?"

"We work together. We're partners." Sonny took a sip of wine.

Bindi raised his eyebrows. "Not lovers?"

Sonny and Faith both nearly spit out their drinks.

"That's hardly appropriate!" scolded Charlotte.

Bindi raised his hands defensively. "No harm meant. I'm afraid I don't always know the ways of America."

"Well," said Faith before Charlotte could respond further, "Why don't we head for dinner."

"Good idea," agreed Bindi. He stood and drained his glass in a single swallow. "Sonny, why don't you pick us up in front?"

Ride to Dinner

Despite Bindi's protests, Charlotte insisted on going with Sonny to get the car.

"See," she steamed over the angry click of her high heels on the pavement, "see the kind of men she attracts? He's a pig! We should get in the car and leave!" She marched a step ahead of him, making no effort to steady herself on his arm.

"He's alright. Just a little loud."

"He's a dreadful boor! I can't believe you're defending him! He actually tried to kiss my hand!"

"Maybe that's how they do it in Italy."

"He's a pig and a fraud! He's taking advantage of her, just like all the other men. Just take me home."

"No. Remember why we're here. This was your idea. You need to ask her about your father."

She crossed her arms tightly and was silent on the remaining march up the sidewalk.

"Nice car," Bindi boomed as he tumbled into the backseat of the BMW next to Faith. Sonny watched in the rearview mirror as the Italian threw a hammy arm around her shoulder and drew her toward him. She limply complied as he yanked her close and smooched her ear.

"So, where to?" asked Sonny.

"We've got reservations at a little place by Navy Pier," Faith answered as she pushed Bindi away. "Italian, of course."

Charlotte, grimly facing the windshield, rolled her eyes so hard that Sonny could almost hear them.

"Lamborghini," pronounced Bindi, dramatically rolling the 'r' and emphasizing the second to the last syllable. "That's the car you should drive, Sonny. That's what I drive in Milan. The finest car in the world." And so began an incessant stream of banter from the oversized Italian, who seemed to be an expert on all things. Although the drive was short, his booming baritone filled the car as he opined on everything from the eminence of Italian restaurants to the superior fitness of European athletes. "Americans are like the English; they have no taste buds ... Soccer is a far more demanding game than American football or basketball ... Lance Armstrong was a drug addict and should be stripped of his victories ... why must Americans join every petty war ... you people should chase money less and chase *amore* more...."

Sonny found the restaurant and pulled up to the valet stand, anxious to escape the relentless monologue. Charlotte sprang from the car before it was fully stopped. He took the valet ticket and opened the rear door for Faith while Bindi wrestled his bulky frame through the opposite door. The four of them headed toward the entrance to the restaurant as the valet pulled the BMW from the curb.

Faith put her arm around her daughter. "I'm so glad you came. I wish I had a picture of this."

"Wait." Sonny pulled out his IPhone. "Line up."

"You have to be in it, too," Faith insisted. She beckoned a second valet to take the picture. The four of them lined up, Bindi on one end and Sonny on the other. The valet took the shot and handed the phone back to Sonny. He took one more of just Charlotte and Faith.

"Oh no!" cried Bindi. He patted his breast pocket, then his hip pocket.

"What's wrong?" Faith asked with concern.

"Here it comes," mumbled Charlotte.

"I've forgotten my wallet! It must be in my overcoat!"

"Oh, no," Faith frowned.

"We must go back," insisted Bindi.

"But the reservation is for seven."

"Good idea, let's go back," Charlotte agreed, a smug smile on her face. "I'm sure Dom feels naked without his wallet." Bindi continued to pat his pockets.

"Don't worry about it," Sonny volunteered. "I'll cover it." Charlotte gave him a withering glance.

"No, you can't," Bindi protested. "We invited you. I insist on paying, and that's final."

"It's alright. Besides, the valet already took the car."

Bindi gave a sigh of resignation. "Well, Sonny, if you insist. But you must let me pay you back."

After Dinner Drinks

Bindi's embarrassment about forgetting his wallet was short lived. Once seated in the restaurant, he took command of the wine list, ordering another bottle of Chianti without consultation.

"Bring me a glass of house Chablis," Charlotte ordered before the waiter could walk away. Bindi shrugged his chagrin and then continued to dominate the table conversation.

When the waiter arrived with the menus, Bindi dismissed him with a wave. "The veal!" he pronounced. "It's the specialty here! The finest in the city! We all must have the veal!" Faith smiled and nodded. Sonny shrugged his assent. Charlotte grabbed the retreating waiter and yanked a menu from his hand.

She gave it a quick scan. "Antipasto," she ordered with a militant expression.

During dinner, Bindi seemed to suck the air from the room with his booming baritone and animated gestures. He smacked his lips and swooned after every bite of his meal. He inhaled glass after glass of wine with gusto, ordering a second bottle when the first was empty. For his part, Sonny found the wine somewhat caustic and the veal tough and tasteless. He'd had better meals at the Olive Garden.

Sonny waited for Charlotte to raise the topic of her father. But Charlotte sat rigid, mechanically picking at her meal, and few words passed between the two women. When they did attempt to talk, Bindi overpowered them with interruptions. The waiter cleared the table while Bindi perused the dessert menu.

"No dessert!" Charlotte told the waiter before Bindi could order. "Just a check."

Bindi looked up, surprised. Then he smiled with understanding. "Ah, yes! I agree! We should go somewhere else for drinks and dessert. I know a place!"

Charlotte kicked Sonny's ankle under the table and made a growling sound. She reached over and pinched his inner thigh hard, right where his rash was healing. "Ouch!" he yelped and gave her an angry stare. She stared back at him, her clenched jaws bulging behind her cheeks.

The waiter brought the check and set it in front of Bindi, who casually slid it across the table to Sonny. "Come, darling, let's get the coats." He and Faith stood and headed for the coat check.

"Sonny, I will *not* spend another minute with that man!" hissed Charlotte when they were out of earshot. "I refuse to go anywhere else with him!"

Sonny wasn't listening. He was staring at the bill --

$502.30. The wine was one-hundred-and-fifty dollars a bottle. His stomach turned as he calculated the tip – one hundred dollars. "Charlotte, the meal was over six hundred dollars!" he exclaimed.

She was unsympathetic. "Don't worry. He'll pay you back! Remember?"

"Sarcasm doesn't help," he protested as he laid his credit card on the bill tray. The waiter swept it up and disappeared.

"I'm not going out for drinks with them! I'll take a cab home!"

"You haven't spoken with your mother yet."

"I can't get a word in edgewise!"

"Charlotte, we came here for a reason. I didn't just spend six hundred dollars for nothing. We're going to see this through. You need to confront your mother!"

"I'll give you the six hundred!" she bargained.

"No! We're going to go for a drink and you're going to ask her!" Sonny commanded.

Just then Bindi and Faith returned to the table with the coats in their arms.

"Everything alright?" asked Faith.

"Fine, fine," assured Sonny. "Shall we go?"

Charlotte stood, snatched her coat from Bindi and headed for the door.

"Sonny," Bindi said as they followed her, "can you tip the coat girl for me?"

Peaches

"Where we going?" inquired Sonny as he pulled from the restaurant.

"A charming place I know," answered Bindi. He directed Sonny back to the Loop and then off again several exits later. They found themselves in an industrial neighborhood of aging brick warehouses and factories. Traffic was light, the streets dark and devoid of pedestrians. Bindi ordered Sonny through several turns, with each street more desolate than the last.

"Up there, on the left," Bindi pointed from the back seat. In the distance, Sonny saw a pool of light. He could make out the movement of traffic and people. They approached a nondescript gray building on the left, its façade lit with colored spot lights. A red canopy led to a shadowed entrance. Across the street was a large gravel parking lot, filling rapidly, it appeared from the line of cars waiting to enter. People, mostly men, were crossing the street to the building. Several cabs were lined up in the opposite direction to drop off fares. A large electric sign on the building said, "Peaches, A Gentlemen's Club."

"My God," exclaimed Charlotte. "It's a strip club!"

"A gentlemen's club," corrected Bindi.

"Sonny?" Charlotte pleaded. But he was preoccupied trying to weave through the traffic and milling pedestrians.

"Drop us here," ordered Bindi. He opened the door and pulled Faith behind him into the street. Then he opened the front passenger door for Charlotte, who gave Sonny a pleading look.

"It'll be fun," assured Faith.

"I'll park and catch up," said Sonny. Charlotte made a forlorn face and climbed from the car, causing a turn of heads from all directions.

Sonny pulled into the lot, where a black parking attendant directed him to a space. "Twenty bucks," the attendant demanded as Sonny emerged from the car. Sonny shook his head, retrieved a twenty from his wallet and handed it to the man, who added it to the thick wad of cash he carried.

Sonny crossed the street and joined his companions in line just as they were reaching the entrance, where a burly bouncer, looking uncomfortably overstuffed in a black tuxedo, eyed the entering line of partiers. Rock music thumped from within the building. The bouncer focused on Charlotte, who wore a grim expression. "No dancing by the audience," he said.

"What?" responded a confused Charlotte.

"No stripping. It takes money from the girls. If you want to dance, rehearsals are on Thursday afternoons."

"What? How DARE you! I have no intention of dancing *or* stripping!"

"Just a warning," the giant shrugged as Sonny nudged a red-faced Charlotte through the door.

They found themselves in a large vestibule. An attractive female greeter, looking very bored as she chomped a piece of gum, stood behind a counter on the left. She wore a black lace bodice, which she amply filled, and a very short red skirt. She was pretty in heavy makeup, but it could not obscure the hard-life features of her face. "Cover's fifteen dollars apiece. Coat check is over there." She gestured across the room to where another scantily clad young woman was checking coats behind a separate counter.

"Sonny?" Bindi nodded toward the greeter, who held out her hand for money. "I'll check the coats."

Bindi peeled off his coat and helped Faith take off hers. Sonny handed over his coat. Charlotte clutched hers tightly about her neck. "I'll keep mine." Bindi shrugged.

While Sonny signed the credit card receipt, trying to mentally track his outlays for the night, Bindi led a cautious Faith and Charlotte through a bead string passage into the main establishment. Sonny followed them to find Faith and Charlotte huddled behind the

Italian, who surveyed the cavernous night club with legs apart and arms stretched wide as if inhaling the universe. "When you find the mother lode," he bellowed, "you must tap it!"

Sonny's closest prior experience to a strip club was a college frat party years earlier where a pudgy middle aged stripper performed. It was a sobering experience, despite the belly of beer he consumed that night. The woman was singularly unattractive with unsightly cellulite on her legs and buttocks. She endured the hoots and taunts of the drunken college students with grim fatalism. Rather than inspiring arousal, her pathetic performance overwhelmed him with pity. He left the party before she finished her dance and was depressed for days afterward.

This was a different scene, an overwhelming sensory experience. Giant speakers in every corner of Peaches vibrated with thunderous rock music. The establishment reeked of a mixture of stale beer, sweat and bold perfume. And everywhere there were lights and motion. A buxom young woman, her body flawless and naked except for a g-string and pasties, gyrated on a raised stage nearby. The stage was surrounded by a bar and chairs, eye level with the dance floor, occupied by a handful of men sipping drinks and ogling the dancer.

Toward the back of the establishment were two

somewhat smaller platforms, each featuring dancers in various stages of undress. Servers, wearing tight peach colored tee shirts and black hot pants, skittered among the circular cocktail tables scattered throughout the room, deftly balancing serving trays of drinks. Along the wall to the right was a long bar lined with young women, everyone a beauty, dressed in all manner of provocative attire. Some chatted with one another. Some preened in the giant mirror lining the wall behind the bar. Some sipped cocktails. Some surveyed the room like leopards spying for prey. Despite the line of people entering, the club was so vast that it appeared nearly empty of patrons. Indeed, there seemed to be more dancers than paying clientele.

Two young women, one in a skimpy sailor outfit and the other dressed as a Catholic school girl, peeled from the bar and strode up to Bindi. He gave them an innocent look and in a syrupy Italian baritone pronounced, "I'm from Milan. I've never been in a place like this and I don't know what to do." They each took an arm and melted against him, then led him through the sea of tables to one in a far corner. Faith, Charlotte and Sonny hustled awkwardly behind them, the row of girls at the bar inspecting them as they passed.

A waitress arrived and took their drink orders. Bindi ordered cocktails for his two companions, now perched together on his lap, and another bottle of

Chianti. Charlotte ordered bottled water and gave Sonny an angry frown as he handed over his credit card.

"Ladies and gentleman," boomed an emcee, "let's give it up for Tanya Hide on stage one!" There was a smattering of applause as the dancer on the front stage gathered the scattered components of her outfit along with the dollar bills littering the floor. She knelt to let a patron slip a dollar into the cash-stuffed garter on her thigh, giving him a peck on the forehead before striding from the stage. "Next up is . . . ."

The girl in the sailor outfit whispered something to Bindi, who leaned forward and stretched out a palm. "Sonny, these girls must eat. Table dances are twenty dollars." Charlotte stared venom at Sonny as he pulled out his wallet and handed Bindi a twenty. "*Two* girls must eat," said Bindi. Sonny pulled out another twenty, his last, and handed it over. A song started and the two girls began an erotic lap dance for the smiling Italian, now practically lying in his chair.

Sonny met Charlotte's stare and nodded toward Faith, who sat demurely and gazed about the room, a pleasant smile on her face, ignoring the performance taking place next to her. Charlotte leaned forward, about to speak to her mother, when a buxom blonde in a sequined gown strutted up and plopped down in Sonny's lap. "I'm Reddy," she smiled. She had a thick

Eastern European accent. "You look like you need some company." She tilted in his lap and reached into his pocket, leaving Charlotte gape mouthed. Reddy pulled out Sonny's IPhone and set it in on the table. "That's better," she cooed.

"No, he doesn't need company!" Charlotte snapped.

"What about you, then?"The girl reached to stroke Charlotte's cheek. "You're hot."

"No!" Charlotte responded emphatically, drawing away. "Please leave!"

The girl pouted, stood and sauntered away toward three men being seated nearby.

Again Sonny looked at Charlotte and nodded toward her mother. "Mom," Charlotte began, her voice raised against the noise in the restaurant. Faith leaned in to listen. Just then Sonny's phone rang. Charlotte eyed it, then picked it up and examined the screen. "Who is Liz?" she asked him.

"I don't know," he answered, confused. He took the phone from her, looked at the screen and answered. "Hello...."

"Sonny, this is Liz."The voice was vaguely familiar and there was a lot of noise in the background.

"Huh?"

"Look behind you -- at the bar." Sonny turned and peered through the growing crowd toward the bar, with Charlotte following his gaze. He noticed an attractive blond waving at him. She held a cell phone to her ear. "Sonny, it's me, your doctor."

"Oh my God," Sonny exclaimed. He stood and walked to the bar, pocketing his cell phone as he went. Charlotte watched in confusion as Sonny shouldered his way between two dancers and greeted Elizabeth Loveland. She was dressed more conservatively than the dancers surrounding him; she wore a white sleeveless blouse and black slacks. Her only remotely provocative accessory was a black dog collar around her neck. Her blond hair was set in a cute page boy. She wore a subtle application of makeup. She looked fetching.

"I didn't take you for a Peaches kind of guy," she mused.

"I'm not. Really, I'm not. I swear, this is my first time in a place like this." She flashed him a skeptical smile. "But what about you?"

"I told you I was a bartender."

"But here?"

"My uncle owns the place. I work when I want and the tips are good." Sonny glanced down the line of strippers along the bar. "I don't dance, if that's what you're wondering. Never have and never would. But I don't judge them, either. They make a good living here. Besides, I would probably go broke with this body."

Sonny noted her petite frame and thought otherwise. "Well, I better get back."

"Who you here with?" Liz peered toward the table, where Charlotte stared intensely back.

"Charlotte, her mother and her mother's boyfriend."

"Charlotte, your partner? The angry one?"

Sonny nodded.

"Wow. I've seen a lot of strange things here, but that may be the weirdest."

"Long story," Sonny shrugged.

"Maybe you can tell it to me sometime." Her smile was captivating.

"Yea," he said. "Got to get back." He made an awkward wave and returned to the table.

"Well?" queried Charlotte.

"Believe it or not, that was my doctor."

"Dr. *Lovelace*?"

"Loveland."

Charlotte, angry now, "Don't you mean Liz? You want to tell me about this?"

"What?" Sonny shrugged. "She's my doctor."

"You have *Liz* programmed into your phone!" Sonny met her angry stare with a helpless one of his own. "That's *it*! I'm out of here!" She stood, grabbed her coat and stormed for the exit, with Sonny in pursuit.

He caught her on the sidewalk out front. "Charlotte, wait. Let me get my coat. I'll take you home."

"Don't bother! I wouldn't want to spoil your evening!" She hailed a cab and was gone.

A Mother's Remorse

Shoulders slumped with dejection, Sonny made his way back through the club. He waved off a black haired beauty who accosted him as he approached the table. Faith wore an anxious look. "Where's Charlotte?"

"She took a cab home."

Bindi, oblivious to Charlotte's departure, emerged from his smothering companions. "Sonny," he said, "they want to show me the Club Room. I need more cash."

"You took my last twenty."

"No problem." He stood and pulled Sonny from his chair, leading him to an ATM in the corner. "I'll pay you back."

"Don't you think we've spent enough?"

"I'm a man of honor," asserted Bindi with a look of indignation. "Do you not trust me?"

Sonny pulled out his wallet and retrieved his credit card. "Another forty dollars?"

"Ha! The Club Room, Sonny."

"One hundred?"

Bindi put a chubby hand on Sonny's shoulder. "These girls must eat. Five hundred. Just a loan, I promise."

Sonny withdrew five hundred dollars and handed it to the excited Italian. "*Grazie*, my friend." Bindi pocketed the money, retrieved his two partners from the table and disappeared through a door across the room.

Sonny returned to the table and pulled his chair close to Faith.

"This was a terrible mistake," she apologized. "I'm sorry, Sonny."

"It's alright."

"No it's not. It's humiliating. Charlotte hates me more than ever. And now she hates you, too. I've missed her so much. And now I probably won't ever see her again."

Sonny nodded toward Bindi's empty chair. "Why do you put up with that?"

She made a pathetic face. "You wouldn't understand."

"Try me."

"Look at me, Sonny. I'm forty-eight. No one is interested in a forty-eight-year-old divorcee."

"That's crazy. Look around, Faith. You're the most beautiful woman in this place." He meant it.

"Nonsense," she waved a dismissive hand. "And I'm twice as old as all of them."

"What is it with you McCardle women? You're beautiful. You're smart. Yet you only can see the one percent wrong in the ninety-nine percent right about you. You don't have to put up with a jerk like Dominic. You can have any man you want, and most of them will worship you."

She smiled and patted his hand. "That's nice of you, Sonny. But I'm not confident like Charlotte."

"She's not so confident," Sonny argued. "Stubborn, yes. Angry, absolutely. But hardly confident."

"What's your relationship with her?"

"What do you mean?"

"You're not just colleagues. A mother can tell."

"I'm not sure I know," he confessed. "She blows hot and cold. I thought for a while that it might get serious. I care a lot about her, but she's distant now."

"I'm afraid I've made it worse for you. Now she hates you, too."

"She doesn't hate you, Faith. She hates your willingness to accept men like Dominic." Sonny related what Charlotte told him on the drive to her home.

"Her father was hard on her," Faith conceded, tears welling in her eyes. "But she's wrong about me not caring. I did try to stick up for her. I did try to protect her. But it was hard. Douglas is very forceful. Have you met him?"

Sonny shook his head.

"He can be intimidating. He's handsome, charming and wickedly smart. He knows how to manipulate people. I was no match for him. You know, I've never told anyone this, but I almost killed him once. Charlotte was thirteen. She had just blossomed from a tomboy into the swan she is today, and he was hell bent on turning her into a super model. The modeling agency wanted to take her to Europe. She was just a kid. She wanted no part of it. She begged and pleaded. Charlotte doesn't know this, but I finally put my foot down and threatened to take her away and leave him. That's when he turned really ugly – to both of us. He told her she could go to hell. From then on, she couldn't do anything right in his eyes.

"One night we hosted a dinner party for some of his work colleagues and Douglas had a little too much to drink. At dinner he told the story. He ridiculed her in front of everyone. He called her his 'idiot daughter.' Everyone was uncomfortable. Charlotte ran from the table and locked herself in her room. I wanted to go after her, but I needed to stay and try to salvage the party. That night, when everyone left and Douglas went to bed, I loaded a pistol from his gun collection and went to the bedroom. I held the gun to his head and wanted to pull the trigger. But then I heard Charlotte crying in her bedroom next door, and it occurred to me that she would have no parents if Douglas was dead and I was in jail." Tears ran down Faith's cheeks.

Sonny stared at her, stunned by the story. "That's awful."

"That's when she started to have her … problems. The anxiety attacks and the eating disorder. That's when my marriage lost its intimacy."

The conversation was taking a turn Sonny didn't wish to follow. "Your husband was an investment banker?"

She nodded and gave a shaky exhale.

"What happened?"

"First Boston went out of business. Everyone thinks the financial crises happened in 2009. It really started a lot earlier, after the tech bubble burst in 2000. Deal making fell off the table and a lot of the smaller banking firms got swallowed by big banks. First Boston was one of them. It eventually disappeared, and Douglas was out of a job."

"What did he do then?"

"He did alright as a banker, but not well enough to retire. He looked for a job, but he was older by then, and the banks were only hiring young MBAs out of college. So he started his advisory business."

"Tell me about it."

"I don't know much to tell. We weren't speaking as he was starting up. All I know is he's doing very well. After the divorce he bought a spread on the North Shore. And a lot of expensive toys. Including a trophy wife."

"He remarried?"

She nodded and took a sip of her wine, which she had barely touched. "He was seeing her when we were married. I caught him. I found e-mails. That's what led to the divorce." She shook her head thoughtfully. "That's not really true. We were headed that way already. It was inevitable after Charlotte started having problems. I began to hate him. It was my fault he had the affair."

"See what I mean?" said Sonny. "You're down on yourself again. The guy asked for it. He was a jerk."

She smiled and wiped her tears, reminding Sonny of Charlotte. "You should be my shrink."

"What kind of consulting does he do?"

"He runs an investment advisory service. He was kind of secretive about it."

"A research firm?"

"Not really. He doesn't publish or invest directly. He doesn't have any employees. He just consults with people."

"Who?"

"Mostly hedge funds, I think. Big, sophisticated hedge funds. I've always wondered what kind of information he's able to give that they don't already know. And he works with some wealthy individuals, too."

"Ever hear of someone named Danny Byrne?"

Her face darkened. "I know of him."

"How?"

"My father was a longshoreman. Danny Byrne came from Cleveland, I think, and worked with the union somehow. Years ago, before he got in the car business. He had a reputation. My father didn't trust the union leadership much and he didn't have anything good to say about Danny Byrne."

"Is he a client?"

She frowned and nodded. "I think so. Douglas had him to the house a couple of times. Say, why are you asking all of these questions about my ex? I feel like I'm being interrogated."

Sonny confided that they were investigating a case involving Danny Byrne. He didn't mention the explosion, the shootings, or the FBI's suspicion that it all might be linked to Douglas McCardle.

"So, Charlotte only called me because she wanted information for your investigation," she concluded, a hurt expression on her face.

"No," Sonny lied. "She wanted to see you. She told me she misses you."

"You're lying, Sonny. Even if Charlotte felt that way, she'd never admit it. I'm her mother. I know her. Never mind, though. What else do you need to know?"

"Do you know any other of Mr. McCardle's private clients?"

"Not personally. But I know he's working for some of Danny Byrne's friends. It's not the most savory crowd."

A familiar baritone interrupted their conversation as Bindi, now drunk and disheveled, stumbled back to the table, the two dancers struggling to steady him. "Sonny, you must experience the Club Room!" he boomed over the blaring music. *"Fantastico!"*

"Sonny, you go now. You don't have to stay here," urged Faith as Bindi plopped down in his chair. The two dancers, having extracted all of Sonny's cash, patted the Italian dismissively on the head and disappeared to find richer prospects in the growing crowd.

"But I'm your ride."

"We'll take a cab. Don't worry. I have money. You go now." She grabbed his hand as he stood to leave. "Whatever you're up to with Danny Byrne, be careful. His type plays for keeps."

Street Fight

The scene out front was busy as Sonny stepped from the club. A growing line of people, men and a few women, was waiting to enter. Cars and cabs inched along the congested street. He found an isolated spot on the sidewalk and tried to call Charlotte. Futile. He left a short message on her voicemail begging her to call back. He knew she would not.

He was walking to the parking lot across the street when his attention was drawn to a commotion near a line of parked taxis down the block. Two men, obviously inebriated, were trying to coax a woman into sharing a cab with them. One man sat in the back seat, the other leaned against the open back door, full of himself, flirting. The woman was politely declining their offer and trying to move away. It was Liz. As she stepped toward the next cab in the line, the man grabbed her arm and held it. He responded to her protests with a teasing smile.

"This night is unbelievable," Sonny mumbled to himself. He jogged to the scene, where Liz was struggling to pull her arm away.

"Hey!" Sonny shouted. "I don't think the lady wants to go with you."

"Who the fuck are you?" The man's mischievous smile faded into a hostile frown. He squeezed her arm tighter, eliciting a grunt of pain. His companion climbed from the car, combat ready. They were young, early twenties, wearing business suits, rumpled from an evening of partying.

"A friend." Sonny kept his eyes on his two adversaries. "Liz, are you alright?"

"I'm fine. Everything's fine, Sonny. These guys were just leaving." She tugged again but could not free her arm.

"Please let go of her," ordered Sonny.

"Or what?" asked the fellow from the back seat as he stepped just inches from Sonny's face. His eyes were bloodshot. His breath reeked of beer. Sonny hadn't been in a physical confrontation since the first grade; his fight or flight instinct was screaming "run." Heart racing, he tried to radiate more menace than he felt as he stared the man down.

Over Sonny's shoulder, something drew his opponent's attention. The young man took a step backward toward the cab. His companion released his grip on Liz, who rubbed her forearm. Sonny turned to find the bouncer from the front door standing behind him, arms crossed against his barrel chest. Without further words, the two men climbed into the cab and closed the door.

"Thanks, Tank," Liz said as the taxi pulled away. He nodded and returned to his station by the door.

"That was brave but unnecessary," Liz said to Sonny. "Tank keeps the peace out here. He wouldn't let it go very far."

"I don't feel very brave. Look at this." He held up his shaking hand.

"I thought you were James Bond." She grabbed his hand and steadied it in both of hers.

"Does that kind of thing happen all the time?"

"Hardly ever, actually. When it does, it's usually young preppies like that, with more testosterone and alcohol than they can handle. Spoiled young assholes on their way to becoming spoiled adult assholes."

"What are you doing out here. I thought you were working."

"Going home to sleep. I've got rounds at the hospital tomorrow at seven."

"You're taking a cab?"

"Unless you've got a better idea."

Conflicting Affections

"Very nice," said Liz as she surveyed the interior of Sonny's BMW. "Business must be good."

"Believe me, when I got this car I could not afford it. I'm still not sure I can afford it. It's a long story."

"We've got twenty minutes."

So Sonny launched into the tale of his first days on the job with Blake & Company, which seemed much longer than six months ago. He told about how embarrassed Charlotte was when they made their first call on a client together in his aging Ford Taurus, how she directed him to a BMW dealership along the way and conned the saleswoman into letting them take the car for a test drive, only to use it for the appointment. And how she coaxed him into buying the car on their way back that evening.

"She sounds like quite a manipulator."

"Oh, not at all! I'm giving you the wrong impression. She's a great person. Smart and funny. And not near as confident as she comes across."

"And beautiful," added Liz. "She looked at him as passing lights painted moving shadows on his face. "She's more than a colleague, isn't she?"

It was the night's second inquiry about his relationship with Charlotte, and again it made him uncomfortable. He shrugged as she studied him. "I don't know what we are." He changed the subject. "So, what's up with you working at that club?"

She tensed and frowned. "This is when you try to save me, right?"

"What? No! It's none of my business."

"Most men want to rescue me from there. The 'Pretty Woman' syndrome."

"I just wondered."

Her face softened. "I'm sorry. I don't mean to be so defensive. It's interesting working there. The tips are good and the work is entertaining. It's like a giant theater. The dancers are some of the best actors you'll ever see. They figure out what turns a customer on and then they become the fantasy. Guys always feel sorry for the girls, but it should be the other way around. The men are the real victims. I've seen guys give up their life savings in a single night."

Sonny thought about his empty wallet. "How much do they make?"

"Depends on the girl. They're all independent contractors, so they work when they want. But the ones that really work at it, the smart ones, can make six figures."

"Where do they come from? How do they get there?"

"All over – the city, the suburbs, Europe, Asia, South America. It's a melting pot. They dance because it's better money than they can make anywhere else. And most of them are entertainers at heart. They like the attention. But it's a short career. By the time they get in their late twenties, they're over the hill. The smart ones save their money and move on to college or another career. The dumb ones blow the money, a lot of them on drugs. That's when I feel sorry for them."

"How often do they meet their husbands in there?"

"Not very. You saw most of the guys that were in there. Half of them are married and the others aren't married for a reason. That's what's impressive; the girls have to entertain some really horrible men – like that guy you were with tonight. A lot of the dancers are lesbians, too."

Sonny smiled. "False advertising. Isn't that illegal?"

"Unfortunately, guys like you don't show up there often."

They rode in awkward silence. "Turn left up here," she directed. She steered him to a working class neighborhood on Chicago's west side. "There, the yellow house on the left. You can drop me at the curb." The well maintained house looked out of place on the street of 1940's-era bungalows and small ranch houses. It was an old two story structure, probably the homestead of what once was a farm. A barn loomed in back, looking completely out of place in the tired urban neighborhood setting. "I rent the second floor of the barn. It's converted into an apartment."

He found this girl baffling. "Okay, you're young, you're pretty, you're a doctor, you bartend in a strip joint, and you live in a barn. You may be the most interesting person I've ever met."

She gave a weary smile and leaned back against the headrest of the idling car. "I'm not interesting at all. Here's the abbreviated version: I grew up in Hinsdale, my father was a doctor. I took ballet and played soccer as a kid. My dad died of a heart attack when I was fourteen. My uncle – my mother's brother – owns Peaches. He helped pay for my college – premed. I've had to pay for medical school myself, mostly with loans. My goals are to get out of debt, have my own general practice someday, and hopefully, meet someone and start a family. But frankly, the clock is ticking on the last one."

"I can't believe you're not involved with someone."

"Think about it. For the past eight years I've spent every waking hour with a bunch of medical students. Nothing against doctors, but most of them have the personalities of melba toast. And the men I've met at Peaches are hardly dating material." She turned to him. "You're the first normal guy I've met in a long time, Sonny."

She hesitated, then leaned toward him. As if drawn

by a magnet he leaned across the console and kissed her – once, twice, three times. Her lips were soft, her mouth moist and inviting. "Do you want to come up?" she whispered.

Every fiber in his being wanted to answer yes. His cell phone rang. He half pulled it from his pocket, suddenly hoping it was Charlotte. "Liar," read the caller ID. He ended the call without answering.

"Charlotte?" asked Liz.

"No. A pest. The reporter from the TRIB. Look, you've got rounds in the morning and I've had a very long evening."

"I understand," she said, disappointed. "Can we stay in touch, Sonny?"

"I'd like that," he said truthfully.

"Mean it?"

"Absolutely," he replied. She leaned in and gave him one more kiss. Then she climbed from the car and walked up the drive, turning to wave when she reached the stairway leading to the second story of the barn.

As he pulled away, Sonny didn't notice the boat-sized red Cadillac Eldorado down the block as it eased from the curb and followed him at a distance. It was the same car that had discreetly followed him the entire evening.

Restless

Sonny spent a restless night. The din of Peaches still rang in his head when he reached his small apartment. His mind toggled between tingling excitement about his encounter with Liz and abject depression and embarrassment as he thought about Charlotte. Wired from the bizarre evening, he found a container of chocolate cookies and proceeded to devour them with a glass of milk as he numbly watched the nightly news on his small television. He left his phone on the plastic beverage crate that served as an end table, hoping that Charlotte would call or text. Finally, the phone announced a text message. He picked it up hopefully. Liz. "Goodnight," was all she wrote.

He was horrified when he reached for another cookie and realized he had eaten them all. How many were there? At least ten. He was overcome by an abrupt awareness of his bloated stomach as it wrestled to digest the rich meal, the edgy wine and the cookie feast he forced upon it. He felt sluggish and heavy. He had made no attempt to run or exercise in more than a week, since the morning he saw the black Town Car parked outside. What was he becoming?

Sleep was elusive. Each time he faded to unconsciousness his sour stomach or an unpleasant dream would awaken him and he would lie, staring at the ceiling, for an interminable time until he faded again to broken sleep. The orange glow of his digital alarm clock slowly ticked off the minutes, then the hours, as if measuring the depth of his misery. At five thirty in the morning he gave up. He climbed from the bed and donned his sweats, determined to make a new start on his quest for fitness and order in his life.

His breath plumed a foggy cloud as he stepped onto the small landing outside his door. Ever wary, he gazed up and down the street out front for any suspicious vehicles before descending the stairs and stretching on the sidewalk. The world was still, the dark sky void of stars. The sidewalks remained treacherous with patches of ice, so he ran on the roadway. He felt fat and slow as he plodded along, turning right at the end of the street and across Cicero. At least his infected thighs were nearly healed.

He huffed heavily as he returned back onto his street, steam puffing from his mouth and nose and rising from his sweating head. He stopped a half block from his apartment and bent down, hands on knees, catching his breath.

Murderous Intent

The driver of the black Town Car stared at Sonny. "There he is. We can get him now." He wiggled the fingers on his injured hand, still bandaged from the blow he took at the Red Swan. He spoke Egyptian Arabic. The car was tucked against the curb past Sonny's apartment. It had pulled into the space after he left for his run.

"No!" commanded Kafele. "We were told to watch."

Bomani stared at Sonny, hatred swelling in his chest. "This isn't Jihad," he cursed.

"Bomani," scolded his sibling, sensing the young man's untamed frustration and knowing how impulsive he could be, "you heard the Imam. We watch for now. Nothing more."

Bomani's eyes narrowed as Sonny straightened and arched his back, stretching. His chest formed a perfect target. Bomani cracked the window slightly to let the chilly air cool his burning anger. But the surge of fresh air only clarified his resolve. He slammed on the gas and shouted, "Praise Allah!"

Attack

Sonny opened his eyes to the blinding glare of headlights and the violent screech of tires on pavement. He stood frozen in disbelief as a car careened toward him, accelerating with every rotation of the tire. He turned to flee, but the vehicle, its engine deafening, had already closed the distance. Sonny made a desperate leap sideways over the curb and thin tree lawn. He felt the rush of the passing car as it barely missed him.

He hit the sidewalk awkwardly on one foot. He took a second long step to keep his balance, but his foot found a patch of ice. He splayed like a tossed spider through the air. He reached to break his fall, but his hand crumpled on impact and his back struck the pavement with the full force of gravity. His breath escaped with a rush and he found himself temporarily paralyzed, gasping for air.

Through the stunned fog of semi-consciousness, Sonny heard the Town Car skid to a stop. He heard shouting from the window. Angry shouting. In a foreign language. He heard the transmission click to reverse and the engine roar. He knew the car was attacking again, but he was powerless to move. He waited for the sound of tires jumping the curb to crush him.

Just then, seemingly from nowhere, a second car roared up the street heading straight for the black sedan as it sped backward toward Sonny. The two cars screeched to a stop, just inches from colliding. The black sedan shifted and sped away, fishtailing around the corner toward Cicero. The other car, a candy apple red Cadillac Eldorado, idled briefly, not twenty feet from Sonny's prone body.

Sonny raised his head to glance at the car and then noticed a shadowy figure approaching him from the stairway of his apartment. It was a bulky figure in a hooded coat. The driver of the Cadillac apparently saw it, too, because the car roared away, its tires spinning. The predawn air, breached by the roar of engines just minutes before, was quiet now except for the ominous footsteps of the stranger.

Still stunned from the fall, Sonny tried to flee the approaching figure, a black silhouette against the streetlights behind it. But he could only crawl backwards on his elbows. He tried to scream, but his lungs would not work. He became conscious of a searing pain in his left hand. The figure walked up to him, raised its hands, and the darkness was pierced by a sudden flash.

Stalker

"Are you alright?"

Sonny peered blindly toward the familiar voice, eyes useless because of the sudden flash.

"It's me, Melody. Melody Gothim." Melody bent to examine him as she pocketed her digital camera.

"No!" he asserted. "Get away from me! You're evil!"

"Are you alright? What just happened?"

"Nothing! Nothing happened! Leave me alone! You're evil!" Sonny, now regaining his senses, sat up on the cold sidewalk. His left hand ached.

"You wouldn't return my calls. I came by to apologize. For the articles."

"Just leave me alone." Sonny struggled to stand. Melody grabbed his right arm and helped him.

"What I just saw was crazy!" she exclaimed. "Are you alright? You could have been killed!"

Sonny took a deep breath, relieved to be on his feet and to feel the cold air reentering his heaving lungs. "I'm fine. Just leave me alone. It was nothing?"

"Nothing?" Melody nearly shouted. "You're like the epicenter of everything! You're a magnet for craziness! That was incredible! You were almost run over!

Who was that? And who was in that second car? The one that saved you?"

Sonny, still dazed, stumbled toward his apartment. Melody went to steady him. "No," he protested, pulling away. "Stay away from me! You're evil!"

"Sonny, I know I've taken a few liberties, but I swear I'm on the up and up now. You're hurt. Let me help you."

"No," Sonny insisted. "I don't trust you."

"Just let me help you to your apartment."

"No!"

"I swear I won't publish any articles about this that you don't approve. Just let me help you to your apartment."

Sonny eyed her, wary of her intentions but acutely conscious of his compromised condition. She gave him a pleading look, which put him in mind of a hungry vulture. "I don't trust you. You've made my life miserable."

"I know," she admitted. "And I'm sorry. I exaggerated some facts. That's why I've been calling you. To apologize. That's why I waited on your steps this morning. Because you wouldn't return my calls so I could apologize."

Sonny eyed her suspiciously. "Cut through the bullshit. You've been stalking me."

She conceded with a shrug. "You're a reporter's

annuity. Trouble follows you like a seagull follows a garbage barge. Now, let me help you up to your apartment."

"Only if you promise that this will not appear in a news article."

She considered for a moment. "Okay," she finally agreed. "I promise that what happened this morning will not appear in a news article. Now, can I help you?" He inspected her, calculating, then put his arm around her shoulder and the two of them hobbled to his apartment.

Nosey

They were halfway up the steps, Sonny leaning on Melody, when an accusing voice interrupted from below. "I saw it all. What's going on, Sonny?" It was Sonny's landlord.

"Hey, Mr. Wilson," Sonny responded in the closest thing to a normal voice as he could muster.

"You saw it all?" asked Melody, excited.

"Who are you?"

"I'm Melody. Who are you?"

"I live downstairs." He turned his attention to Sonny, wagging a finger as he spoke, "This has to stop, Sonny. All this activity: cars screeching about, strange visitors knocking at your door, you coming and going at all hours. And stories in the paper: explosions and gunfights. This is a quiet neighborhood...." He paused as a deafening jet passed low overhead on its ascent from nearby Midway Airport. "This has to stop or you'll have to move out."

"Okay, Mr. Wilson," Sonny responded as he resumed his slow climb with his back to the man.

"Wait, can we talk?" Melody was torn as to whether to continue with Sonny or race down to interview the landlord.

Sonny read her mind. "No!" he answered emphatically. "You promised!" She frowned and followed him while Mr. Wilson disappeared around the corner of the house.

"Cozy digs," she commented as she surveyed his austere apartment. She removed her bulky parka to reveal a thin long frame underneath. "Somehow I expected something more." Sonny sat on the couch, wincing with pain.

She went to the kitchen area and began digging around like she owned the place. "Where's the coffee? Never mind, here it is. So are you alright? Who were those guys? Who was in the red car? It was vintage; had to be from the sixties. How long they been after you? Is this related to the bombing? Or the shooting? That was the coolest thing I've ever seen!"

She awaited a response as she prepared the coffee.

"You calling the police?" she asked.

"No."

"You should call the police."

"No!"

"Any normal person would call the police. Somebody tried to run you over."

"No!"

She thought for a moment. "You're not in a gang," she considered aloud. "You're not mixed up in drugs. You don't seem like the child porn type." She glanced around the room. "You're sure not taking bribes or cheating on your taxes." She snapped her fingers. "I've got it! You're trying to protect someone!"

She turned and faced him. "Who are you trying to protect? A client? A friend? Maybe a lover?" She studied him. "Man, you're really pale." Her eyes gravitated to his left hand. "Oh my God, look at that!" She pointed.

Sonny looked at his aching hand and for the first time noticed that his pinky finger was sticking straight out sideways. He was overcome with nausea.

"That's got to hurt," Melody matter-of-factly observed. She walked over, grabbed his left arm, and with her back to him, pinned it between her elbow and side. Before Sonny could react she gripped his crippled finger and gave it a violent yank. He yelped like a struck dog. "Ta-ta!" she exclaimed as she released his arm. Miraculously, the finger was back in its socket. "That's going to swell," she warned. "You really should get a splint."

She spied his IPhone on the tiny kitchen table. Before he could protest, she grabbed it and searched it for text messages and e-mails. Then she began scrolling through his contacts. "Short list of contacts," she commented. "Charlotte's that hot chick, right? Simon is the guy you saved, right? Who is Liz?" She frowned. "You've got me under 'Liar.' That's not nice."

Sonny's nausea passed. "If the shoe fits.... Say, how

did you do that?" He held up his injured hand. The pinky finger already was swelling and bruising.

"I wasn't real athletic in high school, so I became the football trainer. Dislocations happened all the time." She poured two cups of coffee and joined him on the couch, one leg tucked beneath her. Even through her baggy jeans and sweat shirt Sonny could tell she was all knees and elbows. He pictured her as an awkward adolescent and wondered where she got such confidence.

"Ever try cross country?" he asked.

"Huh?"

"In high school. It didn't take a lot of athletic ability."

"No. Only an idiot would succumb to that torture." She moved on, "Tell me, Sonny, who's trying to kill you and why?"

"Oh no you don't. I don't trust you."

"Ah, give me a break. Those stories were basically true."

"Not even close."

"Do you know how hard it is to get a gig as a reporter? Newspapers are dying. Everybody is cutting staff. The internet is taking over, and you can't make money selling stories on the internet. The only other place that's growing is television. And look at me. I don't have a chance on television."

"But you lied."

"Exaggerated maybe," she conceded. "But the public has a right to know."

"That's bullshit."

"Alright, I was desperate. You're the best story in town, you've got to admit. Come on, Sonny, let me do a follow up."

"No!"

"Please," she begged.

"No!"

She shrugged and drained her coffee mug. "Alright, alright." She stood and put on her parka, pulling the fur lined hood up as she stepped to the door. "You're sure you're okay?" She sounded sincere. "Don't forget to get that finger looked at. Might be fractured."

Healer

Liz held the x-ray to the light. "I don't see any fractures."

Sonny sat on the examination table, shirt off. He bore deep bruises on his back and shoulder. An abrasion gleamed pink and bloody on his left elbow. She took his hand and expertly applied a splint to stabilize his little finger. Then she cleaned and bandaged his seeping elbow. "You're going to be very stiff and very sore. I'm giving you a prescription for Percocet to help. It's an opiate, so be careful. No drinking. No driving." She nodded at his battered watch on the counter. "That's seen better days."

Sonny picked up the Timex, which bore a new gouge on the crystal from the fall. He had to tilt it to find a clear enough view of the hands to tell the time. It was still ticking. He set it back down.

Finished treating him, she took a seat on a low stool and looked up at his face. She leaned forward and put her forearms on his knees. He welcomed the intimacy. "You know, you don't have to go to all this trouble just to see me. You could just call and ask me on a date." She smiled and then her expression turned serious. "This was more than a slip on the ice."

"No," he said, but his expression told another story.

"I hope you don't play poker, because you're a terrible liar. You could dislocate a finger falling on ice. You could scrape an elbow. You could bruise a shoulder. But not all of them. I've seen hit-and-run victims with less damage."

"It's not something I can talk about."

"Sonny, you need to call the police."

He shook his head.

"You know, I'm supposed to report things like this."

He gave her a pleading look. She sighed and laid her cheek on his knee. He reached over and stroked her head. Her skin was smooth and warm, her hair feather soft. After several minutes, she eased away and stepped behind him, her lab coat brushing against him as she passed. He closed his eyes as she massaged his stiffening shoulders. All of his pain and fear temporarily melted away under her comforting touch. All of his tension faded like a shadow in sunshine. She leaned against him and exhaled a warm breath in his ear. "Be careful, Sonny," she whispered. "Please be careful, for me."

Abject Fear

Sonny's trip to the medical center was as much to escape the apartment as to seek medical care, but it provided only a momentary respite from his stark situation. Up until the car attack any threat Sonny felt had been distant and illusive, like a shadowy ghost, a source of background anxiety but not quite real. The car attack turned the ghost into a flesh and blood demon. Sonny's fear was now visceral, inescapable. He knew the attacks weren't merely to scare him. Someone was trying to kill him. He was terrified, for both himself and for Charlotte, who likely was the primary target of the assassin.

Abject fear engulfed him as soon as Melody Gothim left his apartment and the realization set in that his attackers knew where he lived and could return at any time. His apartment, always a sanctuary from the stresses of the world, no longer felt safe. The first thing he did was prop a kitchen chair under the front doorknob. Then he dug an old Chicago Cubs souvenir bat from the closet. He tried to call Charlotte, but she refused to answer. He was reluctant to leave a detailed message for fear of panicking her. "Char, it's urgent. You need to call me right away. And you need to be very, very careful. Please call me."

After leaving Liz and her tender affection, he feared returning home, preferring the security and mobility that his BMW provided. So he left the medical center and drove. He got on I-55 and headed north toward downtown. He drove by Charlotte's, stopping to buzz her intercom, but she did not answer and her apartment appeared dark. He drove east through the city until he reached Lake Shore Drive, then turned south past McCormick Place and through south Chicago. The sun was bright, the air crisp and cold. A brisk wind chopped the water and made the lake look like a glittering blanket.

He thought to call Simon, but he knew it would be futile. Simon detested cell phones, e-mail and virtually all forms of modern communication. He generally turned his cell phone off in the evening and on weekends. Even when it was on, Simon rarely checked his voicemail until someone scolded him because his mailbox was full. Still, Sonny tried to reach him and left him an urgent message to call.

He considered calling the police, as much for Charlotte's protection as his own. But he more feared betraying her again by possibly compromising her father. He never should have forced her to extend the evening with Bindi. He felt her humiliation to his core.

He had hurt her. He had forced a bigger wedge between Charlotte and her mother. Worse, he had damaged his own relationship with her, probably irreparably. He also felt a gnawing guilt about his growing infatuation with Liz, despite Charlotte's recent indifference toward him. He wanted so much for things to return to how they were, when they were best friends and lovers. But that would never be now.

He drove for hours, the baseball bat within reach in the passenger seat, stopping to fill the tank near Calumet on the Indiana border. Then he made his way to I-294 and headed north back toward Chicago. His attention was focused as much on his rearview mirror as his windshield. The roads were peppered with black sedans; his heart raced with each one he spied. He saw no red Cadillacs. If the black Town Car was a mystery, the red Cadillac was a bigger one. How had it materialized seemingly from nowhere? Why had it intervened to save him? Who else was stalking him?

Who Loves You?

He passed the I-55 interchange, which would take him home, and cruised through Ogden, then west on I-88, exiting on Route 59. He turned south off the ramp to where the busy thoroughfare formed the border between Naperville and Aurora and soon found himself in a retail Mecca of strip malls, shopping centers and restaurants. Traffic crawled as holiday shoppers flocked to the stores. Tired of driving, he pulled into the Fox Valley Mall and parked. He grunted with pain as he exited the car; both his shoulder and back were beginning to ache.

Sonny wandered through the packed mall feeling secure and anonymous in the crowd. He watched the many families as parents tried to shepherd their excited children, who were wild with anticipation of the pending holiday. He studied all of the couples, from teens to senior citizens, as they strolled hand-in-hand, some looking comfortable together and others looking awkwardly self conscious. He thought of Liz and her easy affection. He thought of Charlotte, tempestuous Charlotte, and he wished she were here with him now.

His back continued to stiffen so he bought an ice

cream cone and found an empty bench in the center of the mall. On a nearby bench an older man sat with two young children, a boy perhaps five and a girl who appeared to be three. The boy sat quietly, savoring a chocolate ice cream cone. The girl fidgeted about, climbing on and off the bench while the man offered her intermittent bites of ice cream from a cup they shared.

"Eric, who loves you?" the man asked.

"You do, Grandpa," answered the boy without taking his eyes off the cone.

"How much?"

The boy stretched his arms as far as they would go, nearly tipping the ice cream from the cone in the process.

"Jessica, who loves you?"

"You do," answered the little girl, who was now standing on the bench beside him.

"How much?"

"This much!" She stretched her arms wide. Then she grabbed his cheeks in her tiny hands and gave him a kiss on the forehead.

"Don't ever forget that," said the grandfather.

"We won't," the children responded in unison.

Sonny was taken by the tender scene, one obviously practiced often. He reflected on his own life and realized with sober clarity that his parents had never told him they loved him. Indeed, he had never said those words to anyone. He was prepared to once, when he was seventeen and found himself sharing the back seat of a car with Mary Cummings, his first sweetheart. But the gesture proved unnecessary as Mary required little coaxing to share in Sonny's first sexual experience. Now sensitized to his own mortality, he wondered if he would ever get the chance to truly love and be loved by someone.

As dusk settled, Sonny left the mall and made his way back to I-88 East. He stopped first at a drug store to fill his prescription and then at a diner off of Cicero near his apartment. He parked in back by a stinky dumpster to stay out of view. He had little appetite. He ordered a hamburger, fries and a beer.

"You alright? You look like you just lost your best friend," the waitress observed as she brought the food. Sonny took his time eating and lingered long afterward over a cup of coffee. Finally, he headed home, knowing it would be a long and sleepless night and completely unaware of the finned red Cadillac that had followed him the entire day.

Calumet Hideout

While Sonny was filling his gas tank earlier that day, the two brothers sat on folding chairs in a dingy apartment in the gritty mill section of Calumet. The four-unit clapboard building was run down and in desperate need of paint. The shiny black Town Car looked out of place in the weed invested gravel drive and overgrown yard, now brown and matted entering winter. The brothers moved into the first floor unit four weeks earlier, paying cash to the slum landlord who owned it and who asked no questions. The elderly black man living in the unit next door rarely emerged from his apartment except to buy wine and cigarettes. The upstairs units were vacant.

The apartment was empty except for the folding table and chairs at which they sat and the two camp mattresses on the floor, where they made their beds. A small television, off now, sat on the scarred hard wood floor. Near the beds was a pair of matching duffel bags, their contents of clothing spilling out. In the small kitchen, the counters were cluttered with empty fast food bags and boxes of snack food and dry cereal.

Bomani, sullen, angry, slumped in his chair with his arms crossed. He bore a red welt on his right cheek, evidence of the open-handed blow he received earlier from his brother. Growing up, both boys were accustomed to the heavy handed corporal punishment administered by their father, who emigrated from Egypt when they were toddlers. Now that he was dead, shot by a drug addict attempting to rob their convenience store in one of the more infamous neighborhoods on Chicago's south side, Kafele filled the role of disciplinarian. Their mother long ago fled the family after one too many beatings. Since their late teens the brothers had been alone to fend for themselves. Alone except for welcome support they received from the secretive unaffiliated mosque in a Calumet warehouse near their hideaway. The teenagers, angry and disillusioned, had proven to be fertile soil for the Imam's radical mission.

There was a knock. The brothers exchanged apprehensive glances. Kafele went to the door and let in the Imam, who made no effort to conceal his anger.

"You defied me!" accused their visitor when the door was closed. He spoke accented English. He ignored Kafele's invitation to sit. "You were ordered to take no action! Why did you defy me?"

Bomani stared at the floor, radiating contempt. Kafele stepped into the breach. "We're sorry. My brother can be impulsive. The target was there, in front of us. Bomani was only anxious to serve for Jihad."

"Three times you've failed"

"We won't fail again."

"You are embarrassments! I'm angry and others are angry! People who don't tolerate failure!"

Bomani could stand it no longer. "This isn't Jihad!" he raised his voice. "Who are these people? Probably infidels! We came to wage Jihad, not chase around an incompetent boy!"

The Imam glared at the impetuous young man. "That boy has outwitted you three times! Your sloppy efforts have made headlines! And our sponsor has pledged ten million to our cause! There is no Jihad without funding!"

Kafele stepped between them. "Forgive Bomani," he pleaded. "He's not thinking clearly."

"You two need to be more respectful. You don't want to cross those funding us." Fear displaced the anger in his eyes. "You *don't* want to cross them," he repeated.

"What now?" asked Kafele as Bomani trained his stare at the floor.

"You wait. You stay here and you wait until I contact you. You must not fail again." He pulled an envelope from his pocket and tossed it on the table. "Cash for your living expenses. I'll call." He turned and left. As the door closed behind him he heard the crack of a palm striking Bomani's head followed by a thump as his body hit the floor.

Monday Surprise

Sonny was wrong about a sleepless Saturday night. Liz's prediction of stiffness and pain came true with a vengeance; by the time he returned to his apartment he could barely make it up the steps. His back was as stiff as an ironing board; his neck had developed a painful crick that forced him to cock his head; his elbow burned; and his injured finger felt like it might burst from the swelling. He took a Percocet and was out for the night.

Sunday was a wasted day. Between the stiffness of his battered body and the Percocet induced haze, he cared little whether assassins were lurking about. He lounged most of the day on his couch watching old movies on TV. Liz called to check on him in the afternoon and hinted about getting together for dinner, but he was too loopy to drive. He tried again to reach Charlotte, but again his call rolled into voicemail.

He awoke Monday morning, still physically sore but clear minded and restored. He looked outside. The December clouds were low and gray. He saw no suspicious cars on the street. He checked his phone for messages and was hopeful when he saw a text from

Charlotte. But her cryptic comment was not what he wanted to read: "Don't need a ride." Too numb and discouraged to eat, he dressed and headed for work, barely paying attention to the possible threats around him.

He parked in the vacant lot on Harrison and headed for the office, dreading encountering Charlotte after Friday night. As he walked he rehearsed in his mind what to say to her – how to apologize – but he could think of no plausible approach. He stopped in his tracks as he turned down the alley next to their building. Parked near the back was a black sedan. His blood went cold until he noted that the car bore a government license plate. The driver door opened and out stepped Adonis Manos, looking impeccable in a long wool coat. Adonis walked around and opened the passenger door. Sonny's stomach churned with nausea as Charlotte climbed from the car. He watched unnoticed as Adonis put his hand on her back and rubbed it affectionately before the two of them disappeared around the corner.

Sonny leaned against the cold brick building, despondent with despair. He wished the black Town Car would appear and race toward him, so he could step in front of it and end this misery.

Newsmaker

Sonny collected himself and made his way to the back stairway, which was as gloomy as his spirit. His Italian loafers felt like they were made of granite as he drudged up the steps. He felt devoid of energy. He entered the office suite and noted that Charlotte and Simon were not in their offices and the conference room lights were on.

Charlotte, Simon and Adonis were seated at the conference table when he stepped through the doorway. They all stared at him without speaking, Simon with a sober look of concern, Charlotte with eyes swollen from crying, and Adonis with a grim stare of disapproval. Charlotte noticed the splint on Sonny's hand and gave a muffled sob.

"What?" asked Sonny.

Adonis tossed the morning's TRIBUNE at him. Sonny caught it and looked at the front page. There, staring back was a three column photograph of him, dazed and terrified, leaning back on his elbows on the sidewalk. The illumination of the flash gave him a washed out appearance as he lay surrounded by shadow. His left pinky finger, jutting unnaturally sideways, was particularly prominent.

He read the caption as his face flushed with anger: *"Sonny B. Feelright lies injured on the sidewalk Saturday morning after being nearly run down by a car near Midway Airport. It was the third attack on the forensic accountant in as many weeks. TRIBUNE reporter Melody Gothim witnessed the attack and writes about her experience on Page 28."*

He found page twenty eight – the Commentary page. "Should Reporters Make News?" read the lead headline, followed by a bylined column by Melody Gothim:

"'If a tree falls in the forest, does it make a noise?' For a news reporter, this paradoxical question might more aptly be phrased, 'If a news event happens and no one is there to see it, is it newsworthy?'

"Our job as journalists is to report the news objectively and fairly. Usually we arrive at the scene after the event and we tell the story through the eyes of witnesses and officials. Occasionally, we are the witness, a party to the event. Which begs the question, can we objectively report about events in which we unwittingly participate.

"Such was the case Saturday morning when I was eyewitness to a terrifying automobile attack on accounting sleuth Sonny B. Feelright. Feelright heads a forensic accounting firm that investigates accounting fraud. And it apparently is dangerous work. Two weeks ago, Feelright was nearly killed in a bomb attack near his offices on West Harrison Street. The perpetrator has not been identified. The very next day Feelright

foiled an assassination attempt at the Red Swan Tavern, also on West Harrison, when he single-handedly disarmed a gunman, who escaped and remains at large.

"So it was on Saturday morning that I found myself visiting Feelright's apartment near Midway Airport to ask some follow-up questions. Feelright was returning from a morning run – he obviously needs to stay in top physical condition given the perils of his profession – when a late model black Lincoln Town Car appeared from nowhere and sped toward him. Displaying remarkable athleticism, Feelright dodged the speeding vehicle and dove for the sidewalk, landing hard on his back and dislocating his finger. The car sped backwards toward the prone Feelright in a second attempt but apparently was scared off when an older model red Cadillac appeared on the street and blocked its path."

The column proceeded to recite the details of the two prior attacks. It ended, *"Although I am a trained observer, the drama of Saturday's episode affected me. The abrupt violence of the attack distracted me from seeing details, such as the car's license number and the description of the driver. The sight of Mr. Feelright, injured on the ground after diving to save his life, left me feeling vulnerable and aware of my own fragile mortality. But I was most affected by Feelright's calm confidence after the event, which didn't even warrant a call to the police in his estimation.*

"There have been three attempts on Feelright's life in recent weeks. One wonders how many more may have occurred when

witnesses weren't around to make it news. As a reporter, I must admit that it is difficult to remain objective when reporting on a real live action figure like Sonny B. Feelright."

Sonny slammed the paper on the table. "That liar!"

"Is it true?" asked Adonis.

"She swore she wouldn't write an article!"

"Is it true?" Adonis was angry now.

Sonny hesitated, searching each of their faces. "Yes, it's true," he conceded. "It happened Saturday morning."

"Why didn't you call the police? Why didn't you call me?"

Sonny looked at Charlotte, who was crying openly now. He shrugged.

"Have you ever heard of obstructing justice? That's a crime. The courts take it very seriously. And you're about one minute away from being charged with it. Now, why didn't you call the police? Why am I reading about this shit in the papers?" Sonny remained silent as Adonis's anger rose.

"It's my fault," Charlotte squeaked. All eyes turned to her. "He's trying to protect me. He's trying to protect my father."

Adonis went red but he said nothing, abruptly aware of his own complicity in warning Charlotte about Danny Byrne. He turned back to Sonny. "So, start at the beginning. Tell me what happened."

Sonny sat down and related the story of his weekend, including his trip to the clinic and his Percocet blurred Sunday. Adonis took notes but did not interrupt. When Sonny finished he asked, "Are you sure the voices you heard were foreign?"

"I think so. They were shouting. It sounded Middle Eastern."

"And you never saw the Cadillac before?"

"No."

"You didn't see who was driving?"

Sonny shook his head.

Simon, who had been quiet the entire morning, spoke up. "Agent Manos, if someone is trying to scare Charlotte's father, why hasn't she been targeted?"

The agent shrugged. "Probably because I'm keeping an eye on her."

Sonny's breath fled as completely as it had on the sidewalk Saturday morning.

More Visitors

As Adonis crossed the outer office to leave, Inspector Robinson stepped in. He marched purposefully into the conference room and tossed a copy of the TRIBUNE in front of Sonny. "What the hell is this?" he demanded.

Sonny shrugged.

"Is it true?"

"Sort of," Sonny nodded. "That reporter takes liberties, though."

"I'll say, because you're no 'real live action figure.' Why didn't you report this?"

Sonny had no answer.

"Bombings, shootings, car attacks. Combat soldiers don't get this much action. Let me ask you, how's business?"

"Good," Sonny gestured to the piles of files and documents littering the tables in the room. "We've got more than we can handle."

"The first time I came here you didn't have a single client. Now that your name is splashed all over the place you're booming. Is that a coincidence?"

Charlotte snapped to attention. "Are you implying that we staged these attacks?"

Robinson shrugged. Her face went crimson. He turned back to Sonny. "Are you filing a police report?"

"I didn't plan to."

"Didn't think so." The detective searched each of their faces. "I better not find this is all a hoax!" He turned and disappeared.

Simon looked at his watch with an impatient expression. "Look," he said, "we've got a business to run, despite all of these distractions. Obviously, someone is targeting us. I recommend we hire some security here while we're working. Outside of work we have to be very careful. You both should look into security for your apartments – locks and alarms. Try not to go out alone." He trained a penetrating gaze at Charlotte. "Have you confronted your father?"

Tears welled in her eyes again, overwhelming Sonny's emotions. "Don't cry, Charlotte," he pleaded. "Why are you crying?"

"Because I was worried about you!" she lashed at him. "Because Adonis showed up on my door step at six in the morning to tell me you were attacked and injured! Because you never bothered to call and tell me!"

"I did call! Why didn't you call me back?"

"Because I hate you!" she bellowed and stormed from the room.

"I'm sorry, Simon. It's about Friday. We went and met her mother. It didn't go well. I'll go and get her."

"Please," mumbled Simon, who buried his craggy face in his hands.

Charlotte sat at her desk, arms crossed tightly, staring at the ceiling.

"Charlotte, I'm sorry about Friday. I never should have made you go to that place."

"*You* certainly seemed to enjoy it! How is Doctor Lovelace, anyway? I'm assuming she took care of your hand, too."

"I went to the clinic. She was on duty," he defended helplessly. "I tried to call you. I even stopped on Saturday afternoon, but you weren't there?"

"I was out."

"Where?"

"Having coffee."

"With whom?"

She hesitated. "Agent Manos stopped by to check on me. We went to Starbucks."

Sonny was dumbfounded. "He just happened to stop by?"

"He's concerned. It's not a crime. And it's really none of your business."

A woman's voice in the outer office interrupted them. "Hello?" He turned to see Liz entering. She smiled at him, walked up and gave him an affectionate hug, which he received stiffly. "Sonny, I read the paper. I knew it was more than a fall on the ice. Is everything alright?" She turned and noticed Charlotte, who was staring daggers at the couple in her doorway. "This is probably a bad time," she said, backing away from Sonny. "I brought you this. You left it." She handed Sonny his battered Timex. "Call me, okay?" Liz stepped out of Charlotte's view and mouthed "I'm sorry," to Sonny. Then she tiptoed out the door.

Back to Business

The battle waged for fifteen minutes behind Charlotte's closed door before Simon intervened. He poked his head in and shouted, "Enough!" They stopped arguing and looked at him. "You two need to work this out on your own time. We have work to do. And a lot more on the way." He held up his legal pad, displaying a page of names and addresses. "We got six more inquiries this morning, all referencing the article. And the girl at the answering service still wants to meet you, Sonny."

Charlotte squinted a battle stare at Sonny, then grabbed her notebook and returned to the conference room, shouldering him as she passed. Sonny raised his palms and gave Simon a bewildered look before marching after her.

Simon sat between the two stoic combatants, who refused to make eye contact. "Let's start with the divorces. Charlotte, status?"

Charlotte proceeded to provide an update on the divorce investigations, directing her report to Simon as though Sonny was not in the room. "We've got an issue with the Danner divorce. The husband retained us because he believes his wife has stashed some money away and is hiding it from the court. But when we tried to reconcile his payroll stubs with his bank statements, the checks and his deposits don't add up."

"You're saying *he's* been stashing money away?"

"It looks that way. I'm not sure how to handle it."

"How much are we talking?"

"Looks like around fifty-thousand dollars over the past three years."

"Who's his attorney? Do you have his number?" Charlotte retrieved the attorney's business card from a file and passed it to Simon, who dialed on speaker phone.

"Hey Tom, this is Charlotte over at Feelright Intelligence," Charlotte greeted the attorney. "I've got you on the speaker with two of my colleagues, Simon Courtney and Sonny Feelright. It's about the Danner divorce."

"Is that *the* Sonny Feelright, from the paper?" the attorney asked.

"Yes," answered Simon as Charlotte rolled her eyes. "Tom, this is Simon Courtney. You wanted us to track down whether Mrs. Danner is hiding assets from the court."

"Yes. Do you have something?"

"You know, that would be perjury, a felony. It could involve jail time if it occurred."

"I'm well aware of that. I'm sure Mr. Danner wouldn't shed many tears if his wife spends time in jail. According to him, living with her for the past twenty years *was* a prison." He chuckled. "What have you found?"

"Nothing yet," answered Simon. "Given the seriousness of the allegation, we might need some more records to look at. You see, we're seeing a discrepancy between his paychecks and his bank deposits. Probably just a banking error. Or maybe they've got another account somewhere that he forgot to tell us about."

The attorney was silent for a moment. "How much are we talking about?"

"Looks like around fifty thousand. Anyway, we're at a crossroads and wanted some direction on whether to push the investigation further. We don't have enough information yet to confirm anything, but we certainly wouldn't want to testify in court without being absolutely sure."

"Dumb bastard," the attorney sighed under his breath. "You know, it's probably best that we not go down the hidden assets path. I'm sure my client will agree when I speak with him. Why don't you pack up all the records and send them back to my office, along with your final invoice."

"Certainly," answered Simon as Charlotte jotted a note to herself. "We appreciate the business and hope you'll use us in the future."

"And I appreciate your professionalism and discretion. Especially your discretion. Thank you."

"That's one case closed," said Simon after ending the call.

"My God," huffed Charlotte. "That's despicable. He was accusing his wife of hiding assets the whole time he was hiding assets from her. What man would do that?" She shot an accusing glance at Sonny.

Simon ignored her comment. "I closed one more investigation this weekend. I finished my report on the liquor shortages. I'm projecting they'll be able to save over ten-thousand dollars per restaurant per year."

"How?" asked Sonny.

"Simple. I visited all ten of their restaurants. In every case, I was comped at least one drink. Sometimes at the bar, sometimes at the tables. The staff is giving away drinks like water."

"Keeps the customer coming back, I suppose," offered Sonny. "What are you recommending?"

"That any free drinks be approved by a manager. If servers comp drinks without management approval, they pay for it out of their tips." He sighed wistfully. "I'm going to miss that assignment. Let's move on to the Herkmeier case. Have we learned anything?"

Dark Pools

Charlotte pulled out some notes and proceeded to cite the names of the law firms and accountants for each of the six companies that Bill Herkmeier identified as victims of unusual stock trading. She summarized, "Just two of the companies use the same accountants and two other companies have the same law firm. None of the firms have common board members. In short, I don't see any connection among the companies."

"Sonny, what did you find?"

Sonny passed out copies of company profiles he had printed from the internet. "These are stock reports on the main competitors of the six companies. I don't see anything in their trading activity or stock prices that would suggest insider trading. Of course, none of them have had any unusual events recently. No mergers or acquisitions."

Simon pondered the apparent dead end they had reached. "Charlotte, go through those accounting and law firms and tell me where they're located."

She studied her notes. "Chicago. They're all headquartered in Chicago."

"Bingo! We have a connection!"

"I don't get it," offered Sonny.

"I don't get it completely either," admitted Simon. "But we have a thread to work with. We know where to look next. We need to find out who was doing the trading and if there is a connection to Chicago. Who benefited from the inside information? If we know that we may be able to trace it to the source."

"Can we go to public trading records?"

"Ha!" laughed Simon. "If it were only that easy. Mutual funds have to report their holdings semi-annually, so you have some idea of what they're buying and selling. But the private money, the hedge funds and investment banks, go out of their way to obscure what they're doing. Ostensibly, it's so people can't track them and follow their investment strategies. But it also can hide a lot of misdeeds. They often trade in 'street name,' which means placing your trades through another firm. For really big investments they might hire several firms to make the trades so no one can see that they're dumping or accumulating stock.

"The really sophisticated guys use 'dark pool' trading platforms. These are electronic trading companies that operate outside the public markets. It's where big blocks of stock are exchanged outside of public view."

Charlotte, still incensed about the Danner divorce misdeeds, was appalled. "That goes against the whole notion of trading transparency. It's sinister. It's just a tool to manipulate the markets."

"The big institutions would argue that it's a pillar of a free and unfettered market," responded Simon, a hint of sarcasm in his voice.

"That's utter bullshit! It isn't a free market if they can manipulate it!"

"Almost any manipulative or monopolistic scheme can be rationalized under the cloak of the free market mantra," offered Simon. "'Patriotism is the last refuge to which a scoundrel clings.'"

Sonny and Charlotte looked at him blankly.

"A Bob Dylan song. Never mind. Figuring out who is behind the Chicago trades won't be easy."

"How do we do it?" she asked.

"I have a friend who used to work for Georgeson & Company in New York. He's still in the network. I'll call him."

"Who is Georgeson?" asked Sonny.

"It's one of the leading proxy solicitation firms in the country. Proxy solicitors make their living trying to sort through all of the trading obscurity to find out who is really buying and selling stocks. Public companies hire them to keep track of their institutional shareholders and make sure they can get enough votes at annual meeting time so management can keep their jobs. It's a big industry. I'll call him and see what he can tell us."

Date Plans

"Alright," concluded Simon, "that covers the current case load." He studied the list of new prospects on his pad. "Charlotte, can you screen these?" He tore off the page and handed it to her. "Look," he said, "if this keeps up we're going to need some more bodies here. We may have to hire some people."

His partners looked at him with raised eyebrows. Three weeks ago they were starving for work. Now they were looking at expanding. "Maybe we should wait a bit, to make sure it continues," Sonny argued. Charlotte nodded her agreement.

"It's going to continue," Simon stated. "Especially if Sonny keeps making the front page. Which gets us back to where this meeting started this morning." He looked at Charlotte. "Charlotte, when are you planning to confront your father? This violence has to stop."

She said nothing. Sonny spoke up, "I talked to her mother Friday night." She gave him a quizzical look. "She confirmed that Danny Byrne is a client of Douglas McCardle. He also advises a couple of his friends. Unsavory friends. But mostly he works for big hedge funds."

"What did you learn about his business?" Simon asked.

"Not much. Faith said he started the business after he lost his job at First Boston. She said he was very secretive at the time, but they weren't communicating much because of their divorce."

"Does she know what kind of services he provides?"

"No. She said he doesn't have any employees and he doesn't publish research. But they apparently pay him a lot. She questioned what kind of advice he can give them that they don't already know."

"Anything else?" quizzed Simon.

"Yea. I checked out Danny Byrne's car dealership in Schaumburg."

"What?" gasped Charlotte. "When?"

"Friday afternoon, before I picked you up."

"Sonny, that could have been dangerous!"

"I don't know," he responded. "It seemed like a real business to me. The place is loaded with expensive cars. They've got an interactive web site and a real sales staff. It all looked legit."

"Charlotte's right," asserted Simon. "If Danny Byrne is behind all of these attacks that could have been dangerous. It was a foolish thing to do."

"Sunday," Charlotte interrupted.

"What?" asked Simon.

"Sunday. I'll visit my father Sunday. But I'm not going alone. Sonny has to come."

Photographs

Sonny didn't challenge Charlotte after being conscripted to visit her father. The day had been too contentious already; he would approach her later in the week. After the staff meeting she gathered an armload of files and retreated to work alone in her office, the door closed. She declined his offer to step out with him for lunch. At the end of the day he poked his head into her office and asked if she needed a ride home.

"I've got a ride," she answered.

"Adonis?" he asked, but she didn't respond. A short time later she packed her portfolio and left without saying goodnight. Dejected, Sonny retreated to his office to sulk.

"Aren't you going home?" Simon asked as he prepared to depart.

"In a while. I've got some things to do."

"You shouldn't be here alone," warned Simon.

"I'll be alright."

"What about going to your car?"

"Don't worry. I'll be careful." In fact, he didn't care if he lived or died at that moment. Simon ordered Sonny to lock the door behind him when he left.

Back in his office, Sonny retrieved his IPhone and pulled up the photos he took on Friday night. He stared at Charlotte and her mother. Classical beauties both, they could have adorned the cover of any fashion magazine. In the photograph they looked like best friends, both smiling and seemingly happy. Charlotte had smiled at him like that in the past, happy to be in his presence. He flipped to the group photo, where Charlotte's frown radiated contempt for Dom Bindi, who grinned obnoxiously from the page. It was the same hateful look she had flashed at him today. He e-mailed the first photo to his laptop, where he downloaded it to the photo printer in Charlotte's office. He printed three copies. One he placed in the center of her desk. One he put in his portfolio to take home. And one he put in a large envelope.

His phone rang. It was Melody Gothim -- liar. His first impulse was to end the call without answering, but his contempt got the best of him. "How dare you call me!" he scolded.

"What did I do?" Melody asked innocently.

"You lied! You promised me you wouldn't write an article about Saturday."

"I didn't!" she argued.

"Then what was that on the front page of the TRIBUNE? What was that article you wrote? It had your byline, for God's sake!"

"That wasn't a news article. That was an op-ed piece. It was on the Commentary page. Wasn't it cool? It's every reporter's dream to byline an opinion column. Do you know how jealous all of these people are? Some of them have worked here twenty years and never gotten to do a column. You know, they've put a name tag on my cubicle! I'm the only intern here with a name tag on a cubicle!"

"Bullshit!" Sonny shouted.

"Look, Sonny, I was calling for a follow up. Tell me what you're working on. Who's after you and why? I know you know. Give me a break here."

"You've got to be kidding me!" Sonny ended the call, wishing he had a traditional phone receiver that he could slam in its cradle.

His phone rang again. "Leave me alone!" he shouted without looking at the caller ID.

"I'm sorry," Liz stammered.

"No, no, not you," he apologized. "I thought you were someone else – that reporter who wrote the story this morning. I'm sorry. She's harassing me no end."

"It sounds like you're having a really bad day. I called to apologize about this morning. I shouldn't have shown up without calling first. I hope I didn't get you in trouble with Charlotte."

"No, you didn't. I was glad you came. You shouldn't have left so quickly. I was glad to see you."

She chuckled. "No you weren't. You were mortified. And if Charlotte had a gun within reach she would have shot us both."

"No, it's not like that. She was just upset about work and the attacks."

"Like I said before, you're not a good liar. There's only one reason a woman gets that pissed; it's when she's mad at a man she cares about. And Charlotte was mad at you. You can tell me the truth. I know there's something going on between you two."

"I swear, Liz, there's nothing going on. We spent some time together, but she's moved on. She's seeing someone else. In fact, she pretty much detests me."

"If she detests you, she absolutely hates me," she laughed. "Look, Sonny, I like you a lot. I'm not looking for any long term commitments. I'm not trying to compete with Charlotte – I couldn't if I wanted to. But I'd really like to see you again. And I'm worried about you. That article this morning scared me. That's why I came by. I needed to know you were okay."

"I really like you, too, Liz."

"So, can we get together? Maybe go on a real date?"

Sonny recalled his horrible day. He considered the lonely evening ahead and the threats surrounding him. Suddenly, he wanted to see Liz Loveland more than he ever wanted anything in his life. "What about tonight?" he proposed with genuine enthusiasm.

She sighed. "Unfortunately, I have to work. But promise me you'll call me."

"I promise," he answered, feeling as low as the silt on the bottom of the ocean.

Red Eldorado

Sonny trudged to his car, head down, one hand buried in his pocket, the other holding his battered briefcase. He was so lost in misery that he didn't even notice the icy wind that had carried a cold front through, dropping the temperature into the teens. He rounded the vacant building next door to where his car was parked in the overgrown and seldom used parking lot. He froze in his steps. There, idling next to his BMW, sat the long red Cadillac, its parking lights on and exhaust billowing from the tailpipe into the frigid twilight air.

He stared at the car, adrenaline racing. Between the darkness and its tinted windows he could not see how many or who was inside. Fear and confusion consumed him. Should he run? If so, where? Not back to his locked office. Not down the vacant street, where most of the businesses were closed for the night. Should he yell for help? What good would it do; there was no one around to hear him. As he pondered his limited options the passenger window rolled down. He could see a man in shadows in the driver seat, his face faintly illuminated by the instrument lights.

"Sonny Feelright, come over here," the man commanded.

Sonny shook his head.

"I'm not going to hurt you. Come over here."

Sonny approached the car warily, half expecting to be shot at any moment. He stopped fifteen feet away and peered in. "This is close enough."

"Suit yourself," the figure shrugged. While Sonny couldn't make out his features, he could tell the man had a thin face and dark hair. He wore a dark wool overcoat, obscuring his build.

"What do you want?" Sonny demanded, trying to sound threatening.

"After Saturday morning I'd think you would want to thank me."

"What do you want?" Sonny repeated.

"I know somebody who wants to meet you. Soon."

"Who?"

"My boss."

"Who's that?"

"You should know. Danny Byrne. He wants to buy you breakfast tomorrow."

"What if I say no?"

The man sighed. "Kid, if he wanted to hurt you you'd be hurt by now, don't you think?"

Sonny pondered the logic. "I guess. Why does he want to meet me?"

"Because you're so fucking popular," the man answered, his patience wearing thin.

"When and where?"

"There's a Hyatt in Schaumburg, not far from the dealership. You know where that is. Meet him there at seven."

Sonny nodded.

"And Sonny, don't tell anybody. Okay? Especially not that FBI friend of yours." He rolled up the window and disappeared.

Suspect Advisor

Sonny sat in his car until it warmed up, shaken by his encounter with the red Cadillac. He pulled slowly from the lot, indecisive about what to do, whom to call. The street was empty, no red Cadillacs or black sedans. He feared returning to his apartment. He was being pursued by more than one stalker. He worked his way to the Loop and headed toward Lincoln Park. The neighborhood was bright and festive, in contrast to his mood of depression and foreboding.

Faith McCardle greeted him when he rang the doorbell. "Sonny! My God! I read about you in the paper! Are you alright? What are you doing here?" She opened the door and let him in.

"I hope I'm not interrupting. I brought you something." He handed her the envelope containing the photo of her and Charlotte.

She stepped back and inspected him, then grabbed his bandaged hand and examined it. She ushered him into the living room and insisted on taking his coat. "Sit down. Tell me what's going on with you?"

"I don't know what's happening. The paper told the whole story."

"Does this have something to do with our conversation last Friday? About Danny Byrne?"

"I don't know. I don't think so."

She studied him. "What can I get you? You look tired. Have you eaten?"

"No, but I don't need anything."

"Nonsense," she insisted. She put the envelope on the coffee table and disappeared into the kitchen.

"Where's Dominic?" Sonny called.

"He was here earlier for dinner. He left a half hour ago. You just missed him." Sonny exhaled a sigh of relief. Faith swept into the room a few moments later with a tray of Christmas cookies and a glass of milk. "Is milk alright, or do you want something stronger. I've got some of Dom's Chianti in the refrigerator."

"No, milk is fine. Actually," he admitted, "I'm not a fan of that Chianti. It soured my stomach."

"Actually," she conceded, "I don't like it either." She flashed him a conspiratorial grin.

"Where is Dom? Where does he stay when he's not here?"

"He has a suite at the Drake downtown."

Sonny raised his eyebrows. "Expensive tastes."

"What did you bring for me?" She reached for the envelope on the table and withdrew the photograph. "Oh, Sonny!" she exclaimed with heartfelt emotion. "It's beautiful!" She studied the photo intently and then looked up at him with moist eyes. "Sonny, I can't tell you how much this means to me."

"Have you spoken with her?"

Faith shook her head, trying to control her emotions. Her lower lip quivered.

"You should call her."

"No. She hates me."

"She doesn't hate you. Look, Faith, it's none of my business, but it's Dominic she resents. He was pretty overbearing on Friday, you have to admit."

She didn't disagree. "You don't know Dom. He's really very sweet and loving. He's not always like that." Sonny looked unconvinced. "He's also very supportive. He helps me a lot. You don't know how hard it is to be single after being married for so long. I didn't even know how to write a check." She hesitated. "Dom's offered to manage my money for me."

Sonny raised his eyebrows.

"He says I could be doing way better. I've got my money in a bunch of mutual funds right now."

"Faith, are you sure that's a good idea?"

"He's a top investment advisor in Italy."

"But maybe you should do some checking first. Isn't Italy bankrupt?"

She blushed. "Don't say anything to Charlotte, but he's talking about marriage. I think he may ask me on Christmas."

Mystery

Sleep was the last thing on Sonny's mind when he returned to his apartment. His foremost concern was scanning for threats as he parked and made his way warily up the steps. The wind was blowing hard, obscuring his hearing and making the shadows dip and lunge. Once inside, every gust made the old house creak and groan, each sound resembling an invading intruder. Equally unsettling was his pending breakfast with Danny Byrne. The dark stranger was right; if Danny Byrne wished to hurt him it would have happened already. But why did the mobster want to meet with him?

He thought about alerting Simon and Charlotte about his breakfast appointment, but he knew they would object. So he simply sent Charlotte a text message that he would be late for work. She responded back almost instantly, "I have a ride." He groaned.

Sonny also was disturbed by his conversation with Faith. He could not imagine such a beautiful and refined woman marrying a cad like Bindi. He was especially suspicious about Bindi's offer to manage her savings. Watching Bindi blow over five hundred dollars of Sonny's money at Peaches inspired little confidence in the Italian's prudence in money matters.

Sonny booted up his laptop and went online. A search for Dominic Bindi yielded scant hits so he plugged the name into his background research services. Still no connection to the man dating Faith McCardle. Next, he searched through a number of Italian banks and money management firms, scrolling through the lists of their officers and directors. No Dominic Bindi. Finally, he Googled Chicago's Drake Hotel and dialed the phone number into his IPhone. He was informed that no one named Dominic Bindi was a guest.

Gangsters

After a restless night, Sonny finally lapsed into a deep sleep near dawn. He slept through his alarm and awoke in a panic at six thirty, just a half hour from his appointment. He jumped in the shower and restrained himself as he shaved, knowing from experience that a razor nick would only make him tardier. He dressed in a rush and trotted down the steps to his car, taking no precautions to check his surroundings.

So it was that he arrived for his breakfast meeting winded, off balance and fifteen minutes late. He had no difficulty identifying Danny Byrne. He and a companion, the man driving the Cadillac, were the only diners in the restaurant. Byrne sat on a built-in upholstered bench facing the entrance, his back to the wall. His cohort sat in a chair beside him.

Byrne was not what Sonny expected. He wore a light blue cardigan sweater over a white shirt with no tie. His friendly, fatherly face was comfortably pudgy, fair skinned with blushed cheeks. He had a large forehead and blazing blue eyes that turned down in the manner of a grateful dog. He smiled as Sonny approached. He could not have been less threatening.

Sonny nodded a greeting, sat and smiled back. Byrne leaned forward. His smile faded to a threatening frown. His blue eyes squinted with piercing intensity. "Who the fuck is Sonny fucking Feelright and why the fuck are you fucking with my shit?"

It took Sonny a moment to decipher the question, which was the most prolific assembly of profanity he ever heard in a single sentence.

"I'm not," he responded lamely.

Byrne leaned back and studied him. He leaned forward again. "You've got to be the worst fucking P.I. on the planet."

Sonny looked confused. "P.I.?"

"Private investigator."

"I'm not a private investigator," corrected Sonny. "I'm a forensic accountant."

"Whatever you want to call it, you're bad at it." Byrne shook his head with disgust. "You check me and my business out all over the internet."

"How do you know that?"

"Never mind how. I just know. You have your partner ask his police contacts about me; do you really think I don't have friends on the police force? Then you show up at my dealership asking about a ninety-thousand dollar car! Look at you. Nobody in their right mind would see you in that car. Then you leave your real goddamn name but a fake employer. And you never even notice a fucking antique candy apple red Eldorado following you for the past week.

"I told Al not to use the Eldorado. 'You'll stick out like a sore thumb,' I told him. But you proved me wrong, Sonny. I think he could have flown around in a hot air balloon and you wouldn't have noticed.

"And if that's not enough, your mug is in the goddamn newspaper every day! Who's your PR guy anyway? I need to hire him for my dealership."

Byrne's demeanor suddenly changed to cordial. "Oh, I'm sorry. Have you met Al?" he asked with deference.

"Um, not formally," answered Sonny.

"Sonny, meet my friend and partner, Al Cistone. We've been together for over twenty years now."

Cistone leaned forward and stretched out his hand. "Good to meet you, Sonny." In the light Al Cistone seemed far less intimidating than he had the night before. His face was thin and angular with a Roman nose. He had thick black hair and, though clean shaven, the shadow of a beard on his face. He wore a conservative blue suit and a tie, with a gold stick pin in his shirt collar. He appeared lean and at least a decade younger than Byrne.

Sonny shook the man's hand and nodded.

"Now, why the fuck are you harassing me?" demanded Byrne, his hostility returned.

"I don't mean to harass you, but someone's after my partner, Charlotte."

"The hot redhead?"

Sonny nodded.

"Maybe twenty years ago. Hell, maybe ten years ago." Byrne and Cistone shared a chuckle. "Who is Charlotte and why in the fuck would I be interested in her, other than the obvious."

"Charlotte *McCardle*. You know her father."

Byrne thought for a moment. "That's Dougie's daughter? What do you know?"

"You met her once. Years ago. At their house."

Byrne thought again. He shrugged. "I don't remember anybody looking like that! So, why would I be after Dougie's daughter?"

Sonny shrugged. "To intimidate him. To send him a message."

Byrne burst into a guffaw. Cistone joined him in laughter. The two men laughed until they had to wipe tears from their eyes. "Why would I fuck with the best thing that's ever happened to me?" he finally spit out between gasps.

Pursuers

Byrne regained his composure and insisted that they eat. He waved over the waitress, who was leaning against the wall looking bored. Again, he turned polite and deferential. "Shirley, meet my good friend Sonny Feelright. You make sure the guys in back take care of him, alright?"

"We always take care of you and your friends, Danny," she smiled.

On Byrne's recommendation, Sonny ordered the Belgian waffle. "Be sure and get the whipped cream on it," he insisted. "Best goddamn thing you'll ever eat." For his part Byrne ordered a fruit cup and dry toast. "Goddamn doctor," he explained. "Getting my blood drawn tomorrow and need to get my numbers down." Cistone ordered an omelet.

"So, where did you get this notion that I'm out to get your girlfriend?" Byrne asked between bites.

"She's my partner," corrected Sonny.

"Whatever. If I were you she'd be my girlfriend."

Sonny wondered how much he should share. Byrne seemed trustworthy, despite his questionable reputation. "The FBI," he finally admitted. Byrne continued

eating without reaction. "Does that bother you?" Sonny probed.

"No. The feds have been after my ass for thirty years. If you listen to them I'm the biggest crook to hit Chicago since Al Capone. But I'm telling you, Sonny, I swear, I'm squeaky clean. I'm cleaner than Mother Theresa after a bath. You know, I've been audited four times in the past ten years by the IRS. The FBI raided my dealership twice. Every time there's a petty crime in Chicago I get questioned." He sighed, "I guess that's the price you pay for a misspent youth. No, I'm not scared of the FBI. Not as scared as you should be of those punks following you. Who are those guys?"

"You've seen them?"

Byrne and Cistone traded glances and another laugh. "They may be the only guys worse than you at surveillance. They're following you with a goddamn red Eldorado stuck to their bumper and they never even notice. Maybe I should drive a billboard like that," he mused. "Maybe it would make *me* invisible."

Byrne took a bite of dry toast and made a face. "Tastes like a goddamn dog biscuit. Anyway, it's a good thing Al was there on Saturday because those punks meant business."

"Yea, thanks for that," said Sonny. Cistone nodded.

"Who are they and what did you do to them?"

"I don't know who they are. We thought they were you. And I didn't do anything to them."

"Well, you must have done something," Byrne concluded. "At least you're safe at the moment."

"What do you mean?"

Cistone answered, "I haven't seen them since Saturday morning. The car is a rental. It has Indiana plates. I don't know where they went."

Relief washed over Sonny. Byrne sensed it. "Don't take your guard down. They'll be back. Whatever you did to piss them off, they'll be back."

Sonny pushed his plate away, the waffle half eaten.

"You didn't like it?" Byrne asked with genuine concern.

"No, no. It was delicious. I'm just not that hungry."

"You got to be a little tense these days, eh?" asked Byrne. Sonny nodded, the worry etched on his face. "Yea, I've been there. That's what brought me to Chicago."

The Old Days

"You did some research on me," Byrne began. "I grew up in Cleveland – Collinwood. An old school neighborhood. My old man was a dockworker. That's when Cleveland was a growing steelmaking town. The docks had these huge Hewlitts for unloading iron ore from the lake carriers. They were something to behold. There were tons of bars in the Flats where my dad and his buddies would go after work. I never remember him getting home before ten, always loaded. But he was a good man. Never an angry drunk.

"Back then there were more jobs then workers, so people were coming to Cleveland from all over – there were Chinese, Germans, eastern Europeans, Italians, and of course the Irish – I'm Irish," he stated the obvious. "Not a lot of blacks and Hispanics yet, but everybody else. And everybody sort of settled in their own neighborhoods. The steelworkers and dockworkers would mingle during the day, but they chose to live with their own kind. Cleveland was like a mini-Balkans.

"Unions were strong back then. And with all the money flowing, there was a pretty big mob presence. It was all controlled by the Italians and the Jews. Until

Danny Greene came along. He kind of took a shit in the pool for the mob, so to speak. My dad was friends with Danny Greene for a while, before he took over the Local. Greene changed after that and a lot of the members didn't like him. He had no loyalty. He stole from the workers. He extorted from the companies. Later, he turned on his mob employers. He snitched for the FBI.

"Today everybody talks about Danny Greene like he was a rock star, some kind of Robin Hood. All the books and movies paint him as a great Celtic folk hero. But I knew Danny Greene, and he was no hero. He was a psychopath. Certifiable. He would pick a fight with anybody. When he picked a fight with the mob, I don't think he ever intended to take over or build a Celtic dynasty. He was just pissed off. He wasn't smart enough to think it all through. He wasn't even smart enough to run away and save his own ass.

"As a teenager in the neighborhood, though, I worshipped the guy. He didn't take shit from anybody, and he was Irish. I started to do some work for him, mowing his yard and shoveling snow. He paid well and was a good tipper. Eventually, he had me run errands for him. I'd pick up his laundry and his pills at the drugstore. Sometimes he'd take me with him when he collected money from people – garbage truck drivers. I'd sit in the car and wait while he got out and talked to guys. Sometimes he would smack guys around, even guys way bigger. And they never fought back. People were scared shitless of him.

"You ever been in a fight, Sonny?"

Sonny shook his head.

"Well, the last thing you want to do is get in a fight with a guy too stupid to know when he's hurt. That was Danny Greene.

"Greene bought me my first beer when I was seventeen. He took me to this bar in the Flats. I remember it had a lot of dart boards. The bartender didn't even ask for an ID.

"To make a long story short, I got a little too close to Danny Greene, and when the war started, all the bombings and shootings, I was in the middle of it. It became pretty clear that the mob was going to exterminate Greene and everybody associated with him. I was scared shitless – like you are now."

"So you moved to Chicago," Sonny finished the tale.

"I moved to Chicago determined to go legit. And I did."

"Not right away," interjected Cistone. "Remember that faceoff with Lancone?"

"Who could forget that?" laughed Byrne. "You should have been there, Sonny. When I came to Chicago I had nothing, so I was doing some jobs for guys. And one of these guys, Tony Lancone, owned this little two-bit used car lot in Cicero, not far from where you live. I had no money, so I buy the place from him with a note. But the place is a shithole. Half of the inventory belongs in the junkyard. The building leaks. It was a mess. So a couple years later, after I work my ass off getting the place profitable, I decide to withhold the last payment. I tell him why and he gets pissed.

"So one day me and Al are in my office, and in bursts Lancone. And he's got this goon with him." To Al: "Wasn't that the biggest motherfucker you ever seen?"

"Arms like this." Cistone circled his hands as though holding a basketball.

"And they're both holding guns!" Byrne laughed. "Did we shit or what?"

"I thought we were dead!" laughed Cistone.

"What did you do?" asked Sonny.

"Luckily, I had a bigger gun!" Byrne and Cistone both doubled over in hysterics at the memory. Sonny tried to hide his horror.

"In retrospect," Byrne continued, now with a contemplative expression, "I should have just paid the man. Lancone is like an elephant. He never forgets. We spent the next ten years looking over our shoulders, just waiting for the payback. Didn't we, Al?"

Al nodded.

"But you know what that's like. Always being followed. Knowing someone's after you."

Sonny grew uneasy, now conscious of why Byrne picked the farthest table in the restaurant and sat with his back to the wall. "What happened," he asked, half expecting a gang of thugs to rush the restaurant at any moment.

"We got it all straightened out."

"How?"

"I introduced him to your girlfriend's old man. Within six months Lancone called me and said it was all paid in full with interest."

Quail Hunting

"How did you meet Douglas McCardle?" Sonny asked.

"I was introduced by a mutual friend a few years ago. He gives me investment advice."

"Sounds like he's doing a good job of it."

Byrne chuckled. "You could say that. I've never lost money on his advice. He's like clairvoyant. He tells me what to buy and it goes up. He tells me what to sell and it goes down. The man's golden. I've made more money listening to him than in twenty years selling cars. And I sell a lot of cars."

"How well do you know him?"

The Irishman leaned back and gazed at Sonny, reflecting on how to answer. "You ever go quail hunting, Sonny?"

Sonny shook his head.

"Quail will challenge the best hunter. You go out and trudge around the fields looking for them. You know they're all around you, but you can't see them. Every now and then you stir one up and it will fly right at you. It can scare the living shit out of you. If you're lucky enough to get off a shot there's about a one in ten chance you'll hit it. When you make a meal of that quail you know you earned it.

"But there are a lot of guys – I call them 'suits' because they dress up like businessmen and professionals – who pretend to be hunters. They want to eat quail but don't want to go through all the work. They dress up in fancy camouflage and visit the quail farm. Ever hear of a quail farm?"

Sonny shook his head again.

"What they do at a quail farm is hand raise quail in cages, where they never learn to fly. They over feed them so they're fat and slow. Then, on hunting day, they take out a bunch of quail and turn them loose on the quail farm, usually when it's cold. Since these birds have never been outside a warm building, it's a big shock to the system. And just for good measure, they shake the shit out of the birds before they let them go, to disorient them even more. Then the hunters come along and blow them away. The poor birds don't have a chance."

Sonny grimaced. "That's horrible."

"It gets worse. The hunters don't want to get dirty cleaning the birds or picking out the buckshot, so the quail farm gives them dressed quail, freshly slaughtered, all ready to cook and eat. No getting your hands dirty. No breaking a tooth on a piece of buckshot. And the birds they killed get picked up and discarded in the trash. Dead for nothing."

"What's the moral of the story?" Sonny asked.

"You've got to be careful who you hunt with. You always want to hunt with sportsmen, guys who enjoy the game and not just the prize. When you hunt with those other types you can get shot by accident. That's why I don't socialize with Douglas McCardle. What I don't know can't hurt me.

"You know, Sonny, you're not a bad guy. I think there's more going on under that mop on your head than it appears." Sonny didn't know how to take the compliment. "Tell you what; let's keep an eye on each other. You watch my back and I'll watch yours. Alright?"

Sonny nodded, completely unsure of what vague pact he was entering.

Nancy Black

Nancy gazed through sun glasses at the tired urban neighborhood as it passed. It reminded her of her childhood in a gritty section of Toronto after her parents, both college professors, fled Egypt ahead of one of the many intellectual purges following the Second World War. They escaped just ahead of the police, with nothing but the clothes on their backs and their passports. They left behind a life of privileged wealth – Nancy still remembered the servants who coddled her – and replaced it with one of poverty and struggle. For a child the transition was wrenching and she swore she would never go back there.

Yet here she was, riding with the Imam in a pathetic section of Calumet. What few people they passed looked weary and beaten, their eyes as vacant as many of the aging buildings surrounding them. Scattered among the buildings were old houses, most of them serving as slum rentals. Her life had come full circle, which she blamed on one person: Sonny B. Feelright.

Never one to easily acknowledge her own failings, she realized that hiring the Imam for her purposes was a mistake. She learned of him while in Kuwait, where she had traveled to begin courting investors for her next hedge fund. After her fall from grace she knew it would be hard to start anew in the West, where institutional investors maintained a front of propriety. Middle Eastern investors were far less pious. A Saudi businessman, a passionate Muslim, had referred her to the Imam when she expressed sympathy to the cause of radical Islam. In fact, she was indifferent to Islam and every other religion. Since the fall of her firm she had just one motivation – revenge.

The Imam pulled his battered Impala to the curb in front of a dilapidated four-unit apartment. He knew nothing about Nancy other than that she was a very rich and powerful sponsor of the cause. She was traveling under the passport of Jade Crescent, an obvious false identity. When ordered to arrange a meeting between her and his terrorist operatives he was warned that she was angry with his failures. And while they spoke not a word on the drive from Chicago's Ritz Carlton, he could sense her smoldering anger. She frightened him. They both were glad to climb from the car, him to escape her palpable fury and her to escape his filthy rattle trap of a car.

They were greeted at the door by the two brothers, who eyed her suspiciously as they blocked the entrance. "Move!" barked the Imam as he pushed them aside to make a path for Nancy. She strolled into the room and looked around, her face a mask behind her dark glasses. The Imam swept his arm across the card table, knocking a scattering of empty McDonald's clam shells to the floor. He pulled out a chair for Nancy to sit and motioned for the two brothers to do likewise. They reluctantly complied.

"Who is she?" asked Bomani, his voice dripping with contempt.

"Shush!" the Imam scolded.

"It's a woman!" Bomani protested. Kafele cut him off with a raised hand. Bomani leaned back and crossed his arms. He made no attempt to hide his disdain as he studied her. She looked Middle Eastern, with straight jet black hair and a pale complexion. But her attire was Western; a black pants suit over a white blouse.

Nancy sat still, staring at the men, saying nothing. The Imam fidgeted nervously in his chair as tension mounted in the room. Finally, she removed her sunglasses and laid them on the table. Even Bomani was taken aback by the raging hatred in her eyes. "You're incompetent fools," Nancy hissed. "You've made a mockery of this whole affair. I paid to have a job done. You've failed."

The three men watched with concern as she closed her eyes tight and seemed to hold her breath. Her face reddened. She began to shake. Suddenly, she leaped from the chair, screaming. "You're idiots! Fools! Why is he still alive! He stole from me! You've made him a hero!" She lunged toward the Imam and slapped him hard across the face. The brothers watched in paralyzed shock, waiting for the Imam to strike this lunatic down. But he didn't. He simply cowered under her stare as she leaned over him, shaking.

Nancy turned her back to the three men and tilted her head back. She was breathing hard, hyperventilating. She gathered herself and retook her chair, calm again. She gave no apology for her behavior, no explanation. "Why isn't Sonny Feelright dead?" she demanded.

Conjecture

It was nearly ten when Sonny got to the office. Simon and Charlotte were just finishing the morning meeting when he entered the conference room.

"Did Dr. Lovelace have late rounds today?" asked Charlotte.

"Charlotte, I had a breakfast meeting. I haven't seen Dr. Love-*land* since she stopped by yesterday."

"But you've talked to her?"

He was trapped. "She called me last evening. She wanted to apologize. . . ." His explanation was too late; Charlotte had already returned to her office, closing the door behind her.

He dropped into a chair with a sigh. "Simon, can we talk?"

"If it's about the two of you, absolutely not."

"No, it's not about Charlotte. That's over. I'm moving on."

Simon raised a skeptical eyebrow. "What then?"

"I had breakfast with Danny Byrne."

Simon's eyes widened with astonishment. "Tell me."

Sonny shared his experience of the morning in detail. "I'm telling you, the guy seemed on the up and up," he concluded. "I trust him."

"You were reckless to go to that meeting alone," Simon scolded with little conviction. "But at least we know more than we did."

"What do we know?" inquired Sonny, whose mind was a jumble of confusion.

"First, we know that Danny Byrne is not responsible for the attacks, which means that someone else is behind them. It's also possible that this has nothing to do with Charlotte – that you're the target. After all, she was only nearby at the bombing. You're the only one present for all three attacks. Can you think of anyone who would want to hurt you?"

The conjecture was a slap in the face. All along he had operated under the assumption that the attacks were tied to Charlotte and her father, giving him hope that this nightmare could soon end. If it wasn't true they were no closer than ever to ending his ordeal. He strained but could think of no one who could hate him so badly that they wanted him dead.

"They said the Town Car is a rental with Indiana plates. You know anybody in Indiana?" Simon inquired.

"No."

Simon went to his office and came back with Inspector Robinson's business card. Using the speaker phone, he called the cell number listed.

"Robinson here," he answered on the second ring.

"Inspector Robinson, this is Simon Courtney and Sonny Feelright. We may have some information for you about the attacks."

"Oh?" he responded. His tone was skeptical.

"The Town Car that tried to run down Sonny, we think it's a rental with Indiana plates?"

"What do you base that on?"

Sonny shook his head, fearful that Simon would reveal Danny Byrne as the source. "A tip we got. An anonymous tip."

Robinson exhaled audibly. "An anonymous tip, huh? That's the best you can do?"

"I'm serious, Inspector. This isn't a joke. Someone's going to get hurt."

"Have you called the newspaper yet? I'm sure there's a front page article in this."

"Look, Inspector . . . ."

"You look," interrupted Robinson. "When you're ready to tell me the source of this 'tip,' maybe I'll take it seriously. Until that time we're going to devote the department's limited resources to solving real crimes." The connection went silent.

"That went well," Simon said as he ended the call. Sonny slumped. He would get no protection from the police.

"Look," Simon continued, "somebody has done

some planning for this. They're spending money. I think Byrne is right; they'll try again. They're probably laying low because of the publicity. You need to stay vigilant."

Sonny felt ill. "At least this takes Charlotte's father out of the picture. I won't have to go there with her on Sunday."

Simon reflected. "No, you still need to go. I don't like what we're learning about Douglas McCardle. No one bats a thousand in investing. That's impossible."

"That's none of our business, Simon."

Simon gave a frustrated frown. This was just the kind of mystery that interested him. "But he still could be involved in this. What if it's this Lancone character? And we don't know who else he might be advising. We need to find out more."

Sonny slumped further in his chair, dreading Sunday.

"Sonny," Simon advised after a moment of reflection, "I wouldn't tell Charlotte about all of this just yet."

"Not to worry. She's not speaking to me."

Sonny's phone vibrated in his pocket. He fished it out. It was a text from Liz: "I'm off tonight. Can we hook up?" He glanced at Charlotte's closed door. "B by @ 8," he replied.

Seeking Help

They met at the Red Swan for drinks. Adonis swung back after taking Charlotte home from work. Sonny was nursing a beer at the bar when the agent entered. The two men shook hands. Adonis removed his wool overcoat, folded it neatly on an empty bar stool and took a stool next to Sonny. He ordered a Heineken. As always, he was impeccably dressed. Sonny looked down at his spit-shined black wingtips and contrasted them with his own scuffed loafers. He eyed the agent's neatly coiffed hair and became suddenly conscious of his own unruly mane.

"Thanks for meeting me," Sonny began. "I hope I'm not interfering with any plans you and Charlotte have for tonight."

"We don't have any plans," the agent assured him, disappointment in his voice. He seemed unusually subdued to Sonny.

"The reason I wanted to talk to you is about Charlotte – actually about her mother. Has she talked to you about her mother?"

He shook his head. "No. She's never mentioned her family. You'd think she doesn't have one."

"Yea, she can be a little private sometimes." They shared a quiet moment of agreement. "Anyway, I'm worried about her mother. She's seeing a guy right now. His name is Dominic Bindi. He's from Italy. He says he's an investment advisor there. They're talking about getting married. But the guy doesn't seem to have a history. He wants to manage her money for her. I'm worried he might have bad intentions." Sonny pulled a paper from his pocket and unfolded the picture from in front of the restaurant. "That's him." He pointed at Bindi.

Adonis picked it up and maneuvered it in the dim light. "Whoa, that's Charlotte's mother? They could be twin sisters."

"Yea, and that's Bindi on the end."

Adonis studied the picture further. "Don't know him." He put the picture on the bar and slid it toward Sonny. "Why are you asking me?"

Sonny shrugged. "You're with the FBI. I thought maybe you could check into it. See if he's for real."

"Look, Sonny, that's not how it works. We can't just go investigating anybody. This isn't Nazi Germany. We have a Constitution and a Bill of Rights. I can't go snooping around about people without just cause. I'd need a warrant. Even then, it would have to fall within the Bureau's jurisdiction."

Sonny pursed his lips and nodded his disappointed

understanding. They sipped their beers. "Besides," continued Adonis, "I've already crossed some lines."

"What do you mean?"

"I told Charlotte about our investigation of Danny Byrne. I violated my oath. I betrayed my team."

Sonny stared at the agent to see if he was serious. For the first time he noticed the tortured conflict etched in his face.

"It's not that big a deal," Sonny consoled him.

"Yes it is. It's a very big deal. I don't blame Charlotte for telling you and Simon. I blame myself. I betrayed my oath. That investigation was top secret. Now I've put the whole operation at risk."

Sonny recalled Byrne's casual disregard about the FBI. "I'm sure a guy like Byrne has an idea he's under a microscope. I don't think it's that big of a deal."

The agent shook his head. "You don't understand. Ever since I was a kid I wanted to join the Bureau. I spent four years in the Navy; I was a Navy Seal. There, you learn the importance of discipline and loyalty. Loyalty for the team is paramount. You put your duty ahead of everything – friends, family, loved ones. I took an oath when I joined the Bureau, an oath I take very seriously. And now I've violated it. I let my feelings for Charlotte get the best of me. I'm weak, Sonny. I'm not sure I'm worthy."

Sonny reached over and patted the agent's muscular

shoulder. "You've got to put it in perspective, man. It's not that big of a deal."

Adonis faced him. "I wish I were more like you."

Sonny thought he was joking. One look in his eyes told him otherwise. "Me? Who would want to be like me?"

"Look at you, man. You're confident. You're smart. You started your own business. You drive a BMW. And you've got these assassins chasing you and it doesn't bother you a bit."

Sonny was beginning to question the man's sanity. "No, Adonis, it's not like that at all. I'm probably the least confident person you'll ever meet."

They each took a drink. The conversation was growing more and more awkward, so Sonny changed the subject. "Can I ask you something? That shirt …."

"What? Did I spill something?" Adonis urgently inspected the front of his neatly pressed shirt, swinging his tie from side to side.

"No. I just want to know how you keep it so perfect. It's six-thirty and your shirt doesn't have a single wrinkle."

"Oh." Adonis relaxed. "I change shirts, usually a couple times a day. President Kennedy used to do that, you know."

"No. I didn't." Sonny turned and made a face toward the wall.

"Can I ask you something?"

What the hell, thought Sonny.

"Why did you break up with Charlotte? I can't believe you'd let a woman like her get away?"

Sonny nearly choked on his drink. "Well, I don't know. I didn't really drop her. I mean, we were never really together. I guess we just sort of drifted apart."

"You had a good thing going. Your new girl must be something else. See, that's what I mean. You're always in control."

Sonny tipped back his beer and took several gulps. "So, how is it going between you and Charlotte?"

Adonis frowned. "I'm not really sure. I've never met anyone like her. She's really hard to get close to."

"Are you actually dating?" Sonny asked.

"We haven't been intimate, if that's what you mean. Like I say, she's hard to read."

Sonny nodded his emphatic agreement.

"She intimidates me a little," Adonis confessed. "She's so perfect, but she's so damned independent. Sometimes I feel like we're competing with each other. Sometimes I just want to relax and talk, but she's always wound, always trying to prove herself. It's my fault. I guess I'm just old fashioned."

Adonis drained his beer, stood and put on his overcoat. He shook Sonny's hand. Before leaving he grabbed the photo from the bar. "Let me see what I can find out."

Date

Sonny went home to shower and change. By the time he arrived at Liz's he was fifteen minutes late. Her neighborhood was quiet. He passed only one car on her street, a gray Ford Focus heading the opposite direction. No black Town Car, to his relief. He parked in the street and walked up the drive to the stairs leading to the second floor of the barn. The handrails were decorated in garland and big red bows. The decorations warmed his heart as he climbed the wooden stairs. Liz greeted him at the door before he could knock.

Her apartment was a large open space with a high gambrel ceiling. The floor was made of wide wooden planks finished in glossy polyurethane over a century of nicks and scars from when the barn was the hub of a working farm. The far left corner of the huge room was partitioned into a bathroom. Next to it was an efficiency kitchen, including a round wooden table and matching chairs. Furniture and rugs were positioned to form living spaces in the giant room: a double bed, side table and dresser formed a bedroom; a desk, wooden file cabinet and rolling chair formed an office; a couch, Lazy Boy and rocker surrounded a coffee table to form a sitting area.

There was an eclectic collection of furnishings, mostly antiques and period pieces purchased on the cheap. But what struck Sonny was how perfectly they were arranged and decorated. The apartment was a feast of coordinated colors and textures: pillows, fabrics, candles, vases. Everywhere there were throw rugs. And delicious smells; a mixture of scented candles and baking food. Next to the sitting area was a six foot Christmas tree, beautifully adorned in white lights, charming decorations and ribbon.

Sonny stood in the doorway and took in the magazine worthy scene. "My God," he uttered, "this place is beautiful."

"Thanks," she replied, turning to inspect her abode. "I like it homey. It's hard on a budget, but I try." She turned and gave him a hug and kiss on the lips. He gave her a lingering hug in return, savoring the soft warmth of her body. She pulled away and took his hand, pulling him into the room. She looked as charming as her apartment. She wore black wool slacks and a blue cashmere sweater that matched the color of her eyes. Her blond hair was pulled back with a beret on one side, revealing a delicate gold hooped earring about the size of a ring.

"You do more than just try," he marveled.

"Take your coat?" she asked, reaching.

"Did you want to go out? Maybe get some dinner?"

"I thought we could hang out here," she suggested. "I whipped a little something up if you're hungry."

"Perfect," he shrugged and handed her his coat.

"Sit," she said, pointing to the couch. "I'll open a bottle of wine. Chianti, right?"

"Huh?"

"Isn't that what you drink? Isn't that what you had at Peaches?"

"Oh, yea," he answered, not wanting to disappoint her.

He watched her as she went to the kitchen and opened the wine. She pulled two wine glasses from the cupboard, inspected them in the light for water spots, and poured them each a glass. She returned and sat beside him on the couch, slipping off her shoes and tucking her legs under her. "Anything interesting happen with you today?" she asked.

Where to begin, thought Sonny. "Not really. We're buried at work right now. Simon says we may need to hire some people."

"Nice problem to have, I guess." She made a worried face. "What about the trouble. Do they know who's been trying to hurt you?"

"No. And the police have pretty much stopped looking. They think we staged the attacks for publicity."

"That's awful," she sympathized. She reached out and rubbed his knee. "But forget about all that. You're here now. You're safe." A timer sounded in the kitchen. "Give me ten minutes."

Liz went to the kitchen area while Sonny stood and wandered around the apartment, mesmerized by her design skills. Every corner, every table top, every nook and cranny was carefully arranged. "I really can't get over your place," he yelled.

"Thanks. That means a lot. I don't get many visitors. It's fun to share it."

"Are you sure you want to be a doctor. You're so talented." He strolled to the window and looked out. The night was frigid; the ground littered with patches of ice and crusted dirty snow. A car passed on the street out front – a gray Ford Focus. The hair on the back of his neck tingled. Was it the same car he saw earlier? He shook his head. It probably was a different car, or a neighbor coming and going. He was just growing paranoid.

Feast

Liz summoned him to the table, where a feast awaited. She served a roast with vegetables; a lavish salad with homemade dressing; and twice backed potatoes. The table was set with fine china and polished silverware. Real cloth napkins in silver rings sat on the two dinner plates. A homemade cherry pie cooled on the kitchen counter.

"I'm overwhelmed," Sonny commented, meaning it. "You call this 'a little something'?"

She put her arms around his shoulders and kissed him tenderly. "For a special guest," she cooed.

They ate and talked. She shared stories about her childhood and her father, who she still missed terribly. She described her life as perfect when he was alive, and how hard it was for her mother and her after his passing. Sonny told her about his own unconventional upbringing, his feeling of abandonment when his parents split and left him alone to work his way through college and graduate school.

The meal was delicious. Sonny could not recall the last time he'd had a home cooked meal. Since he'd been on his own his diet had consisted largely of prepared foods and restaurant fare. Between the main course and dessert he stood to stretch, wandering to the window. It was empty of traffic. She served the pie ala mode, then they sat and sipped the last of the wine. She urged him to relax in the sitting area while she cleaned off the table. Again, he wandered to the window, staring out at the cold night. He felt content and safe for the first time in weeks. He did not want the feeling to end.

"You're spending a lot of time at that window." Liz came up behind him and put her arms around his waist. He pulled her around and embraced her. They kissed passionately. He was aroused by her warmth, the heat coursing through him like a current. "Will you stay the night?" she whispered in his ear, her breath a warm breeze on his soul. They turned to head for the bed when something outside caught Sonny's eye.

The gray Ford Focus passed slowly. It stopped next to his BMW on the curb. Sonny could discern two figures in the vehicle. He could tell they were inspecting his car. After a moment's pause the Focus continued slowly by, the driver staring up at Liz's apartment as they passed. Sonny's momentary contentment faded, replaced by gripping fear. The car was stalking him. And his presence was putting Liz in danger.

"Sonny, what's wrong?" asked Liz.

He grabbed her shoulders and looked into her eyes. "I have to leave."

"What? Why? What's wrong?"

He did not want to alarm her. "I'm feeling sick," he lied.

"You look pale," she agreed. She put a hand on his forehead. "I hope it wasn't the meal."

"No, no. The meal was spectacular. I don't know what it is, but I have to go."

"Just stay here. I'll take care of you."

"No," he argued. "I need to leave."

"Is it something I did?" she asked.

"Absolutely not," he assured her. "You're perfect. The meal was perfect. Your place is perfect. I really, really want to stay. But I can't."

Stalking

The two brothers watched from down the street as Sonny hurried to his car, his head swiveling from side to side.

"He spotted us!" Kafele exclaimed. "I said be careful!"

Bomani ignored his older brother, his murderous eyes trained on Sonny. "We could take him tonight. We could take him now."

"No!" Kafele argued emphatically. He was exhausted by his brother's impetuousness and did not want to face the wrath of the Imam and that wicked woman again. They could afford no more failures.

Their meeting with Nancy Black had lasted over an hour. After berating them unmercifully for their prior failures, she announced that she would take charge of the operation. She would stay in the area until the job was finished. She ordered them to follow Sonny Feelright discreetly for a few days and to record his every move. They were to rent a different car each day to avoid detection. They were to report back to her on his schedule and habits, and she would dictate how and when they would engineer his demise.

She also dangled incentives. She disclosed that she had already contributed one-million dollars to the cause of Jihad for the operation. She told them she would give them each five-hundred-thousand dollars when the job was complete. After she left, Bomani scoffed at the notion. They served a higher cause then her money, he asserted. But Kafele, never as fanatical as his younger brother, was less strident. A half a million dollars could be life changing.

"Don't follow too closely," Kafele ordered as Sonny pulled away. Bomani waved him off and eased from the curb, his headlights off.

Sleep Inn

Sonny drove slowly, watching his rearview mirror. His fear ratcheted to terror when he saw the shadow of a car, its lights off, ease from the curb down the block. Sonny hit the gas pedal. He sped to the first intersection and turned right, his tires screeching from the torque. He took another fast right, shutting off his lights as he turned. He turned again into the driveway of the first dark house he saw, pulling all the way up to the garage in back and shutting off his engine, hoping that no one was home. He sat low in the seat and held his breath, watching the street behind him in the side mirror.

Soon, a gray Ford Focus passed, going fast. He sat for a long time, engine off, eyes trained on the street. He sat until the interior of the car chilled to the outside temperature and his feet began to go numb. He sat and longed for the comfort of Liz's apartment and the evening of companionship he was missing.

The Ford Focus did not reappear. When he could stand the cold no longer he restarted the car and backed from the driveway with his lights off. He gazed up and down the street but saw no traffic. He deliberately made his way in the opposite direction to which he came, losing himself in a maze of side streets. He eventually found the highway.

He could not go home. They surely would be waiting there. So he drove until he saw a Sleep Inn sign. He exited and booked a room for the night.

Security

He slept poorly at the Sleep Inn due to his sated stomach and exhausted emotions. He arose early and went to his apartment to change. The world seemed less threatening in the growing light of morning. Still, he cruised past his apartment twice before parking and hustling up the staircase. He now made a habit of wedging a chair beneath the doorknob whenever home. He kept the ball bat within reach at all times. After a quick shower and change, he darted back to the safety of his car. He did not spot the Ford Focus on his drive to work, although he still felt that hostile eyes were watching.

He called Liz as he drove. She seemed subdued when she answered.

"I'm so sorry about last night," he apologized.

"Don't be. I understand. You have feelings for Charlotte." There was hurt in her voice.

"No, it's not that," he pleaded. "It's just that … I was frightened."

"You think things are moving too fast."

"No. I saw a car on your street. I think it was following me. I was afraid of staying. I was afraid for you, Liz. My life is a mess right now."

There was a pause. "Are you sure you're not just paranoid?"

He sighed. Even Liz was growing skeptical. He wanted to argue, but the truth, if she accepted it, might scare her. "I don't know. I really enjoyed being with you last night. That was the best meal I've ever had. I didn't want to leave. I'm sorry. I swear I'll make it up to you."

She softened. "Okay. I'll hold you to it. Promise you'll call."

"I promise."

Sonny was grateful to see the security guard patrolling the alley. Simon hired the service to keep an eye on the building during the workday. The guard was somewhat overweight and did not carry a gun, but his uniform was a welcome sight to Sonny after his tense evening. He stopped to introduce himself and was surprised that he recognized the man.

"You're the policeman," he pointed. "The one from the explosion. The one at the robbery."

"*Was* the policeman," corrected former Patrolman Madigan. "I've been suspended."

"What happened?"

"That reporter. She quoted me in those articles. I told her it was strictly for background. She quoted me by name anyway. She's a liar."

"Don't I know," Sonny commiserated.

Global United

"You look like shit," opined Charlotte when he entered the conference room, where she and Simon were preparing for the morning meeting.

Sonny wanted to blurt out the story of the Ford Focus. He wanted to describe the terror of his evening and how he eluded his stalkers by hiding in a driveway. He wanted to share how he took refuge at the Sleep Inn and the fear that gripped him when he returned to his apartment this morning. But it would require him to reveal that he spent the evening with Liz.

So he just said, "Didn't sleep well."

Simon began the meeting by announcing they had four new engagements. They were hired by a bankruptcy trustee to sort through the financials of a failed paving company whose books had been deemed unauditable. The executor of a wealthy businessman's estate retained them to catalog the deceased's assets; sadly, the man was killed in a car accident at forty-two and had made no efforts to organize his affairs beforehand. And Tom Friedman, the lawyer in the Danner divorce, gave them two additional divorce cases to investigate.

Charlotte provided updates on all of their pending projects. It was clear their young firm was taking off, in no small measure due to Sonny's unwanted publicity. "I'm worried about the workload," she concluded. "I'm fearful that something might fall through the cracks, especially with some of us so distracted these days." She gave Sonny a sideways glance.

"Don't start," admonished Simon. She made a pouty frown while Sonny pursed his lips.

"I've got news on the Herkmeier investigation," he continued. "You ever hear of Global United Investments? It's among the top ten hedge funds in the country. Based in New York. My Georgeson contact linked it to the suspicious trading activity in all six of the suspect companies. In every case, Global United bought or sold large positions during the period leading up to the material events."

"Could it be coincidence?" asked Charlotte.

"Maybe, if it was just the six companies. But they also may be just the tip of the iceberg. I went back and looked at other public companies in the region that did major deals in the past several years. I found five more suspicious cases where there was significant trading activity leading up to a public disclosure. In every case Global United was the investor."

"What does it mean?" asked Sonny.

"I think it means that Global United has an inside

source to these companies. It has a pipeline to all of these board rooms."

"But how?" asked Charlotte. "They don't have common directors. They don't use the same law firms. They don't use the same accounting firms."

"Maybe we should just call somebody," Sonny volunteered. "The SEC or something."

"No," said Simon. "Global United will just claim that they're savvy investors and their conduit will lay low. We need to figure out how they're doing it."

"What do we know about Global United?" asked Charlotte.

Simon referred to his notepad. "It's run by a guy named Aaron Morrel." Simon passed Charlotte a photo he'd printed from the internet.

She crinkled her face. "He's disgusting. He's obese." She passed the photo to Sonny. It was taken as Morrel was struggling to exit a limousine. The setting appeared to be New York's financial district. Morrel was grossly overweight, his open suit jacket appearing several sizes too small for his girth. His tie, draped over his belly, barely reached halfway to his straining belt. The buttons of his white shirt were pulled tight, revealing specks of pasty skin underneath. His face appeared bloated, his piggish eyes barely visible above his pudgy cheeks.

"He's also very rich," offered Simon. "He started

Global United eight years ago. Prior to that he was a bond trader for Goldman Sachs and then Citicorp. He grew up in Pittsburgh and got a degree in economics from the University of Pittsburgh. He got his MBA at the Kellogg School of Management here at Northwestern. He moved to Wall Street after graduate school. His career was unspectacular until he started Global United. He's been golden ever since."

"Northwestern; a Chicago connection," noted Sonny.

"Maybe," Simon agreed. "We just need to find out how."

They were interrupted by a commotion on the stairway, a shouting match between a man and a woman. They raced to the ruckus to find a wrestling match underway between Melody Gothim, who was trying to ascend the stairs, and security guard Madigan, who was lying below her on the steps desperately clutching her right foot. His hat was off, his hair askew.

"Let me go!" she demanded. "I'm press! I have a Constitutional right!"

"No, you bitch!"

She wiggled free and shot up the steps to where the three partners were crowded in the doorway, staring.

"Sonny, give me an interview!" she demanded.

"No!" he responded, stepping back. "Get away from me!"

Madigan grabbed her from behind and wrestled her back down the stairs.

"Tenacious young woman," Simon observed as Madigan forced her outside.

Rage

Bomani and Kafele squeezed together with the Imam on a bench seat at a McDonald's in Elgin. The charcoal-haired she devil sat alone across from the trio. Nancy selected this meeting venue; she had no intention of revisiting their disgusting hideout in Calumet. The Imam again served as her chauffeur, picking her up at the Ritz Carlton. Bomani and Kafele arrived in a Honda Accord, their third rental car in as many days.

Nancy was livid to learn that Sonny slipped his stalkers Tuesday night. "You fools!" she hissed. "You let him see you! Now he'll be wary! I said to watch! I said to be discreet! You're idiots!" She gripped the edge of the table with both hands, squeezing until her finger tips turned white. Her face reddened. She trembled with rage.

The Imam looked around nervously, hoping she would not erupt like she had at the apartment in Calumet. Bomani stared at her, insolent and resentful. Kafele watched her nervously, realizing this woman ultimately would determine the fate of his brother and him. If they failed on their mission, she would seek to retaliate with the same determination she now directed toward Sonny Feelright; if they succeeded she would reward them with riches. She controlled the scale of life and death.

She calmed. Tentative, Kafele continued with his account. Their prey was now cautious. He varied his schedule. He avoided moments alone. Some nights he did not stay in his apartment. Worse, a security guard now patrolled the premises of his business.

Nancy leaned back, thoughtful. "That's our opportunity," she said. "We'll strike at his business."

"But there are people there. There's a guard," cautioned Kafele.

"Exactly," said Nancy. "He'll be least expecting it there. We'll take him there. When he's alone. Just him. No collateral damage."

"What next?" asked Kafele.

"Stop following him. Watch the building. Watch the security guard. I want to know his every habit."

Trudging On

The three partners dove into their heavy workload. The immersion was a welcome distraction for Sonny. He felt safe in the office knowing that a guard was on duty. By Wednesday afternoon Charlotte emerged from her closed office and joined them working in the conference room. Her exchanges with Sonny were limited to work; no friendly banter, no general conversation. But at least their relationship had evolved from one of hostility to one of mutual coexistence.

His anxiety rose when the workday ended. Madigan developed a habit of leaving early every day. Sonny tried to time his departure when Adonis stopped to give Charlotte a lift home. It was difficult watching her climb into the handsome agent's car and drive off, leaving Sonny alone in the ally. He felt most vulnerable then, as he made his way to his car in the isolated lot around the neighboring building. With every step he mapped his escape in case a black Town Car or a gray Focus appeared. He searched the traffic for suspicious cars as he drove and periodically peered out his apartment window when at home. But he detected no threats.

On Friday afternoon, as he was making some calls, Charlotte stepped into his office. "Can we talk?" she inquired. She closed the door and sat across from him.

"I want to apologize for being such a bitch lately," she began.

"Don't apologize."

"No, I mean it, Sonny. I want to be brave. But I'm scared. I'm afraid to leave my apartment for fear this Danny Byrne guy will try to kill me. It's been awful. And it's affected me. I'm so stressed I can barely stand it."

It occurred to Sonny that Charlotte still was completely unaware of his meeting with Danny Byrne and the revelation that someone else might be behind the attacks. She still believed that she was the target of the attacks. She was feeling the same anxiety as him.

"Look, Charlotte," he began to explain.

"No," she interrupted. "You don't need to apologize again. Last Friday is in the past. But I want to talk to you about this Sunday when we visit my father."

"But Charlotte, there are some things you need to know."

She waved him off. "My father can be…," she groped for a word, "judgmental. He's very meticulous and can be pretty intolerant of people who don't share his … sense of order."

"What are you saying," asked a confused Sonny.

"What were you planning to wear?" she asked.

"I hadn't thought about it. Pants and a sweater?"

She shook her head. "I really want to make the right impression."

"What do you recommend?"

She hedged. "I was just wondering if maybe we could get you an outfit. Maybe tomorrow. Together."

"You're joking."

She raised her eyebrows expectantly. She wasn't joking.

For the first time he realized just how anxious she was about seeing her father again, how important it was to her. "Sure, Charlotte," he agreed, "whatever you need." Inside he was thinking that she would never need to make such a request of the always fashionable Adonis.

Gigolo

It was just before noon on Saturday when Sonny picked Charlotte up at her apartment. Her vibrant red hair tossed in the December breeze as she approached the car, a discernable bounce in her step. She carried a newspaper. She flashed a smile at him for the first time in weeks, warming his heart. She climbed in the car, flooding it with the scent of vanilla. It was as though assassination attempts, financial intrigue and Adonis had never entered their lives.

"You're in a good mood," he observed. "I hope it's because you're glad to see me," he half joked.

"No," she laughed a bit too enthusiastically, he thought. "It's my mother. She's devastated."

"Why?" Sonny asked with concern.

"It seems that Dominic Bindi was arrested yesterday morning. It turns out he's not Dominic Bindi at all. His name is William Pepple. He's not even Italian."

"You're kidding?" Sonny feigned surprise.

"Apparently, he's a notorious gigolo. He's wanted in seven states for fraud and theft. He makes his living traveling around and preying on wealthy divorcees and widows. He used to be an actor in Los Angeles."

She handed him the paper, folded to reveal an article headed, "Fugitive Con Man Arrested." It was accompanied by a photograph of Dominic Bindi being shoved into a police car by two plain clothes detectives. Sonny quickly scanned the article, which cataloged a decade of misdeeds and indicated that the arrest was the result of an anonymous tip. He was relieved that it did not mention the FBI.

"Faith must be crushed," Sonny commented.

"More embarrassed than anything. He was caught in Lincoln Park, just two blocks away, leaving the home of another woman he was courting. He was sleeping there the whole time he was dating her. Can you believe he proposed to her? He was trying to persuade her to be the custodian for her investments."

"Is she alright?"

"She'll be fine. She called me yesterday evening, practically hysterical. She came over and stayed the night. It was the first time she ever saw my apartment. We talked a lot, about everything." She turned and faced him. "She told me about the photo. That was nice of you."

He said nothing. She stared into his eyes as though searching for a secret.

"Whoever the anonymous tipster is, I could kiss him," she finally remarked.

Shopping

They felt safe among the crowds of busy shoppers in downtown Chicago as they parked in a garage and walked to the clothing boutique. He followed her with trepidation; his first and only visit to the store seven months earlier had been humiliating. She took him there to buy a new wardrobe after hiring on with Blake & Company. The proprietor had been wickedly insulting to Sonny. He spent over four-thousand dollars on his new clothes, money he did not have at the time.

A chime sounded when they opened the familiar mahogany door and stepped into the fashionable men's store. Jared, the thin-faced proprietor, smiled at Charlotte. His smile faded when he noticed Sonny. He lowered his pointy chin as a hawk might drop his head before swooping to kill its prey. "You," was all he offered in the way of a greeting.

Jared stepped around the counter and examined Sonny from head to foot. He pointed at Sonny's expensive Italian loafers, now scuffed and stained from winter road salt. "My God. You've ruined them. Have you no pride at all?"

He walked up and with both hands grabbed Sonny's sides, pinching a handful of skin. "Putting on some weight, I see," he pronounced. What little confidence Sonny possessed when he entered instantly disappeared.

Charlotte took charge. "We're attending a brunch tomorrow. Sonny needs appropriate attire. It will be with an influential group. It's on the North Shore. It's at a horse farm."

Jared raised his eyebrows. He was very familiar with the prestige of the North Shore and the exorbitant cost of real estate there. Only the extraordinarily wealthy could afford acreage in Chicago's wealthiest suburbs.

"He needs to look sporting and tastefully casual," she continued.

"Will he be riding?" Jared asked, as though Sonny was a pet or an inanimate object.

"Possibly," she answered. Sonny gave her a surprised look. The closest he'd ever been to a horse was a miniature pony at a petting zoo.

Jared exhaled deeply. "You're asking the impossible," he muttered. "Follow me."

They left over two hours later carrying four bags of new clothing. After agreeing on an outfit for the brunch – Khaki pants, a western cut white shirt, a beige tweed jacket and low-cut leather boots –

Charlotte and Jared decided to update Sonny's entire wardrobe. He left with an array of shirts and pants, three new sports coats, a half dozen neckties and a new pair of Italian loafers, which Jared insisted Sonny not wear until spring.

For all of the insults and abuse he absorbed, Sonny found the session fun. Charlotte clearly enjoyed shopping for him, and the bickering between her and Jared was wholly entertaining. They stepped from the store smiling and energized, despite the $3,880 credit card receipt in his pocket.

"How about a late lunch?" he asked as they strode along the busy street toward the car.

"That would be nice."

Lunch

After stashing their packages in his car they walked east along West Adams Street, pulling their collars tight against the wind swirling from the lake. On a side street they found a quaint bar and grill. It was crowded, but they found a booth in the bar area. They ordered draft beer while they perused the menu.

"That was fun," volunteered Charlotte.

"I'm glad we did this," agreed Sonny. "I'll admit, though, I don't know what to expect tomorrow."

She made a worried frown. "Me neither, Sonny. This will be hard for me. I haven't spoken with him in over two years. I swore I never wanted to see him again. And yet, I'm excited to see him, too. Does that make sense?"

It made no sense at all, but he nodded anyway.

"I want him to see what I've done, what we've accomplished. I want him to see that I'm self reliant, that I can take care of myself, without his support."

"Frankly," Sonny admitted, "I've never met the man but he intimates the daylights out of me. The way everybody talks about him – he's rich, he's brilliant, and he's handsome. It's like I'm going to meet royalty or something. Let's not forget our mission, though. We need to find out about his business."

She nodded.

They sat and laughed about Jared while they awaited their meal. Their conversation was comfortable again, the recent events and conflicts all but forgotten. They ordered a second round of beers when their meal arrived. The alcohol was relaxing. This Charlotte, the soft and vulnerable Charlotte, was mesmerizing.

"Charlotte, can I ask you something?" he inquired as she picked at her salad. "Who loves you?"

She gave him a quizzical look.

"Who loves you?" he repeated.

She flushed. "Sonny, you're talking nonsense."

He described his visit to the Fox Valley Mall and the affection that was shared between the children and their grandfather. "It made me think, no one has ever said those words to me. And I've never said them to anyone else."

Her expression went dark. "A lot of guys have told me they loved me . . . when they wanted something."

A moment of awkward silence passed.

"What about your father?"

She thought about it. "No," she shook her head. "But I believe he does love me."

"Has anyone said it and meant it?" he asked.

"My mother has. She said it last night."

Another pause.

"Have you ever said it to anyone?"

She shook her head and changed the subject.

They finished their meal and were putting on their overcoats when Sonny's phone chirped. He answered without looking at the caller ID.

"Sonny, it's Liz. You said you would call."

"I know. I'm sorry. I was going to – later today." Charlotte watched him with accusing eyes.

"You promised a rain check on our date. I'm off tomorrow afternoon. Can we hook up?"

He hesitated. "I can't tomorrow. I've got something to do. It's work related."

Charlotte turned and left the restaurant.

"Let me call you later," he said. He ended the call and followed her.

Low Self Esteem

Charlotte was subdued when Sonny picked her up the next morning. At first he thought she might still be angry with him for the phone call from Liz. But when she didn't erupt in the first five minutes of the drive he knew it wasn't anger that bothered her. He stopped at a Starbucks drive thru and bought them both a Grande coffee.

His eyes darted all around as he drove, searching for potential stalkers. When he didn't see anyone he relaxed a little and focused on his pensive passenger.

"You alright?" he finally ventured.

She turned her face and gazed out the window. "Did you go out with your doctor last night?" she asked, resignation etching her voice.

"No," he answered without elaboration.

"She was working?"

He nodded.

"Are you seeing her tonight?" Her tone bore no malice.

He shook his head. They drove on in uncomfortable silence.

"You're lucky to have her," she finally said.

"We're not going together. She's a friend. That's all."

She smiled wistfully out the window. "I could never compete with someone like that."

"What are you talking about?"

"Look at her. She's adorable; she's engaging; she's smart – she went to medical school; she's confident enough to work in a strip club. I'll bet she's really good in bed."

Sonny choked on his coffee, spitting a dribble down his shirt. "Shit!" He clumsily opened the center glove box and found a napkin. "I wouldn't know!" he stated as he dabbed at the beige stains on his new white shirt. "What are you talking about?"

"I just wish I could be so together."

"Just yesterday you couldn't wait to show your father how self reliant you are, how you started your own business and are making it on your own. What changed?"

She shrugged. "You haven't met my father."

North Shore

The BMW's navigation system led them north on I-94 past Northbrook and Deerfield. They exited toward Lake Forest, heading east toward the lake. They drove along curving tree-lined streets of expensive houses, some on spacious estates and others on undersized lots, a testament to the high cost of real estate in the area. Eventually, the streets turned into roads with more extravagant homes and even larger estates. They passed several manicured golf courses. Sonny's BMW five series grew conspicuous as one of the less expensive cars on the road.

They passed a large forest preserve, beyond which the estates grew sparser. After well over an hour on the road, Wanda, the mechanical voice on his GPS system, announced they found their destination. Sonny eased into a wide asphalt driveway which led through a thick line of trees. The drive was lined with ornamental iron lamps with frosted globes, scores of them, spaced every twenty-five feet, like soldiers on guard. Through the thicket of leafless tree branches Sonny could make out the outline of buildings in the distance.

As he headed up the drive, a white panel truck

emerged from the tree line heading toward them. He pulled over to let it pass. "Document Solutions," was painted on the side along with a green recycling logo. Underneath in smaller letters it said, "*Secure shredding and recycling solutions for your document needs.*"

"Looks important," Sonny observed. "Working on a Sunday, too."

He proceeded up the drive, braking again when they emerged through the tree line. "It's not a home," he commented as he stared at the estate before him, "it's a compound."

The driveway continued for another one hundred yards with manicured lawn stretching on either side to wood lines. It then split into a 'Y' and formed a giant tear shape around a two-acre pond. The pound was neatly edged with gravel and several small beach areas. On the far shore of the pond was a large multi-level deck, with a dock extending over the water.

Beyond the deck the driveway led to the main house, a modern lodge-like structure of natural wooden beams, glass and cedar siding. It appeared to have many levels and roof lines as it sprawled across the landscape. Nearby was a long building that appeared to be an oversized garage with five giant garage doors. A couple of hundred yards to the right was a horse barn that resembled a Triple Crown stable. Painted white with green trim, it sported four cupolas along the roof peak and a number of ornamental lightning rods. Behind the barn Sonny could see a section of white paddock fencing. Between the house and stable were a wedge-roofed equipment shed and another well kept building that looked like a miniature Colonial house.

The scene was opulent but also somehow incongruous. All the buildings appeared new and well constructed, attractive in their own rights. But together they formed an unsettling mish-mash of architectural styles and designs arranged to no particular plan. It was as though someone had shaken them in a Parcheesi cup and spilled them into position.

Sonny drove along the lamp-lined drive and marveled at the wealth surrounding him. Charlotte sat rigid in her seat, a look of anxious anticipation on her lovely face.

Douglas McCardle

They parked in the driveway where it curved in front of the house. A winding slate walk led through the professionally landscaped yard to the front door, which was hidden in an alcove among the myriad windows and shingled panels of the front façade. The house was much taller than it looked from a distance.

They stopped before the giant front door. "Are you ready?" asked Sonny.

Charlotte took a breath and gathered herself. "Ready." She banged the door knocker.

The man who answered the door bore no resemblance to the image of Douglas McCardle that Sonny had created during the previous weeks and months. McCardle stood perhaps five-foot-six, slightly shorter than his daughter. He had a fragile build with a boyish chest and shoulders. His hair was a thinning weave of black specked with gray. He was far from the handsome man Charlotte and Faith had described: his look was sleepy, his eyelids half closed over dull green irises, with his left eye sagging slightly more than his right; his cheeks were ruddy and sunken, which extenuated his beakish nose. His lips were thin and slightly pursed, as though preparing for a kiss. He had prominent ears that extended from his head like open car doors. McCardle's face reminded Sonny of the estate itself, with pieces that did not quite fit – like a Picasso portrait or a picture on an etch-a-sketch. Other than the shade of their eyes, there was no resemblance between father and daughter.

"Hi, Daddy," she greeted him tentatively. She leaned forward to hug him but backed away when he did not respond.

"You're late," he stated. "We expected you a half hour ago."

"I'm sorry."

"You know how I hate it when you're late."

"Daddy, this is my friend, Sonny Feelright."

McCardle turned his gaze to Sonny. "I've read about him. Stupid name." Sonny noticed that the man's left eye twitched reflexively.

"My parents were sort of like hippies," Sonny tried to explain. He stretched out his hand. "How are you today?"

"Do you really care?" McCardle bristled. He rolled his lower jaw forward and back and tugged at his shirt collar with his hand, another nervous habit.

"I really care," Sonny joked. "It could have a real impact on the next few hours for me."

McCardle did not laugh but inspected Sonny.

"Do you go by Douglas or Doug?" asked Sonny

"Mr. McCardle will do." He pointed at Sonny's chest. "You couldn't afford a clean shirt?"

"Coffee, I spilled some coffee." Sonny wiped at the dry stains. "The shirt is new. I swear."

"How are you, daddy?" Charlotte interrupted.

"I'm wondering why you're here after ignoring me for the past two years. Am I correct in assuming you want something from me?"

Sonny stepped sideways, awaiting a violent reaction from Charlotte. He expected fireworks between them, but not quite so soon. But Charlotte just cast her eyes downward. "I'm not here because I want anything. I just wanted to see you and wish you a Happy Holiday."

"We'll see," he responded doubtfully.

"Can we come in?" she asked.

He stepped aside. They entered a large open entry hall that extended the entire depth of the house. A suspended staircase made of steel and wood split the space and led up to a second floor balcony that opened into lofts at each side of the room. The far wall was all windows, beyond which Sonny could see a swimming pool and extensive patio space.

"Are they here, Douglas?" called a voice from a doorway to the left. An attractive woman appeared, blond and shapely, carrying a coffee mug. She wore red heels, tight white slacks and a red sweater emblazoned with a green and white candy cane. She appeared to be in her mid-thirties.

"Charlotte!" she exclaimed. She swept over and gave Charlotte a one-armed hug.

"Joyce," greeted a reserved Charlotte. "This is Sonny Feelright. Sonny, this is Joyce, my step mother."

Joyce faced Sonny and gave him a warm handshake. "It's good to meet you Sonny. That's an unusual name."

"Yea," he agreed without explanation, uncomfortably conscious of Douglas McCardle's twitching stare.

"Come," she commanded as she led them through the adjoining dining room and into the giant kitchen beyond. "We have pastries."

Sonny eyed the kitchen, the most opulent he had ever seen. It had multiple everything: two full sized sinks and a smaller bar sink; two stainless steel cook tops; two huge stainless steel ovens, plus a convection oven and matching microwave; a giant two-door stainless steel refrigerator with a matching freezer. It had a pair of large islands and acres of granite counter top. Sonny was no expert on appliances, but he knew the brands on display in the McCardle kitchen – Viking and Thermador – were of the highest quality.

They sat at a butcher block kitchen table next to floor to ceiling windows facing the patio out back. The table was already set with sandwich plates, silverware and holiday-themed napkins, along with a silver coffee decanter with matching containers for sugar and cream.

Outside, the desolate season could not obscure the spectacular pool and patio area beyond the glass. The stone patio was huge and multilayered as it surrounded the giant kidney-shaped swimming pool, now covered in green coated canvas for the winter, and flowed into stone sitting areas, a sunken fire pit and a hot tub, with wisps of steam escaping from the seal of the cover.

"Incredible place you have here," Sonny marveled.

"Thanks," said Joyce. She uncovered a silver tray of pastries on the counter and brought them to the table. "We'll have brunch later, but I thought you might be hungry after the drive. Help yourself to everything."

McCardle poured himself a cup of coffee and, after inspecting all of the pastries, selected a maple roll. Charlotte poured coffee for herself and Sonny, foregoing the pastries. Sonny took a cinnamon roll, detecting a glance of disapproval from McCardle.

Joyce went to the counter and returned with a bottle of Bailey's Bristol Cream. She unscrewed the cap and poured a generous splash in her coffee. "A little holiday cheer?" she offered. Sonny slid his mug over, feeling in dire need of holiday cheer. Charlotte politely declined. McCardle rolled his jaw and tugged his collar.

"That looks good," said Joyce as she eyed Sonny's cinnamon role. She reached for the pastry dish.

"That will go straight to your hips," grunted McCardle. Joyce pulled her hand back.

After an awkward silence, Joyce turned to Sonny. "That picture in the paper didn't do you justice. I love your hair. How is your hand?"

Sonny self consciously ran his right hand through his bushy mane and held up his left, displaying his splinted finger. "It's fine. I should get this off in another week or so."

"It sounds like you two have a very interesting business."

"It sounds like a losing proposition to me," sneered McCardle. "What good was college if you're going to run around playing private detective?"

Charlotte reddened and stared at her plate.

"It's way more than that," argued Sonny. "We do forensic accounting. We investigate financial fraud and sort out accounting issues. It's really very interesting work."

"It's a bunch of bullshit, if you ask me."

"Well," Joyce stood, "why don't we take a tour of the house."

Skeet

Sonny was lost almost instantly when they stepped from the kitchen and entered the labyrinth of hallways, staircases and rooms that comprised the McCardle home. There was a theater room with two dozen theater-style seats sloping to a large projection screen. There was a split-level fitness center, jammed with every conceivable kind of apparatus as well as an adjoining sauna and shower. Sonny stopped counting bathrooms at six. The master bedroom featured his and her walk-in closets, each one as big as Sonny's entire apartment. The giant game room was packed like an arcade. The neighboring billiard room, paneled floor to ceiling in cherry and decorated with richly framed hunt scenes, had both an ornate pool table and a bumper pool table.

"Just the two of you live here?" marveled Sonny.

"I *used* to have a daughter," McCardle responded pointedly.

"And here's Douglas's gun collection." Joyce led them into a medium sized room with a loveseat and two overstuffed chairs in the center. A low wooden work table sat between them, its surface marred from cleaning weapons. The wallpaper was hunter green with a plaid pattern. Along the walls were several gun cabinets displaying an array of rifles and shotguns through locked glass doors. More guns were displayed in hanging cases on the walls – a collection of derringers, an array of antique handguns, and a pistol rack. On the far wall, French doors led to a cedar deck.

"You're a hunter?" asked Sonny.

McCardle pointed toward the ceiling, where the mounted heads of several wild animals were on display. "I hunted just yesterday. There's a quail farm down the road. "

"That's what we're having for brunch," Joyce added.

Sonny pointed to the head of a Bighorn Sheep. "I thought those were protected."

"Not from me," McCardle responded. "Do you shoot?"

"No. I've never fired a gun."

McCardle twitched and tugged his collar. "I'll tell you what, it's never too late to try. I've got a skeet launcher on the deck. How about it?"

"I don't think that's a good idea," Charlotte interrupted.

"Nonsense," he dismissed her. "I'm sure Sonny here will enjoy it." He pulled a key from his pocket and unlocked one of the cases. He thoughtfully inspected the shotguns inside before selecting one. He opened a drawer and retrieved a box of shells. "Follow me."

The four of them gathered on the deck outside. Charlotte and Joyce wrapped their arms across their chests against the cold. McCardle seemed oblivious to the chill, showing enthusiasm for the first time since their arrival.

"Daddy," Charlotte tried again, "I really don't think this is necessary."

He turned and glared at her. "Why don't *you* try first?" he dared. "I'm sure you've forgotten everything I ever taught you."

She shook her head.

"Afraid?" he asked.

Her eyes went steely. "Give me the gun," she demanded. She expertly broke the chamber and inserted a shell in each barrel, snapping it closed with authority. She hiked the gun to her shoulder, ready. McCardle, now wearing a wry smile, loaded a clay pigeon in the skeet launcher mounted to the railing.

"Pull!" she yelled. McCardle launched the disk toward the pasture behind the barn. She fired when it reached the peak of its arc. The pigeon shattered into raining shards. McCardle loaded a second bird. "Pull!" she repeated. She fired a second deafening blast with the same precise result. She shoved the smoking gun back to her father and retreated into the house with Joyce close behind.

"See," said McCardle, "nothing to it." He loaded the gun and handed it to Sonny, showing him how to release the safety catch and work the double trigger. Sonny lifted the gun awkwardly, trying to remember how Charlotte held it. He placed the butt loosely against his shoulder and tucked his chin to align the sights.

"Pull!" he yelled. The clay pigeon sailed from the deck, surprising Sonny with its speed. The gun barrel trailed it badly. Sonny watched without firing as it shattered into the frozen ground.

"This is hard," he observed. "Let me try again."

McCardle loaded another pigeon.

"Pull!" yelled Sonny. This time he fired almost immediately, completely unprepared for the violent recoil of the shotgun. The butt struck his shoulder and chin with such force that it spun him around and almost sent him to the deck. McCardle grabbed the heavy weapon as it fell from Sonny's hands.

"Shit!" he cried as he crouched and clutched his bruised shoulder. "Shit! Shit! Shit!" The pain welled to a crescendo of agony before gradually subsiding. Both his arm and his jaw were numb. He took some deep breaths and straightened. He turned to see Joyce and a frowning Charlotte watching him through the door.

"Ever play billiards?" asked McCardle as his eye twitched excitedly.

Games

It had been years since Sonny held a pool cue. McCardle had to refresh him on the rules of eight-ball. He racked the balls and offered Sonny the break. Sonny's effort was humiliating; he topped the cue ball, which rolled lazily into the racked stack and deflected into the corner pocket.

"Scratch on break. Too bad," said McCardle. He retrieved the cue ball and aligned it, smacking it with authority into the cluster of balls. "I'm solids," he announced when the five ball dropped into a leather pocket. He circled the table, eyeing various possibilities. He shot again, dropping a second solid. Again and again he made his shots until only the eight ball was left for him. It was tucked among a cluster of stripes. "Maybe you can clean up some of your mess," he suggested after missing the shot.

With only stripes left on the table, Sonny had numerous easy shot options. He lined up a straight shot to the corner, but his effort went awry. The cue ball bounced off the curb and ricocheted into the eight-ball, knocking it into the side pocket.

"Game!" said McCardle. "I wouldn't play for money if I were you." He turned to Charlotte, who leaned against the wall watching Sonny's annihilation. "You're next," he challenged.

She wouldn't take the bait. "No thanks."

McCardle shrugged and, turning back to Sonny, asked, "Ever play Foosball?"

He led Sonny to the arcade room where the two men moved from gaming table to gaming table, arcade machine to arcade machine. They competed for more than an hour, with Sonny losing every match. Joyce, who left several times to refresh her drink, offered McCardle encouragement. "Good one, honey ... You're such an expert ... *Excellent* shot!" Charlotte stood sullenly by the door, a look of disapproval on her face.

"I have to say," McCardle concluded after destroying Sonny at pinball, "I've never seen anyone as uncoordinated as you. What did you do growing up? Hide in a closet?"

"Don't let him kid you," joked Joyce. "Douglas is good at everything."

McCardle twitched, rolled his jaw and pulled his collar. "How about a ride before we eat?"

Horses

McCardle disappeared to change while Joyce declined the invitation to ride and retreated to the kitchen.

"Are you alright?" Sonny asked Charlotte while they waited alone in the entry hall.

"Why did you do that?" she asked.

"What?"

"Why did you let him humiliate you like that?"

"Why didn't you play pool with him?" he responded.

"Because if I beat him he goes ballistic. And we have to keep playing until he wins."

"You can beat him?" Sonny was impressed.

"Don't you see he's making fun of you? He's manipulating you."

Sonny frowned with embarrassment. "I'm sorry," he shrugged.

McCardle returned wearing white riding breeches, riding boots and a leather bomber's jacket. Charlotte, who came dressed for the possibility of riding, had on stove pipe jeans and ankle boots. McCardle handed her an insulated jacket to wear over her wool sweater. He offered nothing to Sonny.

The trio made their way the several hundred yards to the barn, their breath forming clouds as they walked. Sonny buttoned his tweed jacket, which offered scant protection from the chill.

"What's in there," he asked as they passed the Colonial style outbuilding.

"My office," McCardle answered.

"What exactly do you do?"

"Consult."

"What about?" Sonny probed.

"Nothing that you would understand."

Sonny was surprised and relieved to find that the barn was heated. They entered through a side door. Stretching before them was a wide concrete aisle. On either side were six large stalls. Between the third and fourth stalls was a wide crossing aisle connecting large sliding barn doors on each side. Partitioned next to one door was a tack room; opposing it across the aisle was a storage area, where bags of grain and bales of hay were stacked. The building was immaculate, brightly lit with Halogen lights overhead and painted white everywhere but the stalls, which were natural wood. Horses peered at them through vertical stainless steel bars that made up the upper portion of the stalls.

"You ride all of these?" Sonny asked in amazement.

"Three are pleasure horses. I breed the rest of them," McCardle replied.

Charlotte pointed to the farthest stall, where a large black horse glared at them with a wild eye. “That’s Majestic. He’s a champion stallion. The rest are brood mares – all with bloodlines.”

“Majestic brings in ten thousand a pop,” McCardle bragged.

Charlotte went to the second stall on the right. “Hey, Hombre,” she cooed. She opened the stall door and stepped in. “You miss me? How’s my boy?” She hugged the neck of a large white gelding, who stepped in place in response.

“I didn’t know you had a horse,” said Sonny. Of course, he realized, he never knew she could shoot or play pool, either.

“You ever ride before?” McCardle asked.

Sonny shook his head.

McCardle pulled a gray mare from a stall and cross tied it in the aisle. He handed Sonny a rubber brush. “Brush,” he commanded. Sonny approached the beast tentatively, intimidated by its mass. “It’s not going to bite,” barked McCardle. Sonny stroked the brush gently across the horse’s heavy winter coat. McCardle grabbed it from him and began to violently brush, sending horse hair flying into the air. “Hard. Like this.” He handed the brush back to Sonny.

Charlotte brushed and expertly saddled Hombre in the stall, talking tenderly to him the whole time. Then she saddled Sonny's horse while he tried to pick the horse hair from his new tweed jacket. Sonny winced when she shoved her knee against the horse's side and yanked the saddle cinch tight, forcing a loud exhale from the massive animal. He winced again when she forced the bridle bit into its mouth, metal clacking against giant teeth. Down the aisle, McCardle saddled his own horse, a muscular brown thoroughbred that dwarfed him. They led the three horses through the barn door into the paddock out back, McCardle first, Charlotte second and Sonny, staying as far as possible from his horse's giant hooves, last.

"Isn't there supposed to be a handle on this saddle?" Sonny asked.

"A horn," corrected McCardle. "And no, that's a western saddle. These are English. No 'handles.'"

Outside, Charlotte stretched her leg high and planted a toe in a stirrup. With two hops of her grounded leg, she leapt and swung into her saddle. She quickly began trotting Hombre in a tight circle, thoroughly engaged with the animal. McCardle led his horse to a step stool by the paddock fence and mounted up. He nodded for Sonny to follow suit.

Sonny walked his horse to the stool, struggling to maneuver it into position as it stepped about nervously. McCardle sat still and watched him with disapproval. Feeling the pressure, Sonny climbed on the ladder and leaped for the saddle of his fidgeting mount. For a brief moment, he thought he made it. But then he felt the horse side step and he began to loll slowly to the other side. He clutched desperately at the thin saddle, but it offered little leverage. When he was nearly parallel to the ground he gave up and let go, landing with a "Humph" on the frozen ground. He scrambled on hands and knees to avoid the horse's dancing hooves.

"Tell you what," offered McCardle as he dismounted and grabbed the reins of Sonny's horse, "why don't you wait for us here." Sonny stood, brushed himself off and followed McCardle back into the barn. All the while, Charlotte rode her mount in tight circles, seemingly hypnotized by the experience.

Stall Duty

Sonny stood lamely by and watched as McCardle removed the horse's tack and returned the animal to its stall. He then walked to the feed storage area and returned with a wheel barrow and a manure rake. He handed them to Sonny and nodded toward the two empty stalls. "Maybe you can make yourself useful."

"This is ridiculous," Sonny muttered after McCardle left. He entered the first stall and looked around. Whatever the horse had been eating, he obviously had eaten a lot. Sonny slid the plastic tines of the rake under the first pile and conveyed it to the wheel barrel, then returned for more. He finished the first stall and went to the next.

"You know, you don't have to do that." It was Joyce. She was standing inside the door, a tumbler in her hand.

"Huh?"

"You don't have to clean the stalls. We have a stall boy. He comes every day. He'll be here in an hour."

Sonny laid the rake across the wheel barrel and approached her. "Why did he tell me to?"

"Because he's like that." She sipped her drink and eyed him.

Sonny shook his head. "No offense, but he's a real jerk!"

Joyce didn't disagree.

"Why do you put up with it?"

She smiled. "Look around."

"For the money?"

She shrugged. "I'm not like you and Charlotte. I'm not smart. I never went to college. I don't mind being a trophy wife."

"Do you love him?"

"I thought I did. Now, I tolerate him," she smiled and held up her drink. "There are times I wish he was dead. Other times he's alright. Never loving, but tolerable. The biggest frustration is the loneliness." She swept her arm about the room. "All of this, and we're here alone most of the time."

"Why did you marry him?"

"It wasn't like this in the beginning. He used to be more social. We would travel and have dinner parties. But he's changed over the past few years. He's become more bitter and reclusive. He doesn't trust anyone. I was so excited you two were visiting. It's been months since we've had guests."

"Why don't you just leave him?"

"There's a prenup. I don't get squat unless he does something really bad. My goal is to outlive him."

"That's awful," Sonny commiserated. "I feel so bad for you."

"I feel worse for Charlotte," she said. "The poor girl had to grow up with him. At least I have a choice." She tipped her tumbler, finishing whatever drink it contained. "Come on. Let's go back to the house. Share a drink with me."

Collections

They walked together to the house, heads bent against the cold breeze. "What's in there?" Sonny asked as they hurried past the miniature Colonial.

"Douglas's office. I'd show it to you but he keeps it locked."

"Even when he's home?"

"He's paranoid about it. He doesn't even let me in there."

"What exactly does he do?"

She shrugged. "He consults. I don't know much. He's very secretive. He has a handful of clients – some here and some in New York. It's stock market stuff. I guess you have to be careful about disclosure laws and things."

"Does he travel? Does he write reports?"

"Not much. He's pretty reclusive. He reads a lot. He's constantly studying. He doesn't travel. I guess most of his client contact is by phone and e-mail."

Sonny eyed the building as they passed.

"You want to see his cars?" she asked. She diverted course and led him to the oversized garage. They entered through a side door. Like the barn, the building was immaculate, painted white and brightly lit. The floor was surfaced in large white tiles. On display inside were at least a dozen collector automobiles.

"Holy shit," Sonny murmured. He recognized a Porsche 911 Turbo Cabriolet, similar to the one from his visit to Exotic World Cars. He wandered among the vehicles, reading the name plates – Aston Martin, Ferrari, Lamborghini. "There are millions of dollars in here."

She nodded. "As you can tell, Douglas likes to collect things."

"Why isn't this building locked?" Sonny inquired. "If he locks the office, why wouldn't he lock this, too?"

She shrugged. She held up her empty mug. "Let's go to the house."

"I'll join you in a minute. I need to take all this in."

She left. He cracked the door and watched until she disappeared into the house. Then he slipped from the garage and jogged back to McCardle's office. He stepped onto the wooden porch and peered through the door window. The building was about fifteen-hundred square feet, bigger than most of the houses and apartments Sonny lived in growing up. It appeared to be sectioned into four rooms: the office directly inside the door, a second room to the back, a bathroom to the right and a kitchenette beside it.

The office was carpeted and appeared to be professionally decorated. A long conference table occupied the center of the room, its polished wooden surface devoid of papers or files. A matching oversized desk was behind it facing the door, its surface tidy. To the left was a sitting area with a leather couch and matching upholstered chairs. The scene was antiseptic, like an arrangement for a magazine photo. The room looked unused.

Sonny walked around to the side of the building. He cupped his hands and looked through the window into the back room. Here was where the work was done. In the center of the room were three stacks of file storage boxes, each four boxes high. Along the far wall was a long work table. An open file box sat on the floor next to it. Files and papers were scattered on the table. He retrieved his IPhone and snapped several pictures through the window.

Sudden Exit

Joyce poured Sonny a second glass of wine while they waited in the kitchen for McCardle and Charlotte to return from riding. They had talked for nearly an hour. Coincidentally, like Sonny, she also grew up in Elmwood Park in a modest, working class family. Her father was an alcoholic who could become abusive when he drank. After securing a promise that he wouldn't tell McCardle, Joyce confided to Sonny that she never finished high school, dropping out in her senior year so she could take a job and escape her stressful home life.

She worked multiple jobs. Her break came when she took a sales clerk position at an exclusive women's clothing boutique in Barrington. That's where she met McCardle, who would bring his wife in to shop for her. As their marriage faltered, McCardle began courting her.

"To this day I feel bad about the affair," she admitted. "I used to think Faith was to blame for the divorce. There was no affection at all. But now I understand her better. I fantasize about apologizing to her someday."

They were interrupted by McCardle, who stormed into the room, enraged.

"What's the matter?" Joyce asked with concern.

"My *daughter*," he hissed. "She's no better than her mother!"

Sonny was fed up with this boorish man. "That's no way to talk about Faith or Charlotte!"

"Faith-*less*!" retorted McCardle.

Charlotte entered. She did not look at her father. "Sonny, we're leaving," was all she said, her voice subdued.

"What happened?" Sonny asked as they left the estate in his BMW. She had been mute since the encounter in the kitchen.

"He called me a whore." She covered her face with her hands and began to weep.

IED

Nancy sat in a folding chair in the Calumet hideaway. While she hated the place, it was the only appropriate location for the business at hand. The Imam sat across from her. Bomani slouched in the chair to her right. Kafele, standing, reverently placed a brown grocery bag on the table.

She sensed the utter hatred radiating from Bomani. But it did not bother her. He would do her bidding. Throughout her life Nancy had bent people to her will, forcing them to abandon their values, principles and sometimes even their loved ones. Her weapon of manipulation was the one constant of human nature – greed. She knew that Kafele and the Imam also detested her and were embarrassed to take orders from a woman. But her promises of personal riches for them overwhelmed their sense of pride. Bomani had no interest in personal wealth. He was greedy for far greater riches; martyrdom and the glory that awaited him in death. Achieving it required that he also be her servant on this mission.

In her entire career, she met only one person who did not behave consistent with this rule of human nature – Sonny Feelright. He was irrational. He had shunned the opportunity to join her in amassing incredible wealth. His mission all along was to destroy her empire. And he succeeded.

Kafele withdrew the contents of the bag and set it on the table. He proudly explained how all of the contents, except for the C-4 explosives, were procured at a local hobby store. He displayed the detonation device – a controller to a remote control toy car – and described how it would signal the receiver on the bomb.

"What if someone has a similar controller? What if someone else detonates it?"

"That's unlikely," answered Kafele. "The signal is only good within one hundred feet. And the location is remote."

She eyed the device with satisfaction. "You'll do it tomorrow. The guard always leaves fifteen minutes early. Wait until he's gone. But make sure you just get Feelright. No collateral damage. And no witnesses. He has to be alone."

"What if things don't go as planned? What if he's not alone," Kafele asked.

"Abort. We'll wait and try again." She looked at Bomani, who refused to make eye contact. "He drives," she pronounced. She nodded at Kafele. "You set the device. I want no more impulsive mistakes."

She pulled a cell phone from her black coat. "This is prepaid. Call me when the deed is done. Then destroy the phone."

Different Approaches

Sonny arrived at work before daylight Monday, hoping to catch Simon before Charlotte showed up. Simon now arrived early most days, invigorated by the challenging workload the firm was enjoying.

Sonny's ride home with Charlotte from her father's the day before was heart wrenching for him. He thought he had witnessed all sides of Charlotte, all of the many textures of the complex tapestry that comprised her personality. But he never saw her so utterly forlorn. She wept quietly while he drove, ignoring his gentle questions. He pulled off at an oasis on I-94 to get gas and something to eat. She obediently followed him in but declined food.

He ordered her a diet soft drink anyway, along with a McDonald's Fillet-O-Fish meal for himself. As they stood by the counter awaiting their order, Sonny got an obnoxious whiff from the man standing nearby.

"That guy really stinks," he whispered to Charlotte. Meanwhile, the man turned and made a sour face in Sonny's direction.

She leaned toward the man and took a discreet sniff. She leaned back and took another sniff. She turned to Sonny and sniffed his jacket.

"It's you. You smell like manure. What did you do, roll in the stalls?"

"No. But your dad made me clean them – until Joyce came and rescued me."

She shook her head sadly. "This is why he did it. To humiliate you. Now do you see how he manipulated you?"

They sat at a table in the center of the busy complex, Sonny self-conscious about his odor.

"Will you tell me what happened?" he coaxed.

"He was horrible. As soon as we set off he began disparaging you and our business. He said you're dull. He said you'll never amount to anything. He accused me of abandoning him in favor of my mother. He said the only reason I came back was because he has money now. He called me a 'gold digger.' He called me a 'whore.'"

"What did you say?"

"I didn't say anything. I never say anything when I'm around him. I let him demean me, just like my mother."

"Listen, Charlotte, I know he's your father, but he's despicable."

She conceded the point with a nod. "He's doing bad things."

"Did he tell you anything? Did he tell you about his business?"

"No, but that place, all that money. We were always comfortable, but he was never that wealthy. People don't just get rich that fast. Like Simon said, if it seems too good to be true it probably is."

She bowed her head. Several moments passed. They were enveloped in the cacophony of the hustling crossroads. Finally, she looked up and gave him an urgent look. "Am I like him, Sonny? Please tell me I'm not like him."

"You're nothing like him," he assured her.

That was yesterday. Now, Sonny was glad to see Simon's light on when he entered the reception area. He discarded his coat and briefcase in his office and then flopped in a chair across from his senior partner in the conference room.

"I'm guessing from your demeanor that yesterday didn't go well."

Sonny described the visit, including the reasons for its abrupt end.

"Charlotte should be a treat to work with today," Simon warned. "Poor Adonis has to pick her up." He shook his craggy head. "Tell me more about McCardle's office."

Sonny pulled out his IPhone and scrolled through the pictures he had taken.

"These are file storage boxes," Simon observed. "They're not all the same; they were made by different vendors. He could have bought them at different times. But why would he be storing files in cardboard storage boxes? With his money he could afford a wall of file cabinets. And what's he doing with them? It's not tax season yet." He stared closely at the pictures. "Some of these have labels, but they're too small to read."

Sonny tinkered with the phone in an attempt to zoom in on the photos. "They're too blurry."

"Forward them to me," ordered Simon. "I'll send them to a guy I know to see if he can enhance them."

"His wife says he keeps the office locked tight. But his car collection is unlocked. I swear, there had to be a couple million worth of cars in that garage. It didn't make sense."

Simon sat back and rubbed his chin. "Maybe we need to approach it from a different angle. Your friend Danny Byrne, do you think he would do you a favor?"

"Like what?"

"See if he'll tell you some of the stocks that McCardle recommended. Maybe we can work backward from that."

"I highly doubt it. He knows McCardle is up to no good. He said he avoids getting close to him because what he doesn't know can't hurt him."

Simon laughed. "He's living in a fool's paradise. If he's trading based on inside information, it doesn't matter that he's ignorant of the exact illegal disclosures. It only matters that he knows he's trading based on illegal information. And if everything McCardle recommends is a winner, Byrne will be presumed to know. Byrne has been an embarrassment for the FBI. They only need a toehold of suspicion to build a case. Not even Danny Byrne can withstand the might of the federal government when it's pissed off."

"I'll try."

Phone Taps

They were interrupted as Charlotte arrived in the outer office. She was accompanied by Adonis, who wore a worried look. Sonny stood and watched them from the doorway. Her expression was grim; her makeup could have been war paint. Adonis normally dropped her off outside, but he felt compelled to walk her up because of her sour mood. He shouldn't have; he put a nurturing hand on her shoulder in an attempt to help her remove her coat, but she shrugged away and disappeared into her office, closing the door.

"What did I do?" asked a frustrated Adonis.

Sonny shrugged.

"I mean, I thought everything was going well. I thought we were making progress. And then this morning I walked into a buzz saw."

"Probably just had a bad weekend."

Adonis left, shaking his head. Sonny went to his office and looked up the phone number for Exotic World Cars. A professional receptionist answered on the first ring.

"May I speak with Danny Byrne?" Sonny asked.

"Mr. Byrne isn't here right now. May I ask who is calling and what it's in regard to?"

"My name is Sonny Feelright. It's a personal matter."

"I'll see that he gets the message."

Not two minutes passed before Sonny's phone rang. The caller ID said "Private."

"Hello?"

"You called?" It was Byrne.

"Mr. Byrne, it's Sonny."

"Yea. I just called you."

"Yea, I'm sorry. I wanted to talk to you. I need some information and I wondered if you could help me."

"If it's not about a car you shouldn't be calling me."

"It's not about a car."

"Then why the fuck are you calling me?"

Sonny was confused.

"Jesus Christ, do I have to spell it out for you? And for everyone else who might be listening? Tell you what, Sonny, maybe we can break bread again someday. I'll call you sometime." He hung up.

Two more minutes passed and Sonny's phone rang again. It was the receptionist from Byrne's dealership. "Mr. Feelright, I understand you recently visited our dealership to inquire about a car."

"That's right."

"Mr. Byrne suggested it might be good for the two of you to meet and discuss it. He'd like to come by at three-thirty this afternoon. He suggested you meet him in front of your building. Would that be alright?"

"Fine. That will be fine."

Trading Tips

The long red Cadillac was waiting in front of the building when Sonny emerged into the winter sunlight. Al Cistone was driving. Danny Byrne rolled down the passenger window and scowled. "You're late. We've been waiting five minutes."

"I'm sorry. One of my partners is being a little difficult today. I had trouble escaping."

"I'm guessing it's the redhead."

Cistone stepped from the driver side and walked around the car. He motioned for Sonny to raise his arms and then patted him down. "Cell phone." He held out his hand. Sonny obligingly turned over his phone and then climbed into the back seat. The cabin of the car was spacious; Sonny was able to stretch his legs completely.

"Sorry about that," Byrne apologized. "The heat's been rising lately. Can't be too careful. In fact, you need to be a lot more careful, too. The cops might be tapping your phones. So might those guys chasing you."

"That would be illegal."

"Fuckin eh! So is killing you." Byrne shook his head.

"Where we going?" asked Sonny after a few moments.

"Let's get coffee."

Cistone drove to a nearby Starbucks and elected to wait in the car while Sonny and Byrne went inside. They ordered coffee and sat at a round table far from the counter.

"So, what is it you want from me?"

"Information. We need to know some of the stocks Douglas McCardle has recommended to you."

Byrne guffawed. "That'll fucking ever happen!"

"We think he's engaging in illegal insider trading."

"No shit, Sherlock. That's exactly why I'm not telling anybody anything. What I don't know can't hurt me."

"Simon says that's not true."

Byrne eyed him suspiciously. "What do you mean?"

"Simon's a lawyer and an investment banker. He said you're vulnerable. Ignorance can't protect you when it comes to securities laws. He said the feds will put you away if they find out. He said you're living in a 'fool's paradise.'"

"Son of a bitch," Byrne muttered. They each sipped their coffees, Byrne with a scowl on his face. "So, if I tell you and McCardle goes down, what does it do for me?"

"I don't know. We can't tell you anything until we find out what he's doing and how. All I can do is promise you that we'll do our best to protect you if you help us."

"That's not enough."

"What then?"

"You've got to keep me informed. And you've got to promise me you won't turn him in without consulting me first. I've got to say it's okay."

Sonny wasn't sure it was a promise he could keep. "Agreed," he replied.

Byrne made a phone call. It was to his broker. He asked for the names of the companies he had traded in the past two years. "Write these down," he directed Sonny and proceeded to read off the names, which Sonny recorded on a napkin. Sonny slipped the napkin into his pocket.

"Alright," Byrne said after hanging up. "Quid pro quo. I've got something for you." He pulled a handful of photographs from his pocket and laid them on the table. Sonny leaned in to look.

"What's this?" asked Sonny. The photos were grainy and taken from a distance. One was of a man and a woman entering a dilapidated apartment. Several were of two dark haired young men dropping off rental cars. Another was a closer look at the woman entering a worn Chevy Impala. She wore dark glasses and had long straight black hair. She looked vaguely familiar.

"The quality is not the best," Byrne apologized. "Cistone in his goddamn land yacht. He can't get close enough for good pictures. Those two guys are the ones stalking you. They have a shithole apartment in Calumet. I don't know who the woman and man are, but they all met there."

Ambush

They waited in the rented Chevy Malibu, Bomani at the wheel and Kafele in the passenger seat. They were parked down the street, a block and a half from the Feelright Intelligence Services building. The paper bag containing the bomb sat in Kafele's lap. He toyed nervously with the controller that would serve as the remote detonator. He patted his jacket pocket for the umpteenth time to make sure he still had the cell phone that the wicked woman provided.

As had become the pattern, the overweight security guard began glancing at his watch at four-thirty p.m. Fifteen minutes later he left his post early and made his way to his aging Ford Fiesta and pulled away, leaving Sonny Feelright's BMW alone in the lot. Bomani started the car and eased down the street and into the lot. As planned, he parked along the untended boundary, backing the car into the overgrown foliage until only its grill and headlights protruded. In the waning winter daylight the car was all but invisible.

From their lair they watched as the handsome man in the black sedan with government plates pulled into the alley, emerging a short time later with Feelright's red headed colleague in the car with him. Even from a distance she appeared angry. Their anticipation grew as they waited for the other two partners to emerge. The cab that would take the crusty old man home arrived as expected, parking in front of the building to wait. Kafele's signal.

He set the controller on the dashboard, making sure it could not tip or slide. He withdrew the bomb from the bag and flipped a switch to activate the remote receiver. He slipped it carefully back into the bag and then eased from the car. He crept stealthily along the brush line to the BMW. Crouching, he placed the bag on the ground next to the driver door, sliding it halfway under the car where it would not be easily noticed and would have maximum impact on anyone standing there. He made his way back to the Malibu. He retrieved the controller from the dashboard and held it as delicately as if it was a butterfly.

The brothers watched intently as the old man appeared. He climbed into the cab and rode away. Their anticipation mounted as they waited for Sonny Feelright to round the corner from the alley. Minutes passed. They traded surprised looks. Where was Sonny Feelright?

"We need to abort," whispered Kafele.

"No!" insisted Bomani.

"You heard the woman. No mistakes. Abort if things don't go as planned. He should be out by now."

"No. We wait."

"Five minutes more."

At that moment a vintage red Cadillac appeared on the street. They watched with pounding hearts as it approached and pulled to the curb along the front of the lot. The back door opened. Out stepped their prey, Sonny B. Feelright.

"We have to abort." Kafele insisted.

"No!"

"She said no witnesses, no collateral damage. We have to abort." He opened the door and climbed from the car to retrieve the bomb.

Quid Pro Quo

Sonny patted his pocket and thanked Byrne for the stock information, which he could barely wait to share with Simon.

"Just remember our deal," warned Byrne. "Quid pro quo. You watch my back and I'll watch yours." His voice was threatening.

Sonny nodded and was relieved to climb from the back seat of the Cadillac. He was twenty-five feet away when Byrne called from his open window. "Sonny, you forgot your cell phone."

Sonny turned and began walking back to the car.

"Hey," Cistone called from the driver seat. "Who the hell is that?"

Sonny swung around and noticed a shadowy figure creeping along the tree line toward his car.

"Hey!" he shouted. "Get away from my car!"

Shadows

Bomani cursed and pounded his fists on the steering wheel as he watched his older brother sneak back toward the BMW. This was their moment to end all the nonsense. Their moment to terminate their frustrating adversary and be rid of the infuriating woman. Until this assignment was complete he would not be free to pursue real Jihad and the glory it promised.

Kafele tiptoed along the tree line, trying to avoid notice from the three men in the car. His clothes were dark. He moved slowly, blending with the shadows in the breeze-agitated foliage behind him. From the corner of his eye he saw Feelright peel away from the car and head toward him. Then Sonny stopped and turned back toward the Cadillac, to Kafele's relief. He began to trot toward the BMW. He had to retrieve the bomb.

Just then he heard Sonny call out. In panic, Kafele took two running steps and launched himself behind the BMW, completely forgetting the toy controller he held in his hand.

Sudden Death

There was a flash followed by a concussion that seemed to drive the air from Sonny's lungs and penetrate the marrow of his bones. He crouched instinctively and watched in horror as his beloved BMW lifted from the ground, expelling pieces and parts as it rose, and then crashed down on its passenger side. A ball of fire and black smoke billowed above it, forming a mushroom in the sky. Debris rained down on the lot.

He turned and faced Byrne, who was staring at the conflagration from his open window. Byrne's eyes met Sonny's. "Jesus Christ!" he shouted. "You're fucking toxic! Al, get the fuck out of here!"

Al hit the gas and the Cadillac roared away. Byrne flung the IPhone from the open window. It soared over Sonny's head and smashed into the parking lot. Sonny turned back toward the burning vehicle, suddenly remembering that a person dove behind the car before it exploded. He inched toward the vehicle, afraid of what he might find on the other side. Just then he heard an anguished scream to his right. A car, headlights off, appeared from the thicket along the edge of the lot. It accelerated straight at him. Just in time, Sonny jumped to the side. He saw the driver's anguished face, tears flowing, as the Malibu sped past. It was one of the men in the photographs. Sonny turned and watched as the car bounced over the curb to the street and fled in the same direction as the Cadillac.

Sonny again turned his attention to the burning vehicle, determined to help whoever was on the other side. He crept forward cautiously. When he was forty feet away the gas tank erupted in a fiery flare. The heat of the blast forced him backward and he realized that there was no hope for the man caught in the explosion. Sonny just witnessed a violent death.

He stood for a moment, watching the scene in horror. Then fear enveloped him. He turned and ran.

Hiding

He ran east on Harrison, in the opposite direction of the Chevy Malibu, toward the Chicago River and downtown. He sprinted at first, fueled by adrenaline, his mind a cauldron of fear and panic. When his lungs felt as though they would burst, he slowed to a steady jog, swiveling his head backward and forward in search of the Malibu. He heard sirens in the distance. He ran all the way to the Chicago River and across the bridge until he found himself among the skyscrapers of Chicago's business district. There he slowed, feeling anonymous surrounded by the rush hour crowds and traffic. He needed a place to hide, a place to think. He walked until he grew chilled in his sweat soaked clothes.

He needed to call someone – Simon or Charlotte. He reached to his pocket before remembering Byrne tossing his phone out the car window. Byrne's warning came back to him; his phone might be tapped. What if the assassins were tapping his phone or tracing his credit cards. He found an ATM and, using both his credit card and his bank debit card, withdrew a thousand dollars in cash. He hailed a cab.

"Where to?" asked the driver.

"Can you recommend a hotel?"

"How good? There's the Trump or the Essex if you want something nice right on Michigan. We've got a Double Tree or a Marriott if you want something less expensive."

"Something close," said Sonny.

"How about the Burnham?"

Sonny nodded to the face in the rearview mirror.

Ten minutes later a doorman welcomed him into the canopied entrance of the Hotel Burnham in the historic Reliance Building, one of Chicago's early skyscrapers. He checked in as S.B. Feelright, showing his driver's license to the clerk, who seemed flummoxed when Sonny insisted on paying in cash instead of with a credit card. The clerk called a manager over, who personally handled the reservation. A bellman shrugged when Sonny told him he had no luggage. Sonny made his way along the mosaic tiled floors to the ornate elevators, which took him to his room on the sixth floor.

The ornate furnishings of the room barely registered to Sonny as he closed the door behind him, double checking to make sure it was securely locked. He sat on the bed and buried his face in his hands. Suddenly struck by the trauma of the evening, he wept. For a full five minutes he wept, until his sobs shook his body and his tears stained his pant legs.

He gathered himself and reached for the room phone. Then it occurred to him that he did not know anyone's number to call. He relied on the speed dial of his cell phone to call his colleagues; he never committed their numbers to memory. The only numbers he knew were the office, which was empty now, and his own. He dialed information and asked for the phone number of Liz's medical clinic.

"Please be there," he pleaded as he waited for someone to answer the phone.

"Is Dr. Loveland on duty?" he asked when the receptionist answered.

"Are you a patient? If you're a patient I'm sure one of the nurses in triage can help."

"No," he insisted. "I have to speak with Dr. Loveland. It's an emergency. A family matter."

"I'll see if she's still here."

A few moments later, Liz answered, "Hello, this is Dr. Loveland."

Sonny was never more comforted by another human voice. "Liz," he said urgently, "I need to see you right now."

"Sonny, where are you?" she asked.

"I'm downtown at the Hotel Burnham."

"Wow! This is a surprise. Romantic, I'll admit, but a little unexpected. I'll need to call off tonight at the club and pick up some things at my place."

"No, no! Something's happened! Something terrible has happened! I need your help right now!"

"You don't sound right," she noted with concern. "Are you okay? What happened?"

"I can't talk about it on the phone. Please, come to the Burnham. Don't tell anyone where you're going. Make sure no one follows you."

"Sonny, this is all kind of weird...."

"Please, Liz!" he interrupted. "I need your help!"

Reactions

Charlotte remained sullen but less belligerent than earlier in the day as she dined with Adonis at a bar and grille near her apartment. He found himself babbling in a one-sided conversation, trying to lift her from her depression. He looked at her longingly across the table. Her beauty was timeless, enchanting. But beneath the skin she was a conflicted soul. Since he began courting her weeks ago she had rebuffed his every effort to get close to her. Now she seemed completely unapproachable. What little encouragement he felt when she accepted his invitation to a casual dinner was fading fast.

He pulled his vibrating cell phone from his pocket and answered it. He furrowed his dark eyes and stared at her as he listened. "Excuse me," he said and stepped from the table to a secluded area in the far corner of the bar. She watched him as he talked on the phone, a look of growing concern on his face. She sensed something was wrong.

When he returned to the table he sat and reached across, grabbing her hands in his, staring seriously into her eyes. "Charlotte, something's happened."

"It's Sonny!" she blurted out, her whole body tensing. "What's happened to him? Tell me!"

"We don't know. But his car, it's gone. There was an explosion."

"No!" she gasped, yanking her hands away and hugging her shoulders. "Where's Sonny? What's happened to him?"

"There appear to be remains at the scene. We don't know who it is or whether it was one person or more. We don't know if it was Sonny."

Charlotte began to tremble. Tears welled in her eyes and tracked down her face. "No!" she screamed, the agony of her cry penetrating every corner of the restaurant. "No! No! No!" She sprang from the table and ran from the building, with Adonis in close pursuit.

The parking lot was aglow, lit with spotlights and the flashing beacons of police cars, an ambulance and two fire trucks as Simon climbed from the taxi. Fifteen minutes earlier, while nursing a Tanqueray and tonic at the bar next to his apartment building in Chicago's Gold Coast area, he received a call from Inspector Robinson. The policeman indicated there was an emergency at the Feelright Intelligence Services office but refused to divulge any details.

Simon surveyed the chaotic scene. A smattering of spectators was gathered in the street beyond a hastily erected fence of yellow crime scene tape. He recognized Billy, the bartender from the Red Swan. Firefighters and police were milling about the smoking wreckage of a burned car on its side. It was charred beyond recognition. EMS technicians conferred next to their ambulance. They clearly were not in rescue mode. Inspector Robinson noticed Simon and approached him from the other side of the crime tape. He wore a grave expression.

"What happened?" Simon asked. "Whose car is that?"

"I'm sorry. It's Sonny's BMW. It was a bomb."

"What? Where's Sonny?"

Robinson lowered his eyes and shook his head. "There's a body. It's burned beyond recognition. The lab will have to confirm the identity. We don't know if it's Sonny. But we found his cell phone in the parking lot about fifty feet from the car. We think it was tossed by the explosion."

Just then a van pulled up from Fox Television's local Chicago affiliate. A female reporter jumped out and began asking questions of policemen and spectators while her crew pulled equipment from their vehicle and conferred about camera angles and lighting.

"My God," Simon uttered.

"Look, Mr. Courtney, I'm very sorry. I apologize for ever doubting you people about the attacks. Obviously, I was wrong."

Simon didn't respond but stood staring at the smoldering wreckage in shocked silence.

"Mr. Courtney, can you give us access to your offices? We'd like to look around. We also want to ask you some questions."

Simon snapped from his trance. "Sure. Yes, of course." He led Robinson away to their offices.

Douglas McCardle was sequestered in the back room of his office. He worked alone, reviewing files and documents from the storage boxes, saving some and stuffing the rest back in the boxes to be discarded. As always, the doors to the building were securely locked. His phone rang. It was his wife, Joyce.

"I told you not to bother me when I'm working," he scolded.

"I'm sorry, but you need to come to the house. Something's happened."

"What?"

"It's on television. You need to come to the house."

Impatiently, he donned his coat and headed for the house, locking the office behind him. He found Joyce in the kitchen staring intently at the drop-down flat screen television beneath the upper cabinets.

"It's Sonny," she said without looking up. "That's his car. It was a bomb."

McCardle pulled up a chair and focused on the screen, where an attractive blond reporter was standing in front of the smoking wreckage of what appeared to be a car on its side.

"Authorities have confirmed that the bombed car is a late model BMW. It is registered to a Mr. Sonny B. Feelright, who apparently worked in the building two doors down. They also have confirmed that at least one body was found in the wreckage, burned beyond recognition. A police spokesman would not speculate on the identity of the body, however, they did indicate that Mr. Feelright's cellular phone was found in the parking lot near the wreckage."

McCardle grinned almost imperceptibly. "Couldn't have happened to a more deserving person," he muttered.

"I can't believe you just said that!" Joyce responded.

"He was a waste. It's a wonder he lived to adulthood."

Joyce burned a stare at him. "Are you going to call Charlotte? To make sure she's alright?"

"Why?" he countered sharply. "She'll just go out and find another loser. Just like her mother." He stood and returned to his office.

Nancy Black had been pacing the living room of her two-bedroom suite at the Ritz Carlton for nearly an hour. The television was on, sound turned low. Her laptop sat open on the desk surrounded by documents, notes and financial statements. She had been using her time productively while sequestered in Chicago, preparing for her eventual return to the world of high finance. She worked most of the afternoon. But she became uneasy as the clock ticked past six o'clock and she still had not received the confirming call. At six thirty she tried calling Kafele on the prepaid cell phone she bought for this purpose, but the call went unanswered.

"Idiots," she hissed. "Bumbling idiots!" She continued to pace, watching and waiting for the cell phone on the coffee table to ring. Something caught her eye on the television. A banner scrolled across the screen: "Car bombing rocks near west side – at least one dead…." She grabbed the remote and increased the volume. When the reporter announced that the car was registered to Sonny B. Feelright she was washed with relief.

"Idiots," she cursed her two hired assassins again for forgetting to call her. She could leave Chicago now. She could move on with her life. She could resurrect her career. She would leave tomorrow. She would leave without paying the extra bounty she promised the terrorist operatives. She sat down at her computer and went on the internet to make flight reservations.

Only Hope

There was a soft knock at the door. Sonny peeked through the security peep hole. It was Liz. It took her twenty-five minutes to get to the hotel after their phone call. She had borrowed a car from a colleague to get there. He opened the door and pulled her into the room, peering nervously up and down the hall before closing and locking the door behind her. She had left the clinic in a hurry; she still wore her white lab coat over a yellow blouse and black slacks.

Liz gazed admiringly around the tastefully appointed room. A look of concern crossed her face when she focused on Sonny's worried expression. "What's wrong? What happened?"

"There was a car bomb. My car is gone. I saw a man get blown up."

She pressed her lips skeptically and reached up to feel his forehead. "Sonny, are you alright? You've been kind of paranoid lately."

"I'm telling you, Liz, I saw a man die tonight! The bomb was meant for me!"

"Maybe you saw something …," she delicately

tiptoed, "maybe the stress of work made it look like something else."

He pointed to the television and raised the volume using the remote. She stepped to the screen, staring in shock. "Car bomb rips near west side," read the scrolling banner. The blond reporter spoke sentences, but Liz could only comprehend fragments of what she was saying: "late model BMW … registered to a Mr. Sonny B. Feelright … unidentified victim … gangland style slaying …."

She turned and stared at him, open mouthed. "What's going on? What happened?"

They sat on the bed while he told the story. She held his limp hand in both of hers, shaking her head in disbelief.

"You have to call the police," she ordered when he finished.

"No. Not yet. The assassins are still out there. Danny Byrne warned me not to trust anyone. He told me our phones may be tapped. He told me they'll keep trying until I'm dead. And that man who was killed, what happens about that? I don't even know who he was or why they're after me. The police may think I was involved somehow. No, before I talk to the police I have to talk to Simon. He'll know what to do."

He gave her a pleading look. "Will you help me, Liz?"

"This is all a little out my league." She stood and began pacing. "I like you, Sonny, but I'm not into getting blown up. And if I help you am I committing some kind of crime? I'm not thrilled about going to jail."

"Please, Liz. You're my only hope."

She continued pacing, eyes to the floor, tormented. "Okay," she finally agreed, turning to face him. "I'll help, but if things get too hairy I'm bolting and you're on your own. And you better not implicate me in anything illegal."

Sonny dispatched her to buy him some new clothes while he showered. He grew fearful she might not return as he sat on the bed wrapped in a plush white hotel robe watching the news coverage about him. He was relieved to hear her soft knock on the door.

"No one followed you?" he asked as she handed over two plastic bags with clothes.

"I don't know. It seemed like everyone was following me. I'm getting as paranoid as you. How have you lived like this?"

He dressed in front of her, feeling no sense of modesty under the dire circumstances. She watched him as he shed the robe, stepped into the new briefs and pulled on the blue jeans she purchased. "It's a shame, really," she said wistfully. "Here we are in a luxury hotel room, you naked, and I don't feel one bit romantic."

He stroked her cheek and finished dressing. The

last items in the ensemble were a nylon bomber jacket and a black stocking cap. He emptied the pockets of his dirty clothes and stuffed the contents into his pockets. Then he stuffed the old clothes into one of the shopping bags. He tucked his wild mane into the hat and pulled it low on his forehead.

"Do I look anonymous?" he asked.

"Practically invisible."

"Let's go find Simon."

Bomani

Bomani sat on the floor of the Calumet apartment, hugging his knees to his chest. The room was dark except for the flickering reflection of the small television. His eyes were red and swollen from weeping. After the explosion, he drove about blindly, his vision blurry from crying and his mind dysfunctional from shock and grief. He eventually found his way back to the apartment, where he had sat in a fetal clutch watching the news coverage for the past hour.

He had never before felt so frightened. Frightened not about the violence he witnessed or the fear of being arrested or even dying. He was frightened by his utter isolation. All of his family had now been taken from him. His mother by the lax norms of Western society, which encouraged her to forsake her duty to her family and her religion by leaving. His father by street thugs. And now Kafele, his only brother, by the devil woman and Sonny Feelright.

Reconnoiter

Sonny could not recall Simon's cell phone number, but he could be at only a few places. They headed first for West Harrison. Liz drove slowly by the crime scene, which still buzzed with activity. The fire trucks were gone but police and medical technicians were busily working on the site. Sonny, hunched down in the passenger seat with his stocking cap pulled low, peered at their offices as they passed. No lights. If Simon had been there he was gone now.

Next they headed to Charlotte's apartment. Her lights were on. Fearing that the assassin might be lurking nearby, Sonny made Liz drive by twice before directing her to park in the lot. He was afraid to show himself. What if the police or Adonis were in the apartment? With the engine running, he pondered how to determine if it was safe and whether Simon was on the premises. He finally sent Liz on a reconnoiter mission.

She buzzed Charlotte's apartment, peering furtively around. "Who is it?" a woman's voice responded. It was not Charlotte.

"My name is Elizabeth Loveland. I'm Sonny Feelright's doctor. I'm looking for Simon Courtney. Is he there?"

The door lock buzzed letting her in. She made her way to Charlotte's first-floor apartment and knocked. She was taken aback when the door opened. The woman inside looked startlingly like Charlotte, only older and with shorter hair. Her eyes were red from crying.

"I'm Faith McCardle, Charlotte's mother."

A grim-faced Simon Courtney stepped from the kitchen and greeted her with a sober hug.

"Where's Charlotte?" Liz asked.

"Lying down," answered Faith. "She's not doing well. She's very upset. Her doctor prescribed a sedative."

"Is anyone else here?"

When Faith answered no, Liz went to the window and waved. She then disappeared into the hallway, returning a few moments later with Sonny.

"My God!" Faith gasped when he pulled off the stocking cap, unleashing his untamed locks. "We thought you were dead!" She rushed forward and embraced him. Simon stepped up and patted him on the back as if to make sure he was not a mirage.

"Where's Charlotte?" asked Sonny.

"She's in the bedroom, sedated. She's not doing well. She was having dinner with Adonis when they got the call. She went hysterical. Adonis brought her here and called me. We were afraid she might try to hurt herself. She blames her father. And she blames herself."

Sonny went to the bedroom. Charlotte was curled

in a ball under the covers. Her sleeping face was etched with grief. "Charlotte," he whispered, but she was out. He stroked her silken hair, desperately wishing he could wake her and sooth her pain. Liz watched the tender scene from the doorway.

"Everyone thinks you're dead," said Faith when he returned to the living room. "Why haven't you told the police?"

"Because I saw the assassins. I saw one killed in the bombing. The other one tried to run me over. He's still out there." He turned to Simon. "And I was afraid to do anything without talking to you. What if the police think I did it?"

"You saw the assassins? Do you know who they are?"

Sonny shook his head. "But I have pictures of them." He pulled out the photographs that Danny Byrne provided.

"Where did you get these?" asked Simon as the four of them gathered around a table lamp, studying the pictures.

"Danny Byrne gave them to me. He had them followed. That's the one who tried to run me down," Sonny said, pointing. "I'm pretty sure the other guy was the one killed in the car bomb."

"So, Danny Byrne isn't responsible for the car bomb?" asked Simon.

"No," Sonny answered. "And Simon, he gave me a list of the stocks that Douglas McCardle advised him about. Wait until you see this." He pulled out the napkin with the list of stocks and handed it to Simon.

Simon studied it, his face alighting with surprise. "My God, these are all of the stocks that Herkmeier identified. And the additional ones we found."

"What are you talking about?" asked Faith.

"Your ex-husband," answered Sonny. "He's in the middle of an illegal trading scheme."

They all took seats, stunned by the turn of events.

"The police think Danny Byrne is behind the bombing," Simon said. "He was the last person you were seen with. They took him in for questioning within an hour of the explosion."

"No!" exclaimed Sonny. "He had nothing to do with it. He was there when it happened. He knows I'm alive. He'll tell the police."

"Maybe not," speculated Simon. "He's not exactly trusting of the police. And the last thing he wants is to draw attention to his relationship with McCardle. I'm guessing he'll tough it out until you turn up."

"I've got to help him, Simon. I promised. Quid pro quo. He helped me and I have to help him."

Simon picked up the photos again. "Who are these two?" he asked, holding up the picture of the Imam and the mysterious woman.

"I don't kno…," Sonny started to stay. "Then he took the picture from Simon and studied it closely. He grabbed the picture of the woman entering the car and stared at it. "My God! That's Nancy Black! I'm sure that's Nancy Black!"

Resurrection

It was nearly seven in the morning when Charlotte stirred. She had slept more than ten hours. Even semi-conscious, her memory barren, she sensed an overwhelming sadness had entered her life. She opened her eyes and the horror of yesterday flooded back. Tears began to flow. She desperately hugged her pillow as her body wracked with grief.

She rolled over. Through blurry vision she saw a figure in the chair by her bed. She blinked to focus, disbelieving. It was Sonny. He was sleeping, his head lolling sideways, his long legs stretched in front of him. She sprang from the bed and into his lap.

Sonny awakened to Charlotte's smothering embrace. She hugged him so tightly he could barely breathe. She wept uncontrollably, tears of joy now. She buried her face against his neck and kissed him again and again. They did not speak, but only hugged and savored the comfort of one another.

They were alone in the apartment. The night before, Liz and Faith began to feel useless as Simon and Sonny schemed and plotted. Liz left before midnight, offering Faith a ride home, too. Simon and Sonny stayed up until two-thirty a.m., when Simon returned to his apartment by cab. He was due back at the apartment at nine this morning.

Sonny lifted Charlotte and carried her back to the bed. They made love with a visceral passion that only a close encounter with mortality can provoke.

Homicide

The Imam was elated as he climbed onto the porch of the Calumet apartment. The television news was still breathless about the car bombing on the near west side. The CHICAGO TRIBUNE ran a front page article, bylined by Melody Gothim, including a photo of the smoldering car and a picture of Sonny Feelright taken after the shooting at the bar. While the police had not yet confirmed the identity of the victim, the article speculated that Sonny was targeted because of an investigation on which he was working.

He smiled when Bomani answered the door. "You were successful, my friend!" He pushed through the doorway, unmindful of the disturbed expression on the young man's drawn face.

"Where is Kafele?" the Imam asked, turning to Bomani.

Bomani stared at the Imam with bloodshot eyes from a sleepless night. His gaze no longer bore the impetuous anger of prior meetings. He now stared at the Imam with fatalistic resolve.

"Where is Kafele?" the Imam repeated, instinctively backing away.

"Dead," answered Bomani in a hoarse whisper.

For the first time the Imam noticed the pistol in Bomani's hand. He moved toward the door.

Bomani took a step sideways and intercepted him. "Where is she?" he demanded.

"I can't tell you."

Bomani raised the gun and pointed it at the Imam's forehead. "Where is she?" he repeated.

"The Ritz Carlton in downtown Chicago. She has a suite there."

"Who is she?"

"I don't know. She's very rich and powerful. She's registered as Jade Crescent."

Bomani fired one fatal round.

He would need to fire at least two more to avenge his brother.

Car Shopping

It was eight a.m. when Simon pulled into the parking lot of Exotic World Cars. He was driving a rented Audi A8. Appearances would be important on this day.

Robert, the salesman, watched with interest from the showroom as the first customer of the morning pulled into a visitor's parking space. He sized up the man who emerged from the car; older, life-worn, probably wealthy. A man with more money than years remaining. A man interested in accumulating expensive toys. He stepped outside to greet him.

"I'm Robert," he said with practiced professionalism. He extended his right hand and held out a business card with his left.

Simon shook his hand and inspected the business card. He fished his own business card from his pocket and offered it to Robert. The salesman's eyes furrowed when he saw Feelright Intelligence Services LLC.

"Actually," offered Simon, "I'm here to see your boss, Danny Byrne."

"I'm not sure if Mr. Byrne is available."

"Perhaps you can check. I'm partners with the late Sonny Feelright. You may have read about his premature demise in this morning's paper. I believe Mr. Byrne will want to see me."

"Wait here." Robert stepped back into the showroom. Simon watched through the glass as he made a cell phone call. He nodded and hung up, slipping the phone back in his pocket.

"As it turns out, Mr. Byrne just arrived," explained Robert as he poked his head out the door. "Please follow me."

Convenient Death

Simon arrived at Charlotte's apartment at nine in the rented Audi A8. Charlotte greeted him at the door while Sonny stood back out of site. Sonny had brought Charlotte up to speed on all of the events of the past several days, including his interactions with Danny Byrne.

He was cautious when he explained their plan to trap her father, for whom she had been relentlessly, illogically protective up to now. But something had changed in Charlotte. The events of the past few days pushed her across some psychological boundary regarding her father. Gone was the fear and intimidation. Gone was the need to please him and win his approval. She listened to their plot with stoic acceptance.

"Are you alright with all of this?" Sonny cautiously asked.

She simply nodded in reply.

Simon had decided that Sonny's death was convenient for their purposes. Exposing his survival would only make Sonny more visible to the assassin, whom they assumed was still hunting for him. Plus, Sonny's demise would serve them in their attempt to discover the source of Douglas McCardle's secret information, as it was apparent that McCardle was the center of an illegal trading ring of significant proportions.

Their time was short; Simon speculated that it would be no more than forty-eight hours before the medical examiner would confirm that the charred remains from the bombing were not Sonny Feelright. That's how long they had to trap Douglas McCardle before he could alert his clients and dismantle whatever information network he was using.

Nancy Black presented a more difficult and lethal challenge. While Sonny now was sure that she was behind the assassination attempts, they had no idea where she was or when her hired mercenaries would strike next. Worse, Simon declared that the grainy photographs would be inconclusive at best in convincing anyone in law enforcement to take their speculation seriously. Nancy Black, while professionally tainted by the fall of her firm, was still a paragon of international business. She was beyond reproach. They hoped that Simon's morning visit with Danny Byrne would help them.

Their first order of business was reinforcing Sonny's status as deceased and sending an alarm to Douglas McCardle. Simon sat on Charlotte's couch and returned Melody Gothim's most recent call, one of many she had placed to him since the car bombing.

"Ms. Gothim, this is Simon Courtney," he said in a grieving tone. "I'm sorry I've not returned your calls. We've all been in a state of shock, as you can imagine."

"Of course," Melody responded, barely able to contain her glee at the returned call. She bulled ahead, "Have the police confirmed that the body is Sonny?"

Simon hesitated. "I'm sorry, but we've been asked by the authorities not to make any statements."

"You can trust me, Mr. Courtney. I won't reveal anything you don't approve."

"I don't know. . . ." He hesitated.

"Tell you what, I won't reveal your identity. You'll just be a reliable source. Would that work?"

"I suppose. As long as you promise."

"Cross my heart and hope to die! Have they confirmed it was Sonny?"

"Yes," Simon lied. "You'll want to confirm it with them, but they told us it was Sonny."

"What about Danny Byrne? They've identified him as a 'person of interest.' They say his fingerprints were on Sonny's cell phone. I'm working on that angle for my next story. Do you think he's responsible?"

"No," Simon answered with assurance. "Sonny was negotiating to buy a car from Byrne. That's all. Byrne had nothing to do with it."

"So, I'm chasing the wrong lead."

"You're absolutely chasing the wrong lead," Simon confirmed.

"Sounds like you have some idea who was responsible."

"Maybe," answered Simon coyly.

"Can you shed some light for me? The public wants to know."

"You promise this is not for attribution? I mean, if anyone asks me I'll deny we ever spoke."

"You have my word."

"Sonny was deeply involved in a case. It was about securities fraud. He was convinced that someone in Greater Chicago was the hub of an insider trading ring. Someone has been selling insider information to hedge funds and institutional investors. We think it's a national conspiracy stretching from New York to the west coast."

"So you're saying it wasn't a gangland murder? Somebody from Wall Street did him in?"

"I'm not saying anything except that Sonny was onto something big. With a lot of money at stake."

"This is huge!" Melody gushed, unable to contain her excitement. "Give me some names."

"I don't know the names. The authorities have Sonny's computer and his files. All I can say is that Sonny's last trip on the investigation was up on the North Shore. We don't know who he met, but he was nervous when he came back."

"The North Shore? A lot of wealthy people live there."

"Like I said, we're talking hundreds of millions in financial fraud."

"Outstanding!"

"Look, Ms. Gothim, I really need to go. I've probably said too much already. I don't want to get on the wrong side of the authorities."

"I understand."

"And you promise you won't use my identity, right?"

"Mum's the word. It's our little secret."

Simon hung up and looked from Charlotte to Sonny.

"How on earth do you sleep at night?" Sonny asked.

"Like a baby," he grinned.

Simon donned his coat and left. He had an appointment in an hour-and-a-half on the North Shore.

Vile Little Man

Simon eased the car to the side of the road and inspected the entrance to the McCardle estate. He waited while a panel truck emerged through the tree line crossing the long driveway. It said "Document Solutions" on the side. Simon and the driver traded nods as the truck turned onto the road and passed the Audi. Simon pulled into the drive and made his way to the sprawling house of Douglas McCardle. He parked the car on the driveway circle and climbed out. He looked around, inspecting the property, taking special note of the miniature colonial building that served as McCardle's office. He made his way to the formidable front door and banged the knocker.

McCardle opened the door and inspected Simon with heavy lidded eyes. His left eye twitched reflexively. He rolled his chin forward and yanked at his collar. "You're Courtney?"

"Yes," Simon nodded. "Did Mr. Byrne make the introduction?"

"He called this morning. A little short on notice, I'd say."

"I'm sorry," responded Simon. "But I'm only in

town for a short while." He sized up McCardle, finding it incomprehensible that the awkwardly proportioned man before him could have fathered Charlotte.

"Well, come in. My office is cluttered. We'll talk in the kitchen."

In fact, McCardle wanted no part of a conversation with this friend of Danny Byrne. He wished he'd never heard of Danny Byrne, especially now that he had a cadre of legitimate money managers seeking his counsel. He was sought out by some of the top money managers on Wall Street these days. He could be selective about his clientele.

But when he first struck out as an expert advisor, times were lean and he was happy to take Byrne's money. In truth, he was afraid of Byrne and his kind. He was especially frightened of Byrne's last referral, Tony Lancone. Where Byrne ran an ostensibly legitimate business – the source of McCardle's growing car collection – Lancone was a true gangster. He was a brute and a thug. McCardle shuttered to think of how Lancone would respond if he ever thought he was crossed. While all of McCardle's investment recommendations were sure winners, he feared how Lancone would react if one ever went sour.

McCardle led Simon into the kitchen, where they sat at the butcher block table.

"Beautiful home," Simon observed.

McCardle ignored the compliment. "So, you're a friend of Danny Byrne."

"More of an acquaintance."

"And you're looking for investment advice? I'm not sure I'm in a position to take on any new clients."

"You run an expert network, correct?" Simon asked.

McCardle nodded.

"Mr. Byrne tells me you never miss. Every recommendation you've made has been a winner."

"I'm good at what I do."

"What is your expertise? Tell me about your network."

"That's confidential," snapped McCardle. "Like I said, I'm not sure I'm prepared to take on additional clients right now."

"Your performance seems impossible."

McCardle's eye twitched impatiently. He rolled his chin and pulled at his collar. "Like I said, I'm good at what I do."

Simon pulled a piece of paper from his pocket and slid it across the table. "These are some stocks I've owned. I lost money on every one. I wonder if you're familiar with any of them."

McCardle read the list. It was all of the companies with suspicious trading activity. He looked up at Simon, his eyes radiating contempt from beneath their heavy lids. "Who in the hell are you?"

Simon produced a business card. "My name is Simon Courtney. I'm partners with your daughter and Sonny Feelright."

"Shouldn't you be at the funeral home right now? How's Charlotte holding up now that her boyfriend is dead?"

"What are you up to?" demanded Simon. "Your investment performance is impossible. You have no expert network. How are you doing it?"

"She put you up to this, didn't she? She can't stand my success. And neither can you. You're at the end of your career working for a two-bit detective agency and you can't stand it that someone is more successful than you!" McCardle was enraged now. "Get out! Get off my property and never come back! And tell Danny Byrne that he better be careful or the golden goose may quit laying for him."

Simon stood and let himself out of the house. He sat in the car, noticing that McCardle was watching from a front window. "What a vile little man," he said to himself as he started the Audi and drove away.

Compromised Principles

It was nearly noon when Adonis knocked on Charlotte's door. He was surprised when she called him earlier and asked him to stop by. She was nearly catatonic when he left her in the care of her mother the night before. When she fled the restaurant in hysterics after hearing of Sonny's death, he was forced to physically restrain her in the parking lot. When they reached her apartment she was so despondent that he had to half carry her from the car.

He was relieved when her mother arrived and he was able to leave. He realized that his pursuit of Charlotte was futile. As attracted as he was to her, he now understood that her heart rested elsewhere. She loved Sonny Feelright. And that love was only heightened by Sonny's tragic death. Adonis feared Charlotte might never recover or, worse, try to harm herself in her grief.

To his surprise she greeted him looking fresh and alert. She wore jeans and a sweater and a light application of makeup. Her mother was nowhere in sight.

She gave him a plutonic hug. "Thank you for coming. And for being there last night."

He nodded, unsure. "Are you alright?" he probed. "I didn't expect you to be up and around."

She took his hand and led him to the couch. They sat and she gave him an earnest look. "Sonny's not dead," she declared.

Adonis stared back blankly. She clearly was delusional. He weighed how to respond. He took her hands in his. "Charlotte," he said softly, "I know this is a hard time for you. I know it's hard to accept."

"He's not dead," she repeated. "And I really need your help. Will you help me?"

"Charlotte, you've got to come to grips with reality. Sonny was killed in a car bombing yesterday. I was at the scene this morning. It was his car. We found his cell phone."

The bedroom door opened and out stepped Sonny.

Adonis jumped to his feet as though shocked. His jaw dropped as he inspected the mirage before him. "My God! You're alive!" His first reaction was to pull out his cell phone. "I've got to call this in!"

Charlotte put a restraining hand on his arm. "Wait! Not yet! Hear us out, please!"

He looked at her, then at Sonny. He put the phone back in his pocket and sat. "I'm listening."

Sonny pulled up a chair and sat. "We need thirty-six hours," he began.

Fifteen minutes later, Adonis shook his head.

"You're asking me to violate my duty as an officer of the law. You're asking me to compromise all of my principles."

"Adonis," Charlotte pleaded. "There have been four attempts on Sonny's life in the past three weeks. He'll be a sitting duck if you reveal he's alive. There will be no place for him to hide."

"He can go into protective custody," Adonis argued.

"You can't protect him indefinitely."

Sonny pointed to the photos on the coffee table. "I'm telling you, that's the guy driving the car. I'm sure the other guy was killed in the explosion." He pointed to the woman in a second photo. "And that's Nancy Black. I'm sure of it. We're giving you pictures of the assassins and their address in Calumet. Special delivery. You just need to go pick them up. Once you put them away it will be safe for me. Plus, it gives us time to break an insider trading ring. Give us thirty six hours, that's all. By then the autopsy will be done and I'll have no choice but to resurface."

"You don't understand what you're asking," Adonis pleaded.

"You don't understand," argued an exasperated Charlotte. "You're giving Sonny a death sentence if you make that call!"

"Look, Adonis," Sonny reasoned, "if you work with us you have a good chance of catching the assassins *and* frustrating a huge investment fraud. If you make the call you're enabling Nancy Black to finish the job and Charlotte's father will go underground. He'll warn his clients and destroy any trace of whatever source he's using. You'll have nothing."

"You need to put more faith in law enforcement," Adonis countered.

Charlotte threw up her hands. "Are you kidding? The police accused us of staging the first three attacks! If we listened to you, we'd still be hiding from Danny Byrne! And he's the one guy on our side!"

Adonis sighed, defeated. "Okay. I'll check out the apartment in Calumet. And I'll try to track down Nancy Black. But that picture could be almost anyone." He turned at the door, "You have no idea what you're asking of me."

Leaving

It was six o'clock in the evening. Nancy Black, a.k.a. Jade Crescent, checked out at the desk of the Ritz Carlton and made her way to the exit. She declined a bellman's offer to carry her bags. She was angry and impatient; because of all of the holiday travel, the earliest flight back to Toronto was at eight this evening, a full twenty-four hours from when she made the online reservation. Thankfully, the Imam had not yet tried to contact her about the final payments.

The mercenaries never called on the secure cell phone she provided. She was not surprised; they were bumbling fools. But Sonny Feelright's assassination was confirmed in the morning paper. She could resume her life and career now.

She stepped from the hotel and headed for the cab stand. A dark figure intercepted her, forcing her to stop in mid-stride. It was Bomani. His eyes were red, his expression lifeless.

"What are you doing here? Where's the Imam?"

"You're leaving?" he asked.

"I have a flight to catch at O'Hare."

He grabbed her luggage. "I'll drive you." He tugged

her suitcase and briefcase from her resistant grasp. He led her to his car and put the luggage in the back seat, then opened the passenger door for her. She eyed him suspiciously as she sat.

They rode in silence. Nancy was relieved when he entered the expressway heading west on I-90/I-94 toward O'Hare.

"Where's your Imam?" she asked again. His silence made her uneasy. "If you're worried about the final payments, you needn't be," she lied. "The money already has been transferred to him. You can see him for your share."

Bomani said nothing. He drove robotically, devoid of expression. He exited at O'Hare, paying the required tolls on the convoluted route to the airport.

"You can drop me off at the United Terminal," she instructed.

But he followed the signs toward long-term parking instead.

"It's not necessary to park. You could have just dropped me off."

Bomani ignored her. He pulled into the long-term parking garage and made his way up the ramps. He edged past a sign that said "Section full."

"This section is full," Nancy huffed, her anger rising.

He drove down an aisle on the far side of the garage

from the terminal entrance. All the spaces were filled with cars, their owners off for overnight business trips and holiday visits. He stopped the car in the middle of the aisle and turned off the engine, pocketing the keys. He walked around and opened her door, gesturing her out. She stood, her anger changing to caution. The parking garage reeked of car exhaust and jet fuel. There were no pedestrians in sight. The roar of jets landing and departing made it hard to hear.

"What's this all about?" she shouted.

Bomani stared at her with emotionless eyes. He pulled the pistol from his pocket and raised it to her face. Nancy stared back, astonished. A primal fear swept through her. Throughout her life and career she had faced confrontations. She had faced the angry wrath of defeated adversaries many times. She had seen otherwise calm men reduced to violent tantrums as she humbled them. But she had never faced a serious threat to her life. She had never faced her own mortality. As she stared at the tiny hole in the barrel of the outstretched pistol she realized that she was going to die.

Al Cistone emerged from nowhere. From behind, he grabbed the gunman's outstretched hand and expertly twisted the wrist, grabbing the gun with his other gloved hand as Bomani involuntarily released his grip. Cistone continued with his wrist hold until

Bomani was down on one knee, leaning back awkwardly, his face contorted in surprise and pain. Cistone put the gun to Bomani's temple and fired one shot.

Nancy stared at the unfolding scene in wide-eyed disbelief. She was shocked by the stranger's lethal efficiency. Who was this angel of death? She looked down at Bomani's still twitching body sprawled awkwardly on the concrete, one leg tucked completely backward, eyes staring in eternal surprise. She looked back up to find the thin stranger pointing the gun at her forehead. Again she faced the prospect of imminent death.

He stepped toward her and above the noise said, "Sonny Feelright, he's protected. *Capiche?*"

She nodded blankly.

Cistone bent down and placed the gun in Bomani's hand. Then he turned and walked away. Nancy waited until he disappeared. She rushed to the car and retrieved her bags before escaping to the terminal.

Discoveries

Sonny, Simon and Charlotte were gathered in her apartment. Half empty containers of Chinese takeout were spread on the coffee table. Sonny and Charlotte had remained sequestered in the apartment the entire day. She worked most of the afternoon, returning calls of condolence left with the answering service. Simon brought the takeout and a twelve pack of beer when he arrived at seven.

He also brought the enhanced photographs that Sonny took at Douglas McCardle's office. Enlarged prints were on the table among the food containers. The photos revealed the labels from the file boxes in McCardle's back office. One set of boxes was from a prominent Chicago law firm. In addition to the firm's identity, the labels indicated the files were confidential and slated for disposal. The other set of boxes was from a top corporate accounting firm. They also were labeled confidential.

"What's he doing with confidential files from major consulting firms?" questioned Charlotte.

"It's obviously where he's getting his inside information. These two firms alone service dozens of publicly traded companies. Their files would be a gold mine of insider information."

"But where's he getting them?" she asked.

They pondered the question in silence.

Sonny sat up straight and snapped his fingers. "The truck! There was a trash hauler leaving the driveway when we were there on Sunday! We questioned why it would be there on a Sunday!"

Simon jerked to attention. "That's it! I saw it, too. It said something about document shredding on the side!"

Charlotte went to her laptop on the kitchen table. Simon and Sonny followed her and looked over her shoulder as she searched for document management services in Chicago.

"Here it is!" she exclaimed. "Document Solutions." She found its website. "'Secure and confidential document management services.' It says they're contracted with some of the largest law and accounting firms in the country. It says they're bonded and independently audited."

"That explains everything!" Simon declared. "He's paying off a driver to give him access to confidential files of all of the law and accounting firms on his Chicago route. That truck probably drops documents off for him to comb for information. Then it picks up what he doesn't need when it brings the next load.

That's why there's no discernable connection among the companies. He's privy to every corporate transaction the firms are working on. It's brilliant in its simplicity."

"We've got him!" exclaimed Sonny. He looked at Charlotte, whose expression was somber. "Are you going to be alright with all of this?"

She exhaled. "Yes. He deserves whatever he gets."

The intercom buzzed. It was Adonis. Charlotte buzzed him in and then turned to Simon and Sonny. "Can we wait to tell him what we learned about my father?" she asked. "Just until we know for sure."

They gave each other a look before nodding their assent.

Adonis entered the apartment looking tired and troubled. They watched him expectantly as he took off his coat and tossed it on a chair. He spied the half-full beer bottles on the table. "You got any more?" Charlotte retrieved a beer for him from the refrigerator.

He sat on the couch and took a long swig. "Well, you were right about the apartment in Calumet," he finally said. "Unfortunately, I got there late. It turns out that the older man in the photos was an Imam at a Muslim temple nearby. He was dead when I got there, a twenty-two caliber shot to the forehead."

Charlotte gasped and covered her mouth in horror.

"As for the guy you identified as the driver of the

Malibu, he's dead, too. He was found two hours ago in the long-term parking lot at O'Hare International Airport, also the victim of a twenty-two shot to the head. Only his death looks like a suicide. We still don't know his identity."

"What about Nancy Black?" asked Sonny.

"We checked with passport control and we have no record of Nancy Black entering this country in the past five months. As far as the world is concerned, she never left Toronto. I sent copies of your photograph to airport security at both Midway and O'Hare, but I wouldn't count on anything."

"It was her," responded Sonny. "I know it was her."

Panic

Douglas McCardle sat to have breakfast with his wife. He opened the CHICAGO TRIBUNE and was left breathless by the headline:

"Forensic Accountant Confirmed Dead in Car Blast

North Shore Stock Fraud Ring Under Investigation"

He gripped the paper with both hands and read Melody Gothim's bylined article in disbelief. It confirmed that Sonny Feelright was killed in the explosion and alleged that he was investigating a Chicago-based insider trading network responsible for hundreds of millions of dollars in illegal trading gains. Supposedly, Feelright made a recent trip regarding the investigation to the North Shore area, home to some of the country's wealthiest communities. "Knowledgeable sources said he returned from the trip troubled and concerned for his safety," the article continued.

"Douglas, what's wrong?" asked Joyce with concern as she watched the color drain from her husband's face and his eye twitch uncontrollably.

"Nothing. Nothing. I have to go to my office."

"But your breakfast...." she responded; he already was out the door, not even taking time to grab a coat.

McCardle entered the back office and frantically began stuffing documents into the stacked storage boxes in the center of the room. He combed through his personal files, culling anything related to his consulting activities. He stepped into the front office and eyed his laptop, which held two sets of books, one reporting modest income, which he used for tax reporting, and the other which recorded all of the illegal payments he received through the years from his insider trading clients. He pondered how to destroy the hard drive. But that could wait; first he had to get rid of the files. He looked out the window and was relieved to see the Document Solutions van approaching down the driveway.

Caught

Simon sat at the wheel of the rented Audi and watched the Document Solutions van disappear through the tree line toward the McCardle compound. Charlotte sat in the passenger seat, Sonny in back. They had been parked on the road outside McCardle's estate for nearly two hours. He looked at his watch.

"We'll give them three minutes."

When three minutes passed he started the car. This time, he sped down the drive, skidding to stop just inches from the front bumper of the van, which was backed up to the front of McCardle's office. Simon and Charlotte jumped out. The driver of the van stood frozen on the porch, a heavy storage box in his arms. McCardle emerged from the office carrying another box. He stopped and glared when he saw them.

"What are you doing here?" he shouted at Simon. "I told you yesterday to get off of my property!" He looked at Charlotte, "And you're not welcome either! You're a disgrace! I'm embarrassed you're my daughter!"

The back door of the Audi opened and Sonny stepped out. "Mr. McCardle," he called. "It's over. We know what you've been doing."

"You're dead!" shouted McCardle with a mix of anger and confusion. "The paper says you're dead!" He dropped the storage box, which opened and spewed its contents across the porch, and disappeared back into his office. He reemerged a moment later holding a pistol. He pointed it at Sonny as Charlotte gasped and the van driver backed away from him. Simon stepped between McCardle and Sonny.

"Think about what you're doing!" yelled Simon. "You've made some mistakes. You'll have to pay. But you're not a murderer. You can't kill us all."

McCardle continued to point the gun, at Simon now. His hand trembled. His eye twitched. He rolled his chin reflexively.

"Douglas!" shouted a commanding voice. "Put that gun down now!" It was Joyce approaching from the house. She held her bathrobe tight about her neck. In her other hand she carried the morning paper.

McCardle lowered the gun and bowed his head. "My God, what have I done?" he stammered.

The driver of the truck, a panicked look on his face, dropped the box he was holding and bounded from the porch. He closed the back door of the truck with a bang and jumped into the cab. He backed the truck far enough to clear the Audi and then sped around it and disappeared up the drive.

Reckoning

"You have to help me," McCardle begged. He was seated on one side of the butcher block table. Simon, Sonny and Charlotte faced him from the other, Simon in the middle. Joyce was off to the side leaning against the cupboard, sipping Bourbon, straight, and staring with disgust at her husband.

"Your options are limited," Simon counseled. "You're going to have to pay a price. Destroying evidence will only make the price higher."

"What kind of price?"

"You've committed serious crimes. There will be some prison time. And you'll have to forfeit any ill-gotten gains."

McCardle buried his face in his hands. "I'm ruined. What have I done?"

"Your only hope is to mitigate the penalties," Simon offered.

McCardle looked up, hopeful. "What do you mean? How?"

"You're small time," Simon explained, enjoying what he knew was a bruise to McCardle's enormous ego. "The feds don't want you as bad as some of your clients. How do you know Aaron Morrel at Global United?"

McCardle looked startled. "How did you know?"

Simon shrugged. "How do you know him?"

"We went to Northwestern together. We stayed in contact. When I lost my job at First Boston he was the one who suggested I start an expert network. It was his idea to tap into the shredding service. He gave me the seed money to get things started. I just had to find a willing driver, which wasn't hard."

"What do you pay the driver?"

"Chump change. I tip him two hundred a load. He has no idea what I'm doing."

"Who else is involved?"

McCardle identified three other hedge funds he had been advising, all referrals from Aaron Morrel. "And then there's Danny Byrne and Tony Lancone. I never wanted to work for them, but Byrne surfaced when I was just starting out and needed money."

"Look," Simon advised, "you've got one chance to negotiate your fate. If you go forward voluntarily and promise to testify against your clients, the feds will bargain. You can probably get off with a two-year sentence; you'll only spend six months behind bars if you play your cards right. But you'll need a good attorney to bargain a deal. You'll only get one chance."

"I can't!" argued McCardle. "Byrne and Lancone will kill me!"

"Are they identified anywhere in your records? Is there any paper trail tying you to them?"

McCardle thought for a moment. "No. There are some cash transactions in my private accounting records, but they're not identified."

"So leave them out of it."

"You don't understand! If they even think I might squeal on them I'll be a dead man!"

Sonny spoke up. "They'll leave you alone. I promise."

McCardle looked at him suspiciously. "How can you make that guarantee?"

"Let's just say Danny Byrne and I have each other's backs."

McCardle looked back at Simon. "What happens if I don't cooperate?"

Simon chuckled. "They'll lock you up and throw the key away. You may never see daylight again. And they *will* catch you. That article this morning already has every agency with jurisdiction digging into the case. You have a very short timeframe to cut a deal."

McCardle sighed. "Can you recommend a good criminal attorney?"

From across the room Joyce spoke for the first time. "And a divorce attorney."

He gave her a contemptuous look. "You can't divorce me. We have a prenup. You'll get nothing."

"Wrong," she smiled. "I'm very familiar with the prenup, and it contains a moral turpitude clause."

Sonny gave Simon a quizzical look.

"It's a clause that negates the terms of the contract if someone commits a crime or immoral act. I'm guessing a felony would qualify."

McCardle bowed his head in defeat. The room was silent. Sonny looked at the paper on the table, the headline confirming his death. He noticed that the date was December twenty third. Two days until Christmas.

Aftermath

Sonny and Charlotte stayed in bed until mid morning on Christmas Day, reliving the chaotic events of the past several weeks, which seemed like a lifetime. Their cell phones were off – Sonny had picked up a replacement IPhone after leaving McCardle's estate. Christmas Eve was mayhem. When it was announced that Sonny Feelright was not dead at all, but involved in breaking a notorious insider trading network, the phones began to ring incessantly. Reporters from all over the country called seeking interviews. They also received numerous calls about prospective assignments; it seemed that every law firm and enforcement agency in the county wanted to hire Feelright Intelligence Services LLC. Driving the rented Audi, he swung by his apartment to pick up some clothes, but a clutch of reporters was waiting outside, so he drove past.

For the second time in two days, he was the subject of a front page article in the CHICAGO TRIBUNE. In fact, he was the subject of two Christmas Eve articles. The headline article proclaimed his resurrection and announced that an unidentified witness of the trading scandal had emerged and was in protective custody. A companion article identified the person killed in the car bombing as a member of an Islamic terrorist cell. It went on to say that two other members of the cell were found dead in an apparent murder/suicide. The article speculated that Feelright Intelligence Services was targeted by the terrorists because it was investigating their finances.

Melody Gothim wrote neither story. She called him on Christmas Eve to inform him that she had been fired. "Imagine getting fired from a nonpaying internship," she lamented. "All because of a few errors in that article. Without an internship I can't even graduate."

Sonny was tempted to scold her for the errors and exaggerations in all of the articles she wrote. But he restrained himself. He actually felt sorry for her.

Sonny also stopped at Exotic World Cars on Christmas Eve to assure Danny Byrne that he and Tony Lancone would not be implicated in the insider trading prosecution, and to seek assurance that no harm would come to Charlotte's father.

"I fucking trust you, Sonny," Byrne responded, patting Sonny on the shoulder. "Too bad, though. I made more money off that son-of-a-bitch. Now what am I going to do for investment advice?"

"I might be able to help you with that," offered Sonny. "I know a guy. He's not a professional money manager, but he's as good as any you'll ever meet. He won't be able to give you winners every time. But he's right most of the time."

"I'm listening."

Sonny went on to describe how Bill Herkmeier uncovered the illegal trading activity through his detailed stock research. He promised to put the two of them together, cautioning that Bill might seem a bit eccentric due to his war injuries.

"I'm a patriot. I'll be proud to know a wounded vet. Besides, any friend of yours is a friend of mine.

"By the way," Byrne said as Sonny started to leave the showroom, "have you seen that bitch lately?"

"Charlotte?" Sonny asked with surprise.

"No, the black haired bitch. The one with the Islamic posse."

"No, I haven't."

"Well you won't," Byrne assured him. "Seems that Al bumped into her at O'Hare the other day. Her and that dumb fucker that shot himself."

Sonny just nodded and left, feeling safer but glad to put distance between himself and Danny Byrne.

Spider Lair

Four-hundred-and-sixty miles away, Nancy "Black Widow" Black stared out the window of her penthouse condominium at the bleak Christmas landscape of downtown Toronto. The sky was overcast. There was little traffic. The city appeared gray and dead. Indeed, her world seemed as gray and desolate as a cemetery.

She was numb on the flight home from Chicago, so shocked with fear after her encounter with Bomani and the dark angel of death who smote him that the stewardess in first class asked her twice if she was alright. Upon landing, she expected to be confronted and arrested by the authorities for her part in the deadly conspiracy, but her arrival went unnoticed. For the first twenty-four hours after returning to her home she waited with dread for the knock on the door that would end her existence as she knew it.

She did not consider fleeing or plotting a defense. Reading news accounts of Sonny Feelright's survival and triumph left her utterly depressed. Indeed, even as time passed and it became apparent that she had escaped culpability in the murderous conspiracy, she felt no relief, only overwhelming despair.

She found herself recalling her horrible adolescence, a turbulent time of frustration and self-loathing as she found it impossible to relate with the world around her. For a period she felt like an alien on the planet, alone and ostracized. She would hurt herself then; her arms and legs still bore the scars of razor cuts that gave her the welcome pain to remind her that she was alive. Many times she held the razor above her wrist, convinced that death was her only route to peace.

In time, though, she realized that her superior intelligence was what set her apart. It wasn't that she could not relate with the world around her; it was that the world around her could not relate with her. That revelation was what liberated her from her emotional hell. And the more she exercised her mental prowess, the stronger she became and the more the world appreciated and respected her.

But Sonny Feelright changed that. Earlier in the year, he had destroyed her company, the monument to her superior intellect. Now he had defeated her again, only this time the damage was worse. He had outwitted her and made her swallow the choking poison of self limitation and humility. She found the taste unbearable. She contemplated the amber bottle of Ambien in the medicine cabinet and, as she had as a suffering adolescent, fantasized about the peace that death might bring.

Back to Work

The three partners gathered around the conference table on the day after Christmas. It was nine-thirty in the morning and they were just finishing their morning meeting. Charlotte was stressed.

She gestured at the several pages of notes from the meeting. "This is overwhelming. We'll never get all of this work done if we work twenty-four seven. What are we going to do?"

Sonny agreed. "We need help. We're behind on everything, and new business is coming in over the transom."

Simon nodded sagely. "I've got a couple of candidates who could probably start right away."

His two partners looked at him expectantly.

"Did you hear that Adonis Manos quit his job?" Simon continued.

"What?" Charlotte remarked in surprise. "He was just commended for his work on the terrorist ring."

"Apparently, he's a man of honor. He felt he betrayed his oath. He didn't feel he was worthy of the Bureau. With his background he'd be a real asset for us."

There was silence in the room. Charlotte looked apprehensively at Sonny. "It's Sonny's call."

Sonny considered what it would be like seeing the "gorgeous" Adonis Manos every day. "I'm good with it," he finally assented. "Who else did you have in mind?"

"Melody Gothim," Simon answered without preamble.

This time Sonny wasn't so quick to acquiesce. "Are you crazy?" he erupted. "She's a parasite, a cancer!"

"She's resourceful and tenacious," Simon countered.

"She's totally unprofessional! She lied through her teeth! She'll say anything to get her way!"

"Precocious, I agree," admitted Simon, "but a damn good investigator. We could use someone like that."

Sonny collapsed back in his chair in disbelief.

"You know, I tend to agree with Simon. We could use someone like that," chimed in Charlotte.

"I don't believe this!" Sonny protested.

"Shall we vote?" Simon asked.

Sonny threw his head back. "Okay, okay! But you'll be sorry! You'll see!"

"So, how do we go about contacting them," Charlotte asked.

Simon looked at his watch. "They'll be reporting for duty in about five minutes."

Two hours later, the five employees of Feelright Intelligence Services were packed in the crowded conference room. Charlotte was briefing the new hires on the caseload and distributing assignments. The process was taking longer than normal because of Melody's continuous questions and comments.

"Can we take a bathroom break?" Melody finally asked.

"Great idea," a frustrated Charlotte agreed. "Let's take fifteen."

The two women left the room, Melody heading for the restroom and Charlotte for her office.

"You're new car is awesome," Adonis said to Sonny, referring to the replacement BMW, nearly identical to the first, provided by Sonny's insurance company.

"Yea, thanks."

"That's the one thing I'm going to miss about the old job – use of a Government Issue vehicle."

"What do you drive now?"

"A Focus," confessed Adonis sheepishly. He looked down at the monogrammed sleeve of his tailored shirt. "I probably overspend a little on my wardrobe."

"You'll be able to afford a nice car someday," Sonny encouraged him. "You'll see."

But Adonis's attention was focused on the outer lobby. "Who is *that*?" he asked.

Sonny turned to see Liz entering the office. She carried a plastic shopping bag. He went out to greet her. Charlotte also saw her enter and stood to lean against her office doorway, wary.

Sonny gave Liz a plutonic hug, under Charlotte's watchful eye.

Liz looked at Charlotte. "Don't worry. I get the picture. I'm just bringing back his clothes." She handed Sonny the bag. "It was fun while it lasted," she sighed.

"Will you still be my doctor?" asked Sonny.

She nodded toward Charlotte. "Fine by me, but you better clear it with the boss."

Liz's attention was drawn behind Sonny. "Who is *that?*"she whispered.

Sonny turned to see Adonis stepping from the conference room. "Oh, that's Adonis."

"I'll say," mumbled Liz.

Sonny introduced Adonis and Liz. He may as well have been absent from the room; the two of them immediately struck up a totally trivial conversation that completely engrossed them.

"Excuse me," he finally interrupted. "Liz, how did you get here?"

"Cab," she answered. "Oh my God, he's outside waiting!"

"You shouldn't take a cab home," Sonny insisted. He pulled out the key to his new BMW. "Adonis, do me a favor and give Liz a lift home. You can take my car."

When Adonis and Liz were gone, Charlotte walked up and hugged him. "Well done, Cupid. She can still be your doctor."

More Than Life Itself

It was mid morning of New Year's Eve. Sonny sat on Charlotte's couch in only his pajama bottoms. Charlotte was in the kitchen making coffee. They had slept in and now needed to plan their day. They were hosting a gathering for the growing staff of Feelright Intelligence Services to celebrate the New Year, and they needed to decide what to serve.

She came into the room carrying two steaming mugs. She wore a silk robe that excited Sonny, even after a night of lovemaking. He sipped his coffee and smacked his lips.

"Yummy!"

"Bailey's Bristol Cream; Joyce gave me the recipe," she smiled. "Did I tell you that Simon's bringing a date tonight?" she asked.

"No!" Sonny was intrigued. He couldn't conceive of Simon having romantic inclinations toward anyone. "Do you know whom?"

"As a matter of fact, I do. He asked me for permission to invite her."

"No! Not your mother!"

She nodded.

"How do you feel about that? I mean, Simon. . . ."

"He's a lot better than all of the other creeps she's dated," Charlotte responded.

She went to the bedroom and came back with two small packages in holiday wrapping.

"What's this?" he asked.

"We pretty much missed Christmas. I got you a couple things." She handed him the first package.

"Oh, my God!" he exclaimed when he unwrapped the Christian Dior watch inside, gold with diamond insets. "You must have spent a fortune! It's beautiful!"

"Now you've got no excuses for being late." She handed him the second package.

"What the heck?" He held up the inexpensive Timex inside.

"For running," she explained. "It's got a stopwatch." She reached out and pinched his naked side. "I don't want you getting fat and soft on me."

He leaned over and kissed her. "Now I've got something for you." He went to the closet and retrieved an envelope from his coat.

"What is it?" She tore it open and unfolded the document inside. "I don't understand. What is it?"

"It's the papers to Hombre, your horse. It's his pedigree."

She looked at him, confused.

"He's yours now. Joyce let me buy him, before the

authorities freeze your dad's estate. He's at a boarding stable in Aurora. We can go tomorrow."

"Oh, Sonny!" She gave him a long, heartfelt embrace. She leaned back and studied the document as though it was a precious love letter.

"I got a message from my landlord," Sonny ventured. "He wants me out. He can't stand all the commotion. He's threatening to evict me."

She looked up. "You can stay here," she offered.

"Just until I can find a place," he pledged.

She hesitated. "I mean, you could stay here. Live here. With me."

He cocked his head, unsure if he was hearing her correctly.

"I mean, only if you want to." She was blushing now.

"Of course I want to," he responded. "But you're sure? I mean, I know how important your independence is to you."

She leaned forward and put her lips next to his ear. "Who loves you, Sonny?" she whispered.

He leaned back and stared into her eyes.

"I do," she answered her own question. "I love you."

"How much?" he asked.

She leaned forward again, brushing her lips on his ear. "More than life itself."

Author's Note

Thank you for reading this second Sonny Feelright novel. If you never read the first book (THE UNLIKELY CAREER OF SONNY B. FEELRIGHT), please visit sonnyfeelright.com for excerpts and links to the best locations to purchase it. And if you enjoyed this book, or even if you didn't, I invite you to take a few minutes and share your thoughts in a review on amazon.com, barnesandnoble.com, and goodreads.com. Reviews can be enormously helpful in marketing books in the social networking age.

Special thanks to my wife, daughter and all of the friends who took time to read the first draft manuscript of this book and gave me valuable criticism and suggestions to make it better. The most substantive suggestion was to provide insight into Nancy Black's mental state after her flight from Chicago, which resulted in the chapter, Spider Lair. Anyone interested in pre-reading the third book, tentatively titled THE TRAGIC HERITAGE OF SONNY B. FEELRIGHT, can contact me through sonnyfeelright.com, my Goodreads.com author page, or on my Outskirts Press author page.

To those who want to know the real life inspirations for the many heroes and villains in the FEELRIGHT series, I must refer you to the disclaimer up front that this book is purely fictional. Of course, if you cross my path at a pub or airport bar, like Simon Courtney, I can be bribed with a cold beverage.

Dwight David Morgan

CPSIA information can be obtained at www.ICGtesting.com
Printed in the USA
BVOW04s1019010813

327503BV00006B/41/P

9 781432 790899